CW01676547

THE MYSTERY

OF

THE MEMORY TIN

Sally Trueman Dicken

stormy petrel publications

The Mystery of The Memory Tin

Copyright© Sally Trueman Dicken 2021

First edition 2021
Second edition 2023
Published by stormy petrel publications

The rights of Sally Trueman Dicken have been asserted by her in accordance with the Copyright, Designs and Patents Act 1988

All rights reserved. No part of this publication may be reproduced, stored in a retrieval system or transmitted in any form or by any means, electronic, mechanical, photocopying, recording or other, without the prior permission of the author or licence permitting restricted copying.

In the UK, such licences are issued by the Copyright Licensing Agency, Saffron House, 6–10 Kirby Street, London, EC1N 8TS; www.cla.co.uk

ISBN: 978-1-7392998-0-4

stormy petrel publications

The vigilant reader might notice that Kingcharlton, a fictional town, bears a slight resemblance to Keynsham in Somerset. None of the characters, either living or dead, are in any way connected to the real characters who live in Keynsham. These fictional characters are purely the products of my imagination.

Sally Trueman Dicken lives on the borders of Somerset, surrounded by dogs and grandchildren. When she can snatch a quiet moment, she picks up paper and pen to capture her wild imaginings.

This book is dedicated to my husband, Rob, without whose unfailing support, it would never have come to fruition.

I have made many wonderful friends on my journey to write a novel. All of these have helped to keep me going on the right path. Bless you all.

A mention must go to my writing group, Writers in Somerset, who helped in all sorts of ways—especially when they decided we must all self-publish our ongoing novels.

A special mention to two grandchildren:

Lilia Everett, a budding artist who brought to life my concept of what the Memory Tin looked like.

Oliver Trueman, who usually takes very impressive photographs of trains-with-steam-up but paused for a moment to help with the photography.

Prologue

As the decades passed, the little tin lost its shine. All sorts of debris gathered under the floorboards of the ancient building. The blue enamel grew dingy and rusty spots appeared. Eventually only fragments of the white lilies-of-the-valley and bright blue forget-me-knots remained. Dents and scratches occurred as various furry creatures crept over the tin scrabbling with their tiny paws. Severe flooding one winter turned the basement into a swirling pool of mud that encased the tin when the waters seeped away. Luckily the tiny tin was watertight and guarded its secret well.

Inside the contents were intact – the memories of a wartime romance were preserved for posterity, protected from the world outside. A moment in time rested in this shell waiting to see daylight again.

Decades passed. Technology took over. Changes were made. Old buildings were pulled down and one day the little tin saw daylight again. The small container was destined for the council tip until it was rescued and prised open.

Could the clues hidden inside this battered old tin reveal the secrets of a WW1 couple and solve the mystery of a missing baby?

Chapter One - 1916

'You have to go now, Daisy,' her mother said, arms akimbo, small children clustered round her knees. 'You'll be alright! It's a good place to be. Plenty of food, your uniform found, you'll be better off there.'

They stood face to face on the sloping doorstep of the end cottage of Woodbine Batch. This terrace of cottages was a damp dismal relict of the past greed of landowners and employers. It appeared to be crumbling away, the fallen stones slipping sideways down the greensward leading to the river. September squalls blustered round the corners and into the leaking doors.

'But I don't want to go, Mother. I like being here with the family. I don't mind sharing my food with the little ones or having to wear my brothers' old boots. I can help you with the washing. Just let me stay here with you.'

'No, it has to be this way. You won't be far away, just up the hill. We need the money with Father out of work again.' Ivy Hollis pushed the small shivering girl out of the door of number six Woodbine Cottages and closed it firmly behind her. Leaning against the shut door, she raised her ragged apron to her eyes and wept.

Daisy turned her face from her home and began the trek to the workhouse perched high on the hill like a hunched vulture.

*

There had been another parting that evening, a much more elaborate affair. The members of the family standing at the front door of The Firs, Park Row, Cardiff were equally affected by swirling emotions, but this was a mixture of excitement for the two younger daughters and misgivings from their parents. Catherine and Annie were departing to take up positions as Voluntary Aid Detachment nurses, commonly known as VADs, in a sleepy little town in Somerset. Beatrice, the eldest sister, stood at the open door exuding clouds of envy and disapproval at the freedom of her two younger sisters to go gadding off away from her parents' restrictions. Beatrice's bossy husband Arthur was elsewhere – studying his account books and profit margins. To him the war was about making money not humouring the ambitions of silly young women.

Annie, the second daughter, stood patiently waiting for the luggage to be loaded, a picture of serenity and good grooming – like a luscious peach waiting to be picked.

Catherine, the youngest child, the instigator of nursing plans, was a fizzing bundle of nerves and energy. With her red-gold corkscrew curls shooting in all directions, spraying hair-pins everywhere, she was darting here and there – checking her bag – directing the chauffeur on how to store the luggage – kissing her mother – asking the time from her father – never still for a moment.

This was her plan coming to fruition at last. She was leaving home on the first step to becoming a modern woman.

Chapter Two - 2016

The day started in the usual way, or so it seemed to Lizzy who awoke in a bleary-eyed mess. Her head ached from troubled sleep patterns and a surfeit of red wine. Life appeared dull, pointless with nothing to get up for. But then she caught sight of Wellington, her ancient chocolate-brown Labrador, peering at her with anxious eyes. When Gerry was alive the dog slept downstairs, but then a lot of things were different when Gerry was part of their lives. Lizzy fought her way out of the tangled duvet and looked at herself in the mirror. Little did she know that this would be the day that her life changed completely – that this bedraggled figure staring back at her would be faced with a challenging adventure.

Bloodshot eyes struggled to focus. An untidy mop of rust-coloured curls interwoven with silver threads tumbled over her shoulders. Not a sight she wanted to look at for very long. She was drinking too much red wine. This was no way to live. She must sort herself out, tidy the house – get herself back to normal. Stumbling to the bathroom, she seized her toothbrush to freshen her mouth. There, that felt better. When she ran her tongue around her teeth, they felt fresh, her gums tingled with cleanliness.

It pained her to see the concern on her daughters' faces at her sorry state. But it was only a year since a speeding driver had killed her husband. The shock of losing him so suddenly, at a comparatively young age, had sent her into a zombie-like daze so that she lived from moment to moment. There had been plans for an early retirement – carefully thought out schemes, which included a retro camper van for travelling abroad with Wellington.

Her daughters, Nicola and Claire, and their partners had tried their best to help Lizzy in a discreet manner. But she had rejected all offers, saying she just wanted to be left alone to grieve and she fully intended to get herself together soon. It seemed to her that nobody could possibly understand what it was like – this enormous crater of loneliness Gerry's death had left in her life after so many years of marriage.

Her clothes were lying in a heap on the floor: crumpled jeans, a once-fashionable top in need of a wash. She pulled on her garments haphazardly, after fishing in her drawer for clean underwear, finishing with Gerry's old socks worn for the comfort they gave her. Staggering down the stairs, she nearly tripped over Wellington, waiting patiently for his walk. She needed to wake herself up with strong coffee and fresh air. Wellington's walk would sort her out. A clear head was needed: she was picking up her granddaughters from school at lunchtime. They had a half-day and their mother, Nicola, was working.

Downstairs, all was chaos. It was getting like a hoarder's house, every surface covered with old bills, letters of condolence to be stored away in a box, and random items of little use. She filled the kettle with water and reached for the coffee jar, but it was empty. A frantic search of the cupboards produced an older jar in which a stiff mound of partially congealed granules festering in the bottom could only be dislodged by hot water and a severe prodding by a knife.

'I'll start the clear up tomorrow,' she mumbled to Wellington as she swallowed a couple of tablets. Her head was a throbbing mass of pain.

Two cups of sugary coffee later, Lizzy reached for the lead and the doggy bags. They would take a little walk, Wellington would not mind, his legs were getting rather wobbly, causing sad thoughts of his inevitable demise. Oh no, she could not bear it if he was going to leave her too. He was the only thing she got out of bed for. He didn't mind how long the walk was, he just needed the routine of leaving the house, walking and sniffing, then coming back for his breakfast. It would have to be the short walk though, round by the workhouse and memorial hospital and back home.

As they approached the entrance to the workhouse, the clanging of machinery started her headache pounding again. She had forgotten that the demolition work was starting today: the nineteenth-century workhouse, together with the small First World War memorial hospital, was being demolished to make way for a new health centre, an improvement so they said. At that very moment, a lorry full of debris from the ruined building paused at the gates of the site, and then zoomed towards her. The battered old lorry was overloaded with its cargo not properly secured. She was going to take a photo of the registration number to report it, but when she felt in her pocket she remembered her phone was lying on the kitchen table. Would she have bothered though? Her indifference to life around her was becoming alarming.

The lorry bounced over a traffic-calming hump, causing a ball of clay to soar through the sky, narrowly missing her head in its arc of flight, as the lorry charged off through the modern estate. A quantity of caked mud flew off as the missile landed at her feet, revealing the corner of a metal object decorated with a faint pattern of old-fashioned flowers. The way it protruded from its mucky shell reminded Lizzy of a children's cartoon film in which a baby crocodile's snout had emerged from a huge, cracked egg.

'Wow, Wellington, that was close. Why do they allow idiots like that on the roads?'

The careless lorry was already halfway down the road, its stony overflow scattering like dusty hailstones bouncing off the tarmac. Wellington, usually a very placid Labrador, was sheltering behind Lizzy's knees. As she stood shaking at her narrow escape, ghostly recollections of a similar object in her granny's workbasket flickered across Lizzy's mind. Happy memories of Sundays at granny's house with home baking and family chit-chat filled her mind. How could she leave the tin there all forlorn? She would take it home with her and inspect it more closely. Maybe there would be sewing items from the past like the ones granny kept in hers.

'Nobody wants the tin. It has no value. Nobody can blame me for picking it up,' Lizzy muttered to herself. She was seized by a mad impulse to possess the tin and carry it off, come what may.

'You know what Wellington; we're going to take this little tin home. I hope nobody round here has a security camera focussed on us.'

As she bent down, she felt the denim of her jeans stretch tight across her backside – too much comfort eating had made her slender figure a thing of the past, not to mention the high sugar content of red wine.

Half a ball of baked clay with a tin sticking out lay in the palm of her hand. Although the outside was hard, the mud inside was wet and sticky, like a chocolate brownie, clinging to its secret. She tapped it on the pavement to get rid of the coating, wondering why she was bothering with this useless object. She could not relax her grip to allow it to fall out of her fingers. Every time she made to let it go, it spoke to her of mystery and times past. Somewhere in her tired and grieving brain, a spark of curiosity was igniting – a fleeting flash of interest in something apart from her daily misery.

Lizzy glanced around to see if anyone had seen the tin fall or watched her pick it up. The road was deserted apart from the parked cars that cluttered the streets everywhere. Slouching figures clad in florescent jackets topped by plastic helmets stood within ancient walls lovingly constructed by skilled stonemasons. The attention of the demolition team was focussed on their early morning brew and sneaky smoke, not debris falling from a mucky lorry. She felt a momentary pang of loss for the imposing workhouse. Too many landmarks of her childhood were being destroyed; ones similar to this grey stone building that had brooded over the river valley for two hundred years.

The varied history of Kingcharlton had always been its attraction. Workhouse Lane was one of her favourite walks: this area where ancient and modern met. When she and Gerry walked to the allotment, they had always chosen this route, enjoying the feeling of walking through history. The workhouse had been built at the top of a steep cobbled hill on the outskirts of the town well away from the good people of Kingcharlton. The town had grown up around it. The old building, transformed into a maternity hospital, now looked out through its back windows at an estate of modern neat little houses and through its front windows at the remnants of a medieval village: a packhorse bridge, a historic water mill and Elizabethan cottages subject to flooding from the river, shamed by a tumbling heap of shoddy later cottages ripe for demolition.

Feeling for a handy doggy bag, it only took a minute for Lizzy to hide the muddy tin inside and bury it deep in the pocket of her anorak. A childhood misunderstanding at a jumble sale had given her a fear of being suspected of stealing. She shivered in spite of the sunshine. The notion that she was being watched persisted. She tugged on Wellington's lead. They set off for home, moving as fast as Wellington's wobbly legs would allow.

In one of the sixties' houses, unknown to her, somebody was watching the incident with growing curiosity. Behind the grimy curtains of thirteen All Saints Road, Peter Catchpole chuckled softly and ran his long bony fingers through his unruly black curls. A smile worthy of Machiavelli transformed his face. It looked as if an object of interest had been gleaned from the ruins of the workhouse. Somehow, he would have to discover what it was.

Chapter Three - 1916

While Daisy was battling against the wind and rain, a hunting owl was taking advantage of the dark to find food for a nest of owlets. Battered by the wind, the owl swooped low over the houses, over the workhouse, across a small huddle of cottages on the green, over the ancient church, standing stalwart since Norman times, finally swooping down over the rails leading to a relatively new train station where two men and a lad were awaiting the arrival of the seven-forty-five from Bristol Temple Meads. They had been told to expect two young ladies from Cardiff who would need transporting to the workhouse where Matron would be waiting to receive them.

'Two nurses – VADs they do call 'um. Got to be trained by Matron to look after wounded soldiers. You better look after them well or you'll be getting a telling-off from Matron.' The stationmaster straightened his hat and looked fierce.

A young lad shuffled his feet feeling mutinous, but he kept his eyes to the ground, for this job was highly sought after and he had ambitions to climb the ladder of success. A carter stood close by patting his ancient horse, with all the time in the world. He was happy to be away from his crowded cottage, crammed with squealing children.

The owl flew away from the noisy station, following the train tracks towards Bristol, where the expected train was waiting for the lines to clear. The stationmaster took out his pocket watch and held a lighted match over the timepiece.

'Not long now, men. Is the cart ready?'

*

Annie had closed her eyes to shut out the world. It had been a long day, but Catherine was fully alert, intent on not missing a single moment of her first step on the road to becoming an emancipated woman. She peered through the window, scanning the landscape for sight of their destination.

The train slowed as the familiar outline of Brunel's magnificent buildings at Bristol Temple Meads station loomed against the granite night sky. Catherine recognised the dim shape of the splendid restaurant where she had often taken a refreshing cup of tea with her mother and sisters on shopping expeditions.

Their coach halted momentarily alongside a platform crowded with troops whilst the train driver waited for the signal to proceed to a quieter platform further on. As Annie dozed, Catherine rubbed the glass clear with her pocket-handkerchief to get a better view. She was looking out for the station clock, but the light was so bad that the hands on the large round face could not be seen. It was a pity as Father always said that railway stations kept impeccable time; she wanted to check her own timepiece.

The main platform was filled with men stamping their feet to keep out the cold. The mist was seeping up from the river, dark and mysterious. It mingled with the smutty smoke from the engine to veil the rows of men waiting patiently. Khaki-clad figures, coat collars turned up against the wintry weather, cupped their cigarettes in the shelter of their palms as a brisk wind hurtled down the platform from the docks and the open waters of the Bristol Channel.

There was not much conversation, but a cacophony of coughing and spitting filled the air as the smoke from their Woodbines and the steaming trains filled their throats and choked them.

In the lowered lights, no features could be seen until a rogue match flared and a solitary face was illuminated. Catherine's green eyes met a pair of brown eyes that twinkled at her in the gloom. The match died and all was black once more but not before she saw a hand raised to a cap in a friendly salute.

She was startled at the intrusion on her belief that no-one could see her inside the carriage. His face, even in the dim light, was imprinted on her memory, like one of those peculiar negatives used to produce photographs. As her train gathered steam and moved off, she felt a strange sense of loss; now she would never meet him again. He was obviously on his way to war and she would be marooned in a small market town in Somerset.

Their train rounded the bend and puffed slowly alongside the stationmaster and his crew who stood to attention as the carriage door opened to reveal the two younger daughters of the Waterman family from Cardiff. Catherine and Annie had finally arrived at the small station of Kingcharlton. A chill wind threatened to carry off their hats, even though they were secured with hatpins of a ferocious length. The stationmaster helped them down from the train and the young lad carried their baggage out to the yard where a rather uncomfortable-looking cart was waiting for them.

'Not the usual form of transport for ladies like you, but best we could do at short notice.' The stationmaster frowned as he watched the lad heave the trunks onto the farm cart in a careless manner. 'However, the workhouse is not far away, and I am sure Matron will have the kettle on the range. She is a very hospitable sort of person.'

As they trotted through the village, the carter maintained a respectful silence until they reached the foot of a steep hill where a row of dim golden globes placed at random intervals revealed stone walls on either side of a cobbled road.

*

Meanwhile Daisy was shuffling over the packhorse bridge away from the tiny cottage filled with children and warmth. Her boots were much too large for her; they went one way and her feet the other, making every step painful. No warm thick socks could be found for her: her older working brothers had pinched them all as their right to have first dibs at everything, being as they brought home their wages from the farmer. They were talking of joining up though so maybe she would be first in line soon. It was not far to go in terms of miles but to a hungry twelve-year-old it was a struggle. She shifted her tiny bundle of clothing to her other hip and sighed. Tears slid silently down her cheeks at having to leave the comforting huddle of humans at home.

As she passed the row of cottages at the foot of the hill and started to stumble up the steep incline, the bitter rain invaded her worn tattered clothing, whipping her wet bonnet strings across her face with a painful slap. Above the howling of the wind, she caught the faint sound of the clip-clop clatter of a horse's hooves interspersed with the harsh tones of the carter, by now ready to get home for his tea.

'You must get down, ladies, and walk the rest – don't know as how the old mare will manage the cobbles in all the wet weather. She should have been retired this last year but with all our decent horses taken, we've been forced to "make do" the best we can.'

The carter, his somewhat surly appearance belied by his eagerness to impart unsolicited information, offered his passengers a grubby hand of assistance to clamber down. His experience of life had more to do with shifting loads of mangelwurzels to feed the sheep than dealing with high-society folk. The two young ladies were glad that they had heeded their mother's warning and worn their heavy tweed coats instead of smart outfits, not suited for inclement weather. The cobbles were treacherously slippery, especially in fashionable boots; their mother had not been successful with her advice there. Chestnut trees dripped relentlessly on their sodden coats. It had seemed such a short journey from the railway station to the workhouse when they had looked it up on

Father's Ordinance Survey map, but now it felt endless. The dim glow from each gaslight they passed did little to alleviate the gloom.

A stone wall bordered the road to their left where bushes towered over them trailing clusters of berries, black in the dim light. What lay beyond the travellers did not know, but the soft splish-splash of a water mill could be heard when the horse was rested for a moment "to save her wind". Indeed, her breathing sounded very laboured and Catherine felt sorry for the poor old nag dragged out on a night like this.

'This feels like the end of the world,' muttered the smaller of the women.

'Don't be so dramatic. It's the cold dark rain that is making you think that way. They always built workhouses on the edge of the town to keep the bad from the good.' Catherine was trying to keep their spirits up.

'I don't like being away from Cardiff at all. I'm a city girl. I know it doesn't bother you, Catherine, you're fearless.'

'It's the countryside, quiet and peaceful. It will be different in the daylight. Don't you feel excited?' Catherine's pace slowed down as the hill got steeper, 'We are away from home with so much freedom without Mother and Father continually restricting us.'

Annie stumbled and nearly fell. 'No, I am cold, wet and weary. I liked living at home, all the tea parties, shopping in town, tennis and going about.'

'Don't worry,' Catherine's voice was soothing. 'There'll be plenty of young men for you to talk to when they come home on leave. Think what a jolly time we'll have; dancing and going to the theatre.'

A silence fell on the two sisters left alone in the gloom with their own thoughts about their situation.

'Look, Catherine, over there – a ghost. It's a lost spirit, risen from the grave.' Annie's voice trembled with fear.

Ahead of them, a small figure plodded slowly upwards, like an apparition from another age.

'No wonder she is trudging, those boots look at least two sizes too big. Poor little mite. And just look at her bundle. Where on earth is she going at this time of night?' Catherine's excitement had turned to sadness at the sight of the child ahead.

'Watch out, Daisy,' the carter bellowed, causing the mare to pick up her ears. 'Horse u'll have 'ee over. Her's not too steady on her feet with the wet.'

The face that turned to them was pinched and despairing. The thin girl with stringy hair looked too frail to be out in such weather. What she needed was a good meal; she looked like a drowned mouse.

'Where are you off to at this time of night, Daisy Hollis?'

'To the hospital, Billy Sawyer. I'm to be Matron's little helper, her maid of all sorts. My meals provided and a uniform and new boots if I'm lucky,' the child sobbed.

Catherine glanced over at Annie, to see if they shared the same feelings, suddenly ashamed of their trivial complaints. They had left a comfortable home of their own volition. Here was this insubstantial creature off to earn her living at half their age. She didn't appear to be strong enough to do much work.

*

Daisy snatched a shy glimpse at the two ladies who were looking her up and down as though she was livestock at the market. She knew they were ladies because every child in the village knew from an early age who was gentry and who was one of them.

The gentry wore lovely warm clothing, had shiny hair, beautiful hats and spoke posh. They asked all sorts of questions, expecting you to give them answers: just like the parson's wife before she gave you a charity bundle. She had to make sure you were deserving, not scoundrels or heathens because they did not deserve charity.

Not that these ladies were particularly dressed up. But still, they had that manner about them as if they owned the air that you breathed, and that if you didn't do as they said, they would take it away.

Daisy shivered with cold – she could not move till they dismissed her. Matron would be getting cross. She should have been there this morning but Father had been ill again and Mother needed her to mind the little ones whilst she went to her charring job at the Big House, dealing "with the rough" - the mucky side of housework, leaving the lighter stuff such as dusting to the housemaids.

'Come along – let's get going,' the taller lady's voice sang out against the wind, 'we'll catch our death out here.' She pulled off her mohair shawl and placed it around the small girl's shoulders before instructing Daisy to take a place between them where she would be sheltered from some of the howling wind and rain.

*

Matron strutted up and down the hall, looking out now and again through the peephole in the door, to see if she had missed the knock, leaving the expected visitors waiting forlornly on the doorstep. She inspected her ledger: two newcomers, Voluntary Aid Detachment recruits, to help with the new hospital and one local girl to train as her maid in Matron's own little cottage across the yard. This was her own private project – to take a deserving girl from poor circumstances, train her up to be a competent maid, then send her out into service where she could move upwards. She had helped many unfortunate girls in this way, all at her own expense.

There was a sudden commotion in the courtyard. The brass doorknocker clanged. The huge, blackened door was heavy and cumbersome to open; damp weather had made the wood swell so that it scraped the floor. The creaking hinges made a high keening noise as though protesting at having to admit any visitors at such a late hour. Matron's sharp black eyes assessed the dripping travellers, making a swift decision as to which one was in the most need of immediate attention.

'What time do you call this, Daisy Hollis? Off you go to the kitchen straight away before Cook goes to bed. Tell her you are to have some bread and soup – a big bowlful. There's some dry clothing warming on the fender in front of the fire. You are to change into it immediately and towel your hair dry. Sit close to the fire whilst you eat. I have enough on my hands without having my new maid in bed with pneumonia. You are to sleep in one of the dormitories tonight. We'll see to your boots tomorrow. Off you go now. Cook will tell you all you need to know.'

Matron turned her attention to the two young ladies dripping on the tiles. Some of these Red Cross volunteers were nothing but trouble. They had no concept of discipline and obedience to rules. Fortunately, these two were showing no signs of the impatience natural to their class. Muriel Hardcastle studied these recruits very closely for they were going to have to prove their aptitude and commitment over the coming weeks. The sisters looked totally unalike; the younger one with red-gold unruly tresses in abundance and a serious intense expression in her green eyes. It was interesting to see they were speckled with flecks of gold so that they twinkled in the lamplight. *My grandmother would have called those witch's eyes*, thought Muriel. *She would also have said that they indicated an unstable temperament. Willing to please but often "away with the fairies"*.

This was a dangerous one to handle, thought Matron. She looked fiery like her hair; an avenging angel in the flesh. Numerous hair clips had been employed to keep the curls in place, without much success. One had already dropped to the floor and Matron stooped to pick it up. *Look at you, Muriel Hardcastle, she's already getting you to pick things up for her. Better watch her carefully.*

The older one had a more restrained hairstyle, smooth golden waves framing hyacinth blue eyes with long sweeping lashes and already wearing an expression of being slightly bored. She would be the sort of deceptively meek and mild woman who could command anything they wanted from men by flashing those enormous eyes. What a combination of havoc those girls could wreak on her quiet little corner of the world. It would be interesting to see how they performed in the coming weeks. This might turn out to be a disaster. Major Bowmaker did not realise what he had started when he decided to build his new hospital and send these two young women to help her set it up.

'Come this way to my office. The carter will bring in your boxes.' Matron led the way, her stiff skirts rustling as she walked. The room was welcoming with a sturdy-looking fire in the inglenook fireplace. The weary faces of the sisters shone with relief at the sight of a huge tea tray prepared for supper. A kettle warmed on the hearth and a toasting fork stood ready primed for the slices of bread on a nearby plate. A cauldron with an enticing mist rising up hung on a tripod chain over the glowing coals. Matron peered in and gave it a stir with a huge wooden spoon.

She pointed to a row of hooks alongside the fireplace. 'Hang your wet coats to dry over here. I'm afraid the lateness of your arrival means you have missed the main meal of the day but I think you will find that Cook's homemade soup is both filling and nutritious. There is plenty of bread for toast and a big pot of tea.'

'Lovely,' Catherine sighed, 'just right for a cold September evening.' Her woollen dress was already steaming gently in the heat.

Chapter Four

As the sisters sipped their soup and crunched their buttery toast, Matron used the lack of conversation to make clear what would be expected of them.

'You will have been told that Major Bowmaker, a very important figure hereabouts, has put up the funds for a memorial hospital in the grounds of the workhouse. An old isolation building has been transformed into a modern working hospital to serve soldiers returning from the Front, wounded or in need of rest and recuperation. He was offered the use of part of the old workhouse as we have fewer inhabitants. But the Major came to the conclusion that he preferred this hospital to stand alone as a tribute to his son.'

The two young women munched away, seemingly pleased not to have to make conversation for they looked so tired and hungry. Matron smiled at the sight of colour seeping back into their chilled cheeks.

'It is to be dedicated to the memory of his oldest son, killed in the retreat from Mons. You will understand that he feels very proud and very sensitive about it. Please remember that if you have the occasion to speak to him at any time. He often rides over to inspect progress. Your task will be to set up all the beds and equipment needed to nurse and revitalise the soldiers who will soon be arriving. We are hoping for more recruits to arrive soon to help you. They are being called up as we speak. I will walk you across to my cottage where you are to stay in my spare bedroom whilst the memorial hospital is finished off. Daisy will be assigned to you tomorrow to help you settle in. She can join in with hospital duties whilst I feed her up for more sturdy work.'

Her instructions completed to her satisfaction, Matron took the opportunity to sit quietly, surreptitiously studying the hands of the girls to see if they were used to hard work. Both of them had well-cared-for hands: hands that had lifted china teacups to their mouths, played pianos, and created elaborate hairstyles. Miss Catherine's were particularly elegant with long slender fingers tipped by nails that looked as if they had been fashioned out of mother of pearl by a master craftsman. What a pity they would soon be red and damaged by the constant washing with carbolic soap to keep infection at bay. Matron compared them to her own hands, busy with the poker to keep the coals glowing. It had been a long time since she had to perform the arduous duties of a young nurse, but her hands would never recover from the days when she had sluiced out equipment and scrubbed floors.

She had a feeling that Catherine would not mind the loss of her perfect hands as much as Annie, for the light of enthusiasm to be "out there" nursing shone so brightly from Catherine's eyes that they seemed to sparkle like fairy lights. It was obvious that the gold flecks on the green irises glowed when she was happy. This girl would never be able to hide her feelings. Her whole body showed a desire to "get on with it"; to plunge into her duties. She reminded Matron of the young colts on her father's farm back on the mountainside in Wales. When the doors were open, they shot out with no regard for danger or other people. They galloped themselves into all sorts of problems and then waited patiently for someone to rescue them. They were loving and faithful but jolly hard work. Was Catherine going to emulate them in all these things? Her hands were restless, constantly moving, tucking stray strands of corkscrew curls back behind her ears. The fingers fidgeted: stirring her tea with a teaspoon long after the sugar had been evenly distributed, smoothing her collar, waving in the air to emphasise her feelings.

The other girl, Annie, sat quietly, in total command of herself, her whole body composed and still. She sipped her tea elegantly; she took tiny bites of toast and chewed slowly. She was relaxed and confident in her manner, but it was not easy to tell whether she was as keen as her sister to train to be a nurse or was just following Catherine blindly.

It was going to be interesting, to see how long they would stay with her. Now that those in power had decided to allow voluntary nurses to join in the duties of regular nurses, even to cross the Channel into danger zones, many more girls might come forward. But not all of them would stay when they experienced the reality of nursing in wartime. Images of floating through clean wards carrying a lamp and uttering soothing words would quickly fade and they would begin drifting back home. The summer holiday camps all VADs had attended to learn many different types of voluntary war-work, would have given them false illusions. No doubt they had practised binding injuries with bandages and learnt about nutrition for invalids and splints for broken limbs, but these skills would not be much use in healing the war wounds she had seen, such as the terrible gas gangrene, that came from fighting on farmland that had been constantly fertilised with manure for decades. When that mud got into the wounds, they could not be cured by any medicine so far discovered. All they could do was amputate and hope the gangrene would not spread and bring a terrible lingering death. The nurses had to be made of stern stuff to deal with situations like that.

Such was Matron's cynical opinion, but the sisters seemed to be pleasant company and she resolved to do all she could to help them achieve their aim to become competent nurses. *You never could tell how people reacted in a crisis*, she thought. Who knew how these two would turn out?

Once their supper was finished down to the last buttery crumb and drop of tea, Matron indicated that she was ready to show them to their sleeping quarters. Catherine and Annie followed Matron across the paved yard to a small cottage enclosed in a tiny garden. It looked like a scene from days gone by. This was not what they had been expecting. When a hospital had been mentioned, they had imagined modern plumbing and fixtures, gleaming white tiles, hygienic surroundings. This place looked as if it could be harbouring all sorts of small creatures. *How would Annie cope,* Catherine wondered, *she hated mice?*

'Welcome to my humble abode, ladies,' Matron turned the key in the lock and gestured for the two sisters to follow her. 'It's much older than the surrounding buildings, part of a bygone era. This cottage was already here when the village elders decided that a workhouse was needed. They thought that separate accommodation for those who were to run it would be useful, so they simply enclosed it when the high stone wall was built.'

The wooden door opened onto flagstones, spread with brightly coloured peg rugs. Catherine wondered if the inmates of the workhouse had made them. There was an open fireplace not as large as the one they had just left but similarly equipped to provide tea and nourishment. Matron rattled a poker in the coals of the fire to produce a sparkling red glow.

'Now, let's show you to your bedroom, ladies. Then you can get some rest.'

She pulled open a narrow door in the shadow of the inglenook fireplace, to reveal a twisting wooden staircase. There was little room for manoeuvre. The girls were unused to such a lack of space on a staircase and Catherine began to feel panic at being so enclosed. The bedroom at top of the stairs was only a quarter of the size of the sisters' bedrooms in Cardiff. Rustic windows were framed with waving fronds of a creeper; bearing red hips, produce of the summer red roses. Matron explained that the space under the beams was divided into two bedrooms, each accessed by the cupboard-like staircases on either side of the inglenook fireplace downstairs.

'My room is the other side of that partition wall. I hope we do not disturb each other. It is probably not what you are used to, but I have tried to make it comfortable.'

Despite some drawbacks it looked a pleasant enough room, better than they had been expecting when climbing the stairs, though it was rather disappointing to find that they would have to use chamber pots and carry them down to the backdoor privy in the morning. Perhaps they could ask Daisy to perform this function. *Still,* Catherine thought, *it would prepare them for the rigours of the battlefield.* A rose-patterned china washbasin with matching ewer stood on a table with tiled top – no doubt Daisy would have to carry up the water though she did not look strong enough.

The two sisters unpacked a few things and tumbled quickly into bed; it had been such a long day. Annie was soon snoring, but Catherine lay awake for some time, thinking about her plans for the future. In the drowsy moments before her eyes were fully closed, listening to hooting noises from the trees outside, Catherine's thoughts turned to the curious incident of the soldier at Temple Meads station. It had been such an eerie experience. *Would she ever see him again? There was no reason to think he was local; troops were moving about all over the country.*

Chapter Five - 2016

Thank heavens for central heating, Lizzy thought, as she hung the dog lead on its hook. The kitchen was warm and welcoming after the gloomy day outside. She found a newspaper, separated the sheets to spread across the table, pulled the secret parcel out of her anorak pocket and placed the mud-crusted tin squarely in the centre.

'Why on earth did I bring this home, Welly? It's just an old tin.' Wellington looked hopeful at being included in the conversation though he had not heard the word "biscuit". He waited patiently for his bowl to be filled.

Lizzy rummaged in a drawer, searching for a pair of rubber gloves. Pulling them on, she turned the tin, shaking it gently – tapping it on the newspaper to get rid of any lingering mud flakes. More of the faded pattern appeared – faint lettering and flowers, lilies of some sort. It looked like a cough-drop container – blue, green and white patches of speckled enamel stood out against dull grey metal. Lizzy made out the words by filling in gaps – *Hunters Pastilles, good for catarrh and inflammation of the throat.*

She fetched a J-cloth, dampened it to carefully dab at the muddy surface. A swish of the cloth and the initials C W stood out in steel letters. Her post falling on the mat in the hall broke her concentration. Glancing at the clock, she realised that several hours had passed without her thinking of Gerry. It also reminded her that she had promised to pick up her granddaughters from school and she was going to be late if she didn't leave soon.

Lizzy was reluctant to leave her task. What did *C W* refer to and what was in the tin – just ancient pastilles or something interesting? Had the contents survived? The lid would not budge. It would have to be put away for later as it was too dirty to leave out whilst the granddaughters were around. Their little fingers fiddled with everything when least expected. She found a cake tin, not used now Gerry was no longer around to eat Bara Brith. The treasure was wrapped in clean kitchen roll and hidden at the back of her pantry. From then on, it was a very busy afternoon: the walk to school, the journey home with the girls riding their silver scooters.

'Don't get too far ahead; stop at the end of the road. Wait for me!' She imagined all sorts of accidents occurring whilst these precious little girls were in her charge. They looked incredibly vulnerable, with all the other children streaming out of school without a fear in the world, their whole lives before them.

Fish fingers and chips for Lily, ham in a wrap for Evie. Modern children had choices. They ate a concoction of yoghurt and jam for afters. All consumed on trays on their laps whilst they watched cartoons. It was not the way Lizzy would have chosen but it made it easier for her as she was feeling tired after the exertions of the morning. Her doctor said it was mild depression this continual fatigue, a natural reaction to the loss of her husband, not to worry about it. Try these tablets for a while. Would she like talking therapy or group sessions for older people? On the whole she thought she was winning the battle, but the lack of energy and interest in life was annoying. A few months earlier, she would have kicked the tin into the gutter and walked away. Now, she had been interested enough to bring it home with her. It was a start.

By the time her daughter Nicola arrived to pick up the girls, Lizzy felt ready for some mindless television and a glass of wine.

'How are you today, Mum? Feeling any better?'

'All the better for seeing you and the girls. Work go okay?' Lizzy gave her daughter a hug and hoped she would not linger long. The girls were getting lively and Lizzy wanted to be alone with her thoughts. She opened a bottle of red wine for just one glass and awoke in the early hours of the morning with an empty bottle and a thick head. It was cold and dark outside, so she pulled a crocheted blanket over her body and cuddled up to Wellington who, in the absence of any telling off, had heaved himself up on the sofa beside her.

Lizzy woke to the sound of birdsong and the crashing clinking horn-blowing noise that meant the recycling lorry was holding up all the traffic in the road. Lying motionless on the settee, she remembered her mystery object hidden in a cake tin on the pantry floor.

She plodded to the kitchen, her eyes fuzzy with sleep, automatically reaching for the kettle, the milk and the newly purchased jar of instant coffee to wake her up. After several sips of strong Colombian brew, she drew on her rubber gloves and fetched the tin from the depths of the larder. She tried once again to wrestle off the stubborn lid that felt almost welded on.

'What shall I do, Wellington, it's too stiff? What can we use to pry it open? I wonder if Gerry had a tool for this sort of thing. Shall we go and look? There must be something suitable in the shed for dealing with incalcitrant tins' At the sound of the magic word "shed", Wellington stood up and went to the back door.

She marched down the path in her slippers and housecoat, oblivious to the neighbours' curious eyes, clutching the key for the enormous padlock. Wellington ambled along behind her, happy to be out in the garden with his mistress once more. The bolts on the door were stiff and obviously needed a few drops of oil. They won the battle as skin was torn and blood started to flow. Lizzy sucked her wounds thoughtfully – Gerry had always worried about security. Hung on a series of hooks, the tools gleamed in the dark interior. She could see Gerry working, mud scraped off, surfaces buffed with an old rag. His father had used these tools, maybe even his grandfather, sturdy, old-fashioned but very functional, a bit like Gerry himself, not like those modern, fall-to-bits tools you saw in shops now. She heard her husband's voice declaiming the impossibilities of good gardening with modern tools.

He had been a good man, a good provider. Though he was far more practical than romantic she loved him dearly. There had never been any money worries. If sometimes she wished they could have been more adventurous about travelling abroad, it had not been a problem for them. The sight of the tools ready for the allotment dismayed her. How could she have forgotten about the allotment?

'Oh, Wellington, we forgot about the allotment. I never once thought about it. What about the fees, I haven't sent any money?' Wellington pressed against her knees, recognising her distress.

A year had passed so it must be completely overgrown with weeds. How could she have forgotten all about Gerry's allotment, his personal paradise where he had spent happy hours nurturing his tiny frail babies to vegetables of gigantic proportions? Would the committee have reallocated his plot? Surely they would have written to her first? Maybe the letter from the committee was amongst the pile of envelopes she had pushed into a drawer.

Her daughters had fished out the important ones to settle them, and maybe they had dealt with the allotment as well. Could it be that they had allowed the committee to reallocate the plot to someone on the long waiting list? After total apathy for months another spurt of adrenalin shook her totally awake. She was overwhelmed by an urge to go immediately and see for herself what the situation was.

Chapter Six - 1916

Catherine's parents had been horrified when she announced her intention to join a Voluntary Aid Detachment and learn to nurse the war-wounded. The fact that her mother and father believed that she had inveigled Annie into going did nothing to soothe the situation.

Mama had wept, pleaded, demanded, ordered her father to take measures but had to give way in the end. War fever had gripped Great Britain, leaving all those left at home with the feeling that they were missing something exciting.

Her father, Frederick, was assailed by divided loyalties: he wanted to "do his bit" for his country and to be seen to do so but he also needed to appease his wife, or life at home would be unbearable. Besides which he had niggling doubts of his own, as he was not quite sure that this was an appropriate occupation for two young ladies of genteel upbringing.

'This nonsense will all be Catherine's doing,' Frederick spluttered. 'I'm sure she has persuaded her sister to join in, since Annie is usually such an obedient girl. We shouldn't have let them join those VAD summer camps. It's given them wild ideas.

When will this madness end? Thank goodness we have one sensible daughter settled and married. Beatrice can look after us in our old age if that bossy husband will allow her to.'

His oldest daughter Beatrice was an ideal wife in his opinion, always attentive to her husband's wishes although she did look rather unhappy at the moment. Some infants to fuss over would sort that out but there had been no sign of grandchildren so far.

'I did say at the time, Frederick, that I didn't like the idea.' Florence looked distraught. 'You never seem to realise what Catherine is up to until it's too late. She has been telling me all about the suffragettes; how much she admires them. We do not want her going to any of those meetings.' Florence sighed and wrung her hands in a theatrical manner. 'And there was me thinking that the suffragettes had given up their struggle for the vote whilst we are at war with Germany.'

Fred looked thoughtful; perhaps this was a dangerous situation. He tried to reassure Florence but almost upset himself in the process. 'Mrs Pankhurst and one of her daughters have given up for the duration. I believe they are living in Paris now, but there are still groups of wild young women going to meetings and protests in Cardiff, keeping the spirit of revolution alive until the war is over. Without a firm leadership, who knows what they will get up to. Perhaps our daughters would be better employed putting their energy into the war effort after all.'

The young men at Fred's office put his mind at rest eventually. They had assured him that "all the chaps" had sisters who were joining the VADs. It was quite "the thing". Besides, "they wouldn't be in France, would they? They would be quite safe in England, learning how to wind bandages and make beds, ministering angels and all that."

Frederick Waterman thought perhaps nursing would give Catherine something to focus on – maybe deflect her mind from these insufferable suffragettes. Catherine was a whirling bundle of energy – it might allow her to get this restlessness out of her soul. A couple of years doing this – fellows would be coming home. Then she could take her pick. Once she had a household to run – a few babies to supervise – all wild notions of independence and votes for women would disappear. A young woman's fancy. She couldn't come to any harm. Annie would calm her down; she was a more placid soul – feet on the ground.

Frederick informed his wife that he had made the most of his contacts at the club to find out as much as possible about the area their daughters would be going to. According to the members, Kingcharlton was a very quiet Somerset town, close to Bristol and Bath. Good place Somerset – nothing wrong with doing a spot of genteel nursing there – good hunting to be had. There was no chance of the girls being sent to France. They were merely helping to equip a new hospital for recovering soldiers.

*

The anxious soul-searching and late-night conversations between Fred and Florence had not passed unnoticed by Catherine. Although she was not privy to these comments, Catherine was astute enough to realise there would be opposition.

'I have a plan, Annie,' she told her sister whilst they were practising hairstyles for the mayor's summer ball, 'I think Father is more worried about us joining the suffragettes than learning to be nurses. If I keep mentioning how brave the suffragettes are and that women ought to have the vote, he might think that letting us enrol as VAD nurses was the better option.'

'He might,' Annie replied, her attention focused on pinning a particularly bothersome curl into place. 'I suppose you could try it and see what happens. Trouble is I don't think he likes the idea of us nursing actual soldiers.'

'I don't think we will encounter any causalities from the front for a long time yet. But it would be nice to get away from the restrictions at home for a while.' From that moment on, every time Catherine encountered her father, she neatly turned the conversation to court proceedings, hunger strikes and prison cells with force-feeding.

'I do so admire those women, Father, I have heard there is a branch of the movement starting up in Cardiff. Annie and I thought of attending one of the meetings, if we could have your permission to go.'

Finally Fred relented, allowing the girls to go for a period of VAD training. Little did he know that this was to be the first step on Catherine's imagined journey. She had no intention of returning to a life of domestic chores when the war ended. Her goal was to lead a more meaningful life – to have a career.

As she revealed to Annie when they were walking into Cardiff to pick up some material swatches for their mother. 'There is a whole world out there, Annie. I believe this war will present women with the opportunity to be more adventurous than their mothers. When the war ends, I want to train for a proper career – nursing or teaching.'

'You are such a dreamer and a planner, Catherine. I hope you won't be disappointed when we reach Somerset. The town where we will be working seems pretty rural to me.' If Annie had glanced at her sister, she would have seen a cheerful grin on Catherine's face. Leaving Cardiff was only the first step on her quest and that she had achieved. But in the end it was not Catherine's cunning plan but Annie's big blue eyes that persuaded their father to let them attend summer camp and the placement in Kingcharlton. He was certain that Annie would keep her reckless younger sister out of harm's way.

*

When Catherine awoke in a strange room, her first thought was of the mysterious soldier and his silent yet merry salute, which had haunted her restless dreams. She was not sure if this was a happy feeling or a worrying one, but one thing was certain. There must be no distractions from achieving her ambitious goals. Life had all seemed so simple until this strange encounter at Bristol Temple Meads, for no man had made such an impression on her. If it were Annie who had been so unnerved, it would be understandable because her sister was always falling in love with handsome young men.

Sun streamed in through the window as the clouds cleared. Catherine stretched out her limbs and wriggled her toes experimentally. She felt full of energy suddenly, eager to start the day, to embrace the newness of it all. This was to be a day for exploration. Last night whilst they ate their supper, Matron had spoken of their duties, ending by saying that they would be allowed time today to acquaint themselves with their surroundings. Her sister was snoring gently, her breath lifting a tiny tendril of gold hair up and down. Annie looked like a sleeping angel; the very image of a Pre-Raphaelite painting but Catherine knew from bitter experience that Annie, woken suddenly, could be a veritable devil.

Catherine could explore by herself if she was quiet. She fumbled for the clothes she had placed on the chair and hastily dressed. A few moments later, creeping down the twisting stairs towards the cottage door, she realised that Matron might be downstairs, but the room was empty. Matron must have woken very early and was now about her duties. She looked for her coat hanging on the wall but the coats had gone. Catherine shivered in the cold. There were no signs of any breakfast here, but she thought she could remember the general direction of the workhouse kitchen, pointed out to her the previous night in the moonlight.

'I'll go and see if I can find Matron to see where our coats are and if there is any breakfast to be had.' Picking up the mohair shawl she had swathed Daisy in, she wrapped it round her shoulders, grateful that she had picked it up from the hall stand at the last moment before leaving home. Her attitude to packing had always been haphazard.

By dint of trying one way and another, she found what must be the back door of the workhouse. There was nobody about to ask so she was left with no alternative but to let herself in. Once inside, she found herself in the back kitchen with numerous old coats on hooks, and a shining row of brass bells on the wall to summon help when bell pulls were operated elsewhere.

'It's just like *Alice in Wonderland*,' Catherine murmured, 'except that all the doors are the same size,' as she spotted yet another door, which surely must lead to the Cook's kitchen. Tempting aromas of something cooking, and warm wisps of hot air were wafting through the cracks in the wooden door, enticing her forward. Lifting the iron latch, she stepped over the threshold. A plump smiling woman bundled up in a huge white apron and brandishing a bowl full of batter turned to greet Catherine.

'Come in, my dear. Welcome to my kitchen.' The cheerful cook set down her bowl, pulled out a chair and dusted it down with a tea towel. Her greeting plus the warmth of the room was most welcome after the chill of the bedroom, stairs and yard.

'How are you feeling after your long journey in all that bad weather? I would not be surprised if you had taken a chill in those wet coats. I'm trying to dry them off on the clothes warmer.'

Catherine followed Cook's pointing finger, raising her eyes to a wooden rack suspended high above the kitchen, laden with drying clothes. She was surprised to see their coats carefully spread out amongst a multitude of household linen.

'Matron said to put them there, else they would never dry in all this damp.'

Catherine looked aghast at seeing her expensive garment treated this way. Would it end up smelling of porridge and cabbage?

The cook chuckled; her chubby face wreathed in wrinkly smiles. 'Don't worry, my dear. It will dry beautifully with not a crease to be seen. It's the steam that does it – as good as ironing it is.'

'Thank you, Mrs…? I had forgotten all about our coats, I was so tired last night. I think you are right about the chill. My throat feels very sore – raspy and uncomfortable. Maybe that delicious looking porridge will soothe it a little.'

The cook reached up to the mantelpiece over the fireplace to fetch down a tin. Catherine was alarmed that Cook would topple over and fall into the blazing coals, but all was well and she placed the tin in front of Catherine. 'Call me Mrs Jones; got no hubby, but they always call cooks "Mrs". Here you are, my dear. These u'll do the trick.' The cook's soft West Country burr was foreign to Catherine's ear and at times she found it difficult to understand.

Catherine opened the tin lid with its ornate pattern of delicate lilies-of-the-valley and blue forget-me-knots, unfolded the greaseproof paper inside and took a jelly cough sweet encrusted with sugar. She placed it delicately on her tongue and grimaced as the pungent flavour filled her mouth. It tasted so foul that she judged it to be very effective. No germs could possibly linger alongside it. When Cook turned to stir the porridge, she eased it out of her mouth into her handkerchief and carefully buried it in the pocket of her skirt. Two places were laid on the kitchen table, on a coarse checked cloth. The table was so vast that there was no problem taking one end of it to use as a dining area. On the other two thirds, Mrs Jones had laid out all the implements needed for the day's cooking in a very neat order.

'I expected to see Daisy helping you with the chores, Mrs Jones,' Catherine added in a conversational tone. 'We met her last night on our journey from the station.'

'Daisy's off to get some boots that fit her, poor mite. The boot store is right at the other side of the workhouse, where the men and boys work. It's kept separate you see.'

The friendly tones of the Cook and the general cosiness of what was a cavern of a kitchen impelled Catherine to ask a question that had been worrying her since she had set eyes on Daisy. 'Why doesn't Matron just use one of the girls from the workhouse to be her personal maid? There must be plenty here needing occupation.'

'Not as many nowadays, not like the old days. Since those up above changed all the rules about workhouses, the numbers have dwindled. Besides which Matron has her own ideas about how life should be organised.' Cook poured herself a strong looking brew from the teapot and sat herself down in what must be her personal chair by the warm stove, willing to impart more knowledge and have a bit of a gossip.

‘Matron doesn’t want to use girls from the workhouse because they come and go. In the summer the females can get work in the fields. In the winter they enter the workhouse to help them survive the lean months when there is no work to be had. Matron prefers to train one girl up properly, like Daisy to a certain standard, and then find her a permanent position in a suitable household nearby. They have to be committed; you see. It’s Matron’s form of charitable work.’

Cook ladled steaming porridge into a bowl and pushed a brimming sugar bowl towards Catherine.

‘There’s golden syrup if you prefer,’ added Cook. ‘Best Tate and Lyle.’

‘Ooh syrup sounds lovely, just a spoonful though.’ Catherine trickled the syrup onto the porridge in lacy patterns, bringing back memories of her childhood. She continued her interrogation between tentative mouthfuls.

‘So, she cares a lot about her charges then? One hears such awful tales about these girls.’

‘She looks after the girls well, does Matron. She gives them a good start in life. Daisy will be alright when we’ve put a bit of flesh on those bones.’ Cook returned to her vigorous beating of the batter as Catherine’s sister, Annie, staggered in, sat down and accepted a bowl of porridge. After exchanging greetings with the cook, she sat silently eating, leaving her sister to do all the talking in her usual animated manner.

Once Catherine had finished her bowl of creamy porridge, she felt much better. The warmth emanating from her well-filled belly seemed to soothe away her aches and pains. The steam issuing from the kettle, constantly simmering on the range, eased the stuffiness of her possible cold. Catherine placed her spoon tidily in the bowl and stood up. She stretched her spine and squared her shoulders as if she was eager to be off on her adventures.

'Thank you for the porridge – it was delicious. I think the pastille must be working; my throat seems a little better now.' Catherine made to hand the tin back but Mrs Jones waved it away.

'You keep hold of that, Miss. You may need it later on. All the mist in the valley makes for coughs and colds. I've got plenty of tins in the store cupboard. Matron swears by them for keeping infections at bay.' Cook winked at Catherine who wondered if this was a joke or not. She decided to ignore the comment and leave the kitchen.

'Could you fetch my coat down please? I think I might take a walk.'

The rack was hauled down with much squeaking and groaning. Catherine pulled on the warm garment and made ready to leave the kitchen to the workers and her yawning sister.

'I'll see you later, Annie, when you are wide-awake. I trust you had a good night. I know you are not one for conversation first thing in the morning. I won't bother you now – I'm off to take a brisk walk.'

Annie said nothing, only managing a slight smile before returning to her porridge.

Chapter Seven

Catherine returned to the cottage for her favourite angora beret. She found her way to the magnificent iron gates and stepped into the road they had travelled the night before. Out of the shelter of the high stone-walls, she felt a gusty breeze threaten to whip away her hat, which she had arranged at a stylish angle. She had not realised that the wind would be so strong outside in the open countryside.

'What a nuisance,' Catherine muttered, her words whisked away by the wind. 'What I need is a hatpin or even two, but I can't be bothered to go back now. I shall just have to hope it will stay on.' She pulled the offending item more firmly over her rebellious curls, hoping for the best.

From the distant fields came the clamour of hoarse unearthly cries, which she supposed must be the animals called mules that Cook had spoken about. 'Queer creatures they be, miss, a mixture of horse and donkey – that is why they make that awful noise you can hear. But they are really strong – good at pulling wagons and heavy equipment – guns and food. The Americans sent them over to help us win the war.'

Catherine made up her mind to take the path to the right so that she could see these strange mules. Their raucous bellowing voices were loud enough to guide her to their field. Striding off, the path took her along a passage between more high walls, which suddenly disappeared to display a breath-taking view of the sprawling countryside.

'This is rather different to the city streets of Cardiff, my girl,' Catherine murmured. 'It's a new experience.' With this thought uppermost in her head, she followed the rough road that slowly dwindled into a bridle path with tall hedges of hawthorn and blackberry bushes on either side. Catherine trudged along, watching carefully for swinging brambles that might catch in her hair. Underfoot, sharp stones were causing her to stumble and she almost fell a couple of times. She became so absorbed in keeping her footing that she failed to notice the two horsemen about to cross the bridle path ahead.

'Whoa there, missy! Watch out – you'll scare the horses.'

Catherine looked up to see two young men on huge, spirited beasts much too close for her liking. She took several paces back, losing her footing in her haste and almost fell backwards into a bramble bush. One of the men hastily dismounted and stood ready to help her as she was still wobbling on the uneven stones. A kindly voice expressed concern.

'Careful – slow down. I was joking. These horses are quite steady really. It would take more than a "little miss" to scare them.'

‘Who are you calling a “little miss?”’ Catherine could feel her face go rigid with indignation; she was not used to being addressed in this patronising way, much too familiar for her liking. Did these men have no manners? They looked fairly well clad, but no gentleman would address an unfamiliar lady in such a way. Not in Cardiff, they wouldn’t. These must be country bumpkins.

‘You nearly took a tumble there. Are you lost?’

Catherine pulled herself together, struggling to stand upright in a stern pose on the path that had deteriorated to a jumble of uneven stones. When she put up a hand to pat her hair into place, she realised that her beret was missing. The brambles must have grabbed the light woolly hat with their thorns and whisked it off without her realising.

Her hand encountered small twigs and leaves entwined in her curls. She could feel stray tendrils swinging on either side of her face. She grew hot; she could feel her cheeks crimson with shame. She must look so dishevelled. They would think she was a gypsy or a travelling pedlar with no facilities to keep clean or tidy. No wonder they had addressed her in such familiar terms. Words were lost to her – how to explain that she was a respectable woman.

‘Is this what you are looking for?’ One of the men was untangling her beret from the bramble hooks. He retrieved it and with utmost care, took off the debris clinging to the woollen strands. ‘Why, my sisters at home would simply love this bonnet, it’s so soft and what a pretty colour.’ He handed the beret to Catherine and smiled.

No longer afraid or affronted, she raised her eyes to his face to study him properly. She knew those brown eyes, and the friendly smile. She realised with a shock that the face grinning down at her was none other than the mystery face she had glimpsed the previous night in the flare of a phosphorous match at Temple Meads. He looked even more handsome, now that she could see more than just his twinkling eyes. Her voice wavered as she spoke.

'I confess I might be lost. I was looking for the mule field and must have taken the wrong path as I was merely following their cries. These paths are unfamiliar to me. I have come to help set up the new memorial hospital in the grounds of the workhouse. I fear I might have been a little too ambitious for my first day.' Her words tumbled out riddled now with embarrassment.

'Don't worry; we will look after you, see you back home safely. Ben Trueman at your service, Mam.' The mystery man saluted and clicked his heels together. 'This here is my friend Charley. We are back on leave staying with Charley's family. You must forgive us. It's such a different world, being in the army, living with lots of men continually on special manoeuvres, it's hard to readjust to formal ways back home.' Ben's voice had a strange lilt to it, not very strong, but there all the same. 'It's more formal back here in England,' he continued. 'I emigrated to Canada as a baby with my parents and life is so different over there. Please forgive any lack of manners on my part. I did not mean to upset or offend you. Would you like us to take you to the mule field right now? We are close by as you can tell from the noise.'

Catherine's eyes were fixed on the man's face, despite the embarrassment of their meeting. His voice sounded so repentant and kindly with its strange accent, that Catherine recovered her usual good humour and consented to walk with them a little further. She thought she better introduce herself before walking alongside them. 'My name is Catherine I'm a VAD nurse, here to help in the new hospital.'

Her body was trembling with surprise, her legs struggling to support her. Fancy meeting like this. She had believed that she would never see him again and yet here he was walking beside her. She hoped he would not interfere with her plans to be independent of all men, even if they were extremely handsome and charming.

When they reached the mule-field, she was glad she had not allowed her brief interlude of irritation to spoil things, as the first sight of the animals was truly amazing - a huge pasture full of ugly-looking creatures braying and whinnying with gusto. Who would have believed they could gather so many creatures together and send them across the sea?

'They will soon be off to France,' Ben said. 'They are really sturdy, so useful for pulling the guns and heavy equipment. But they are very cussed creatures; they need a very firm hand to get them to behave.'

'It seems you are very familiar with handling animals' Catherine shouted, striving to make herself heard over the noise of the hungry mules who had just caught sight of the hay nets being handed out.

'I come from farming stock. My family has a few acres of land just outside Vancouver – we grow all sorts there on that lovely rich soil. Good fishing there for salmon.'

'How interesting. You have had a long sea journey as well as the mules. I would love to hear more about Canada – I know so little about it – but I must be getting back. It's my first morning.'

'We'll walk you back to the hospital then, wouldn't want you getting lost again.'

The two men walked their horses alongside Catherine and left her safely back at the gates of the hospital with promises to "see you again". They remounted and trotted off to continue their ride over the fields.

Catherine watched till they were out of sight. Butterflies were "looping the loop" in her stomach with the excitement of meeting her stranger again. He was so handsome and he seemed to like her. Happiness bubbled up inside her as she thought of the days to come. As Catherine hurried through the kitchen, she passed the small girl from last night wrapped in an apron so long she looked likely to trip over it. Catherine raised a hand in greeting which the child acknowledged with a shy smile.

*

Matron who had been watching through an upstairs window, remarked to the cat with the amber eyes, 'Wonders will never cease; Miss Catherine has already made the acquaintance of two of the Major's guests. She is a very independent person and no mistake. We are going to have our hands full with this one, Hector.'

She then returned to her task of placing lavender bags between the clean sheets in the linen press and turned her thoughts to more important matters concerning the running of the workhouse such as whether she could persuade the village elders to allow her more money for books for the children and daily milk for the toddlers to help build them up for the coming winter.

Chapter Eight - 2016

'Right Wellington, there is only one option now. We have to go to the allotment field and find out what has happened to Gerry's patch.' Lizzy reached for the dog's lead. Wellington had become accustomed to the random system of walks. Slowly emerging from his hidey-hole in the tunnel between the sofa and the radiator, he shook his head with pleasure at the rattle of the chain lead and the sound of the keys being lifted off the hook.

The iron gates to the allotment stood open. Number thirteen was Gerry's patch. Lizzy was quivering with fear that Gerry's allotment would be a disgrace to his memory. All his years of hard work would be ruined.

'Nearly there, Wellington, what will we find?' Suddenly Lizzy stopped abruptly, bewildered at what she saw. Number thirteen was a model allotment of neatly dug furrows, an oblong of reddish-brown soil, not a weed in sight. What a surprise! This patch was definitely not neglected. It was neat, tidy and ready to be planted in the spring. The freshly turned rows of earth were evidence of somebody's backbreaking work over many months. All looked in order – how could it be? She checked the sign again – thirteen.

They must have already given it to someone else. Lizzy had let Gerry down. She had not cared for his prized possession. As tears rolled down her cheeks, she let the lead drop and Wellington began to plod towards to his favourite patch by the shed at the back to lie down and bask in the autumnal sun.

'No, Wellington, stop,' she called, stumbling after him almost blinded by her tears. 'Come back, it's not ours any longer. Come back.'

'Nay, lass, don't fret so – let him be. He'll do no harm. He knows which way to go.'

Lizzy gazed through tear-filled eyes at the man standing in front of her, a man with a kind face offering her a neatly folded handkerchief. He seemed about her age, stocky with broad shoulders. She stood transfixed – unseated – bereft – unnerved – stripped of pretence – just grieving for the space where Gerry should be. Above her the pigeons cooed and things skittered in the hedgerows of hazel and hawthorn. A distant hum from a log-sawing machine blurred the air. Somewhere at the top end a bonfire was burning, its smoke evoking memories of bonfire nights and autumn days.

'Nay, lass, come along, come by here, follow the dog; he knows the way. There's a seat.'

Lizzy allowed herself to be guided, as there really was no other option. All willpower had gone, no need for action. She was dependent on the kindness of a stranger.

'Sit there – it's clean – sit and drink this. Don't worry – it won't poison you.'

Don't care if it does, thought Lizzy, *I'd be glad to go now to join Gerry.* The proffered cup contained coffee; hot and very sweet but strangely comforting. She stared at the cup.

'It's my little luxury – condensed milk – a trick of my dad's, left over from the war. They used it because it was sweet as well as milky. Came in tins. Bad for you, I suppose, but my little luxury. Keeps me going – a little treat now and again. Drink it down – won't do you any harm. Biscuit here if you want it. There you are, Wellington – a bit for you too.'

The continual patter of words uttered in a soft North Country burr combined with the hot sweet coffee soothed Lizzy's jangling nerves. Her heart slowed to a gentler beat. She dabbed at her eyes with his hanky, soft and sweet-smelling like a baby's muslin-square fresh from the laundry.

'But the allotment! It's so neat! Who did they give it to?'

'Nay lass, it's thine still – paid up till February.'

'But it's tidy - all that time since Gerry died – should be all weeds, should be messy.'

'I've been keeping it together, alongside your family who helped where they could. They paid the fees. Knew you'd want it kept neat – "shipshape and Bristol fashion" just like Gerry kept it. We all knew you would come eventually. There, there, lass, don't take on so.'

A fresh flood of tears engulfed Lizzy. All this love, all this care, even though she had been unaware of it, was still there working away.

'Let me introduce myself properly. The name's Tom, Tom Weatherspoon,' the kindly man informed her as he poured more of his fragrant brew into her cup. 'That's my allotment next door. Took it over a few years ago, when my Alice died. Your Gerry helped me, so it was only right that I helped him by looking after his allotment.' His blue eyes lit up with a smile that emphasised the laughter lines of his face.

Lizzy sat silent sipping her coffee, enjoying the September sun's heat on her face. The warmth was seeping into her bones and filling her whole being with a feeling of contentment. Looking around as she relaxed, she could see a familiar face in the distance beaming at her and waving frantically. She racked her memory to place him. It was Ken Roberts, one of Gerry's partners at the Bridge Club. Since Gerry's early demise he had offered to take her out for a meal a couple of times but had given up when she'd showed no sign of joining him.

How rude she had been. She would have to invite him round for coffee to make up for that rudeness. *This would be an ideal opportunity to speak to him,* thought Lizzy, *on neutral ground.* She pointed him out to Tom.

'I really ought to have a word with Ken over there, Tom, if you don't mind. He was a friend of Gerry's. He was trying to be kind to me but I kept rebuffing him. Time to make things right again.'

'You go over, lass. It's a good place, the allotment, for chatting and making things right. You stay here, Wellington. Here, have another bit of biscuit.'

*

Lizzy strode down the narrow grass path and up to Ken who was watching her progress. He was leaning on his spade, watched by a cheeky robin hopping closer in anticipation of a tasty worm.

'How are you, Lizzy? Haven't seen you out and about for a long time. So sorry about Gerry, we had some great evenings at the Bridge Club. I thought of calling in, but you always seemed so distant.'

Ken's face was so creased with concern that Lizzy felt uncomfortable. She had no idea why this happened whenever he was trying to be kind. She steeled herself to engage in conversation.

'I feel I've been rather rude, but I needed to be on my own. I'm feeling better now. Perhaps we could meet up for coffee and cake in Costa, my treat for all your kindness.' She didn't feel like inviting him to the house.

'I have a better suggestion.' Ken beamed.

Of course, he would, Lizzy thought, *he was that kind of man, always in control of any situation. I think we are talking as equals and then he takes charge.*

Ken continued. 'I'll treat you instead, how about a slap-up meal at The Old Forge? They do a fantastic steak and chips there with all the trimmings. Superb puddings. Liqueurs afterwards. It's been so long since we talked. I can bring you up to speed about all my news. My son's emigrated to Australia with his family – wonderful lifestyle they have out there – huge bungalow and pool.' Ken chortled at his brilliant idea and seemed to be waiting for her approval.

Lizzy felt instantly overwhelmed. *That's why he makes my spine prickle,* she thought, *he has to be in charge even when he's trying to be kind and thoughtful.* She could not go for a long-drawn-out meal and have to listen to his monologue for hours.

She was not eating much anyway. She could not face more than a bowl of soup and a piece of toast. Why did some people think that what would be a treat for them would also be a treat for her? Ken was totally lacking in empathy. How could she extract herself from this situation with kindness?

'That's very thoughtful of you, Ken.' She forced herself into a radiant smile to ease the pain of refusal. 'But I'm afraid I am not up to such a grand affair just yet. That's why I suggested coffee and maybe a doughnut.'

'Yes, yes, I quite understand, dear lady. What say we compromise and make it afternoon tea in The Copper Kettle in Bath? One of those glass towers with sandwiches, scones and cakes. They give you a doggy box for anything you can't manage, so no problems there.'

Ken was obviously fond of his food and of getting value for money. Lizzy grimaced inwardly and felt tempted to hit him. Why do people ask you what you want and then try to change it? Why had she started this conversation when she'd been feeling so happy chatting to Tom? Why this constant compulsion to do what was right and not what she really wanted to do?

Lizzy glanced back at Tom, sitting happily on his battered old chair, sipping that syrupy coffee – a picture of contentment. She thought she would rather spend a day in his company than an hour with this irritating man. Her thoughts shut out the drone of Ken's voice: *wouldn't it be nice to work on Gerry's allotment with Tom for company whenever I want. He has been so helpful; I feel much more cheerful.*

Gerry's old flask must still be at the back of the cupboard, I must look it out to use for coffee breaks. Wellington likes it up here as well. She surveyed the great expanse of freshly dug ground ready for the winter frosts to break it down into friable soil. The crumbly earth ready for planting turned her thoughts to seed packets with brightly coloured pictures – that would give her something to plan out and ponder over on the long winter nights to come. Yes, taking care of Gerry's allotment would do her good – stop her brooding and get some of that weight off.

But first she had to sort out her present problem: Ken Roberts. Why had she started that conversation? Why had she not left it all alone? She had never taken to him before. But she had started it, so now she would have to make the best of it and ease away gently.

'Cream tea would be lovely. When would you like to go?'

'I'll have to check my diary and give you a ring. Busy, busy, busy, dear lady. You know me!'

'Yes, I do,' Lizzy muttered under her breath, 'and I shall know to avoid you in the future.'

She strolled back to Tom and accepted his offer of another cup of coffee. Sitting in a sagging battered chair sipping nectar, she put all thoughts of her dentist's issues with sugar to the back of her mind and said to Wellington, asleep on a potato sack, 'Maybe life's not so bad after all – perhaps I could make some flapjack to share.' It had been a long time since Lizzy had felt like baking.

Lizzy bent down to clip a reluctant Wellington onto his lead, he was not keen to leave his spot in the sun and looked hopefully around to see if another biscuit might appear. As Lizzy turned to thank Tom for all his hospitality, she was suddenly struck with a thought so blatantly obvious she could not believe she had been so dense.

'Tom, I don't suppose you have some tool that could prise open an old tin? I know this sounds silly but a rather unusual object has come into my possession: an old-fashioned pastille tin.'

Tom stopped what he was doing to give her his full attention.

'I expect I could find something; depends whether you want brute force or gentle handling. Is it precious?'

'I don't know. It's not precious to me. I found it lying battered in the road. I think it might be Victorian or Edwardian, part of the rubble from the demolished workhouse. An overloaded lorry taking the debris away dropped it in front of me. I wondered what was inside when I spotted some initials scratched on the tin. I felt compelled to take it home.'

She laughed, feeling her cheeks grow hot with embarrassment. 'Of course, after all this time passing, the lid was jammed on so tightly that I could not shift it at all. I went to look in the shed for Gerry's tools and then I remembered the allotment. I was afraid it was neglected or gone to a new owner so I left the tin on the kitchen table and rushed up here. Now I feel at a bit of a loss as to how to proceed.'

Tom made no effort to tease her about her strange fancies. He looked very serious. 'I could have a try, lass, if that would make you happy. You say Gerry left a shed full of tools? Bet I could find something there to open that tin. I was going to toddle off home soon. How about I pack up now, come back with you and I'll see what I can do? No urgent tasks waiting at home for me.'

Lizzy sat down again whilst Tom closed up the shed and picked up his bag. As she and Wellington wended their way down the gravel path with Tom, something made her turn to look back. Ken Roberts was watching her with a bewildered expression.

'Do come on, Wellington, you can't possibly want to sniff anymore.'

Progress was slow as Wellington's legs wobbled along but it was a bonny morning, a taster of St Luke's little summer that would grace them in October. Lizzy was enjoying the walk home at first, but she was gradually taken aback by the numerous changes around her. New houses had sprung up in back gardens and enormous ultra-modern extensions clung to the side of older buildings, both of which seemed out of place in this neighbourhood. Kingcharlton was no longer the quiet little town she had grown up in. Her childhood home had been sold to fund her mother's stay in the nursing home. Her father had a plot in the cemetery. There were no brothers and sisters to share the burden. Oh, how she missed Gerry!

'It's not like it used to be when I first moved here from the north.' Tom's gentle voice shook Lizzy out of her reverie. She thought he must have guessed that her mood was becoming sombre. *I must snap out of this,* she thought. *I must think about the happy time at the allotment. I can't let my mind travel down the sad path.*

'No, it's not, Tom, times change. We have to accept that. Not far now and we can see what is in my tin. I appreciate you helping me like this.' She turned to give him a sunny smile to reassure him that she was back on track.

'It's no bother. I'm looking forward to seeing if there is treasure in this find of yours'.

Tom sounded rather sad himself and she hoped she had not infected him with her low mood. She sensed the loneliness in his voice, feeling ashamed of her selfishness when she had family to visit her. Ushering Tom into the kitchen, she pointed out the tin, sitting on a piece of newspaper in the middle of the table. Her confidence dipped at the sight of the small rusting object. Was she being foolish? Would it be full of dirt? Was it a health hazard? A million questions fluttered around her mind like butterflies round a buddleia. Her confidence ebbed; she was nervously waiting for him to say something. Was she being silly? It wasn't junk, was it? Not a harbinger of happiness but merely a discarded item? Should she just put it in the bin and get on with something useful? Why had she brought this kind man all the way here? He must think she was mad. Perhaps she was.

'Here we are, Tom. This is the mystery object. It looks rather small and insignificant all of a sudden. But when I saw it fall off the lorry, I felt for a brief moment that something magical was happening, something good for a change, if you know what I mean…' Her voice trailed off wistfully.

Tom picked the tin up and tried to pull the lid off. It was stuck tight.

'Don't give up hope of there being hidden treasure inside. Wait till we have wrestled it open. At the very least we have made friends, had a lovely chat at the allotment, good start to the day, I would say. Is that Gerry's shed at the bottom of the garden? Is it unlocked? I'll wander down and see if I can find a suitable tool for the job. Come on, Wellington, you can show me the way.'

Lizzy watched Tom and Wellington toddle down the path, open the shed door and disappear inside.

'He has a reassuring presence,' she muttered, 'a sort of gravitas and yet I know nothing about him.'

A few moments later, the companions emerged. Tom was chatting to Wellington and encouraging him along. Lizzy took a good look at her new friend. He had the sort of face that was genial in repose so that he seemed to look happy all the time. His face was tanned – he must spend a lot of time at the allotment or have been on a foreign holiday recently. He wiped his feet on the mat, tidy as well.

The tin was stubborn; it took a lot of persuading and some oil round the edges, to ease the lid off. Tom persisted slowly with able fingers. Wellington fell asleep in his basket whilst Lizzy watched and relaxed. Finally Tom was able to ease the lid off with no damage. Lizzy cleared away the debris and mud fragments, making a newspaper parcel and dropping it in the bin. Clean paper was spread out underneath the tin whose contents were now exposed.

'Go on, lass, take it all out and we can see what we've got here. At least it's not just mud and stones.'

Chapter Nine

One by one, Lizzy lifted out the contents with the utmost caution and laid them gently on the kitchen table. The tin must have been lined with tissue paper, now mere shreds. There were sepia photos, very small – they fitted snugly inside the tin without being folded, a beige postcard with a printed stamp of King George, one or two letters on thin paper, and something more solid – black, metallic and ugly.

'Look, Tom, I've no idea what this can be,' Lizzy placed the mystery object carefully to one side. 'We'll leave it for last, shall we?'

They peered at the photos one by one: three mini pictures. Lizzy had to find her reading glasses to see them in detail. The first one showed a girl with a solemn look, wearing what must be a nurse's uniform, a huge white apron with a red cross on her apron front and a headdress like an enormous white tablecloth. It looked very uncomfortable and rather impractical. Next was a photo of a young man, also solemn – the photographer must have told him to look serious when wearing his uniform.

'That doesn't look like a British soldier standing there. It's the cap I think, a different shape altogether to what our lads wore.' Tom uttered thoughtfully.

The soldier had complied with the order to look serious but there was a twinkle in his eyes plus the hint of a smile on his mouth that belied the pose he had adopted. This man had a sense of humour. The last photo showed the couple together in civilian garb. They were both smiling broadly, almost laughing as if the photographer had told a joke. There was something about their faces and body language that spoke of intimacy and friendship.

'Don't you think, Tom, that they look like a couple, even though they are not touching. But it's not easy to see their features in these small photos. I think what we need is a magnifying glass.' Lizzy looked disappointed.

'Hang on a minute – cheer up. I think I have something here that might do the job. I need this little beauty to read all the small print, nowadays.' Tom produced a folding magnifying glass from one of his many pockets. 'Let's see if it's any use.'

'She's very pretty and he is equally handsome,' Lizzy scrutinised the couple, 'they make a smart looking pair. She looks rather familiar but I don't know where I've seen that face before. Maybe she has some relatives in the town. Some families can trace their ancestors back through many generations.'

She turned over the photos to see if anyone had written on the back. 'Look, Tom, this is so interesting.' Lizzy's voice squeaked with excitement as she moved the glass over the writing. 'The nurse is called Catherine Waterman – the year nineteen seventeen – the location Kingcharlton. Do you want to try with the next photo, Tom, as it's your magnifying glass?'

'No, it's your tin, you look. I expect your eyes are better than mine.'

'The soldier is called Ben Trueman, same date in Kingcharlton. They look as if they were all taken at the same time. I wonder if it was a professional studio or whether an amateur took them with his own camera and developed them himself? People were very keen on photography at that time.'

On the back of the third photo where the two characters stood together, was the message*: With the compliments of Charley Bowmaker*.

'Looks like a friend who had an interest in photography, someone who took these photos for two sweethearts being parted by the war.' Tom was still studying the man's uniform. 'It's the hat that's wrong, definitely not British. I have family photos of relatives in WW1. If we could blow this up a little, it might become clearer. Or we could look it up on the Internet – search for soldiers wearing uniforms.'

Next for inspection was a thin white postcard with a sentimental message of some sort, most of it faded beyond legibility. All that remained was "your loving Mother". The address on the front was better preserved – Miss C Waterman, The Memorial Hospital, Kingcharlton, alongside a red stamp. The postal mark over the stamp showed "Cardiff" quite clearly.

'How very odd,' Lizzy muttered, a puzzled look on her face, 'I have a very faint recollection of distant relatives in Wales called Waterman. There was a falling out. I've never met them, my father denied all knowledge of any disputes, long before I was born, and as my grandparents were based in Manchester, the matter was never resolved. It can't be them, too much of a coincidence.'

Lizzy's slender fingers reached out for the ugly black object. 'What on earth is this? I've never seen anything like it – it looks so black and dirty. What is it?

'Wait a minute, Lizzy, it might be silver, let me buff it up a bit. Lack of attention would turn it black. We need a proper silver cloth really, but we could see if it is worth working on.' Tom turned it over and over very gently in his capable hands.

Lizzy said nothing but reached for the roll of kitchen paper and they set to work rubbing the tiny trinket as if to produce a genie out of a lamp. 'I think you're right, Tom. It might well be silver. But what is it? There's this little ring on the side. Is it meant to be hung on a chain or something?'

'It could have been hung on a chain. I have an idea what it might be but let's continue. I don't want to raise your hopes unduly. It needs that silver cloth to bring it to its original condition. I'll pick one up when I go shopping.' Tom was still patiently working away. His efforts gradually revealed engraved patterns and the edge of a lid at the top near the ring.

'Look, we should be able to open it but it's stuck at the moment. Let me try some oil to loosen it.' Back to the shed again he went for something suitable for dealing with stubborn lids. Tom's careful fingers finally eased the object open to reveal tiny matches with white stems and red heads.

'I know what it is,' Tom beamed with recognition, 'I've seen one of these before. It's a *Vesta* case to wear on a pocket watch chain. Soldiers used them in wartime to protect their matches from the damp. That wouldn't be your average Tommy. This must have belonged to an officer. It's not only functional but ornamental as well, it can be worn as a fob on a gentleman's watch chain. You often see them in old photos, like the ones you have there. But what's it doing in this box? You've uncovered a real mystery here, Lizzy.'

Lizzy was impressed – not only was Tom extremely practical but knowledgeable as well. 'Wait a minute, what about this letter, it's got hidden under the newspaper,' she said, holding out the page to Tom. 'It's got a signature – "Your Canadian chum, Benjamin Trueman." The letter had been written on January fifteenth, nineteen seventeen. The middle message was indecipherable, the letters rubbed out by the folding and creasing of the paper and the debris gathered inside. This was truly a mystery from the past, one hundred years old.

'Wow, I never expected to find all this,' Lizzy gasped. 'It really is a challenge – a tin full of clues. If you study those little black and white photos, it appears to be a correspondence between a Welsh nurse and a Canadian soldier. This letter is dated nineteen seventeen – what happened to them in the war? Did they survive? We have addresses and some names.'

Lizzy spread all the photos and letters out in front of her and studied them intently.

'How can we find out more, Tom? I want to know why this tin with personal possessions ended up in the debris of the workhouse. Did it belong to one of these people? Why did they leave it there? I know the workhouse was changed into a maternity hospital in 1948 when the National Health started. But is it possible that there was a hospital or a recuperation facility there during the First World War? Those sorts of places sprang up all over the country to help the wounded soldiers. And did these two people meet up again?'

Tom looked up from his perusal of one of the letters. 'You could start by joining the local history group. If they don't know the answers, they could point you in the right direction. Would you like me to take you along and introduce you?'

'Would they let me join though?' Lizzy's face drooped.

'They would welcome you with open arms, especially if you show them the tin. They're a very friendly bunch. The members know all sorts of interesting stuff about the First World War, like the history of that field where the allotments are now. That was where they kept the mules sent over by the Americans to help pull the war equipment.'

Tom kept working as he talked, equally absorbed in his physical task and the sharing of local knowledge. The shabby *Vesta* case began to glitter in the sunlight. Lizzy sat silently watching, soothed by the northern burr of his voice and the motion of his hands bringing the matchbox to life.

'They sent hundreds over, but many died on the boats – they did not fare well on the long sea journey.

The ones that survived walked from the station to the allotment field where they rested and were fattened up ready to travel to France. I know you probably don't want to know about mules, but it demonstrates how the history club members delve deep into the First World War.'

Lizzy smiled. 'Poor mules. I wonder if they were there when that nurse in the photo was there, working in the hospital? Yes, I'd love to join, if they'll have me. What day do they meet? Who would I have to contact?'

'They hold their meetings in the village hall, the old one, near the recreation ground. What do you think? Do you want to come along with me next Monday? Do you need my support? I don't want to intrude but I'm willing to help.'

'It's a start, Tom. I'd love you to come with me; I hate going to places on my own. Another thing I could do to solve the mystery is to pay my mother a visit in her nursing home. Her memory comes and goes but I could try to find out about those relatives in Cardiff. It's odd they have the same surname. I might go this afternoon. Do you fancy a run out, Tom?'

'I think not. Mothers and daughters get on best on their own. Another time perhaps, if you want company.'

Lizzy fetched an old shoebox to keep her treasure safe. What could she remember about that longstanding feud? If only her mother was in a good mood and ready to be helpful. As a child, Lizzy overheard whispered conversations about family matters that ended as she entered the room. Who could she ask, now that her mother was losing her memory?

When Lizzy reversed her car down the drive with Wellington sitting on the back seat, she felt familiar fear rippling through her stomach. How would her mother be? Would she be lucid and kind, or vague, aggressive and horrible?

Chapter Ten - 1916

'Catherine, I would like to speak to you and your sister. Please come to my room when you have finished your breakfast.'

Matron's face gave no indication of what she wanted to discuss – whether it would be good news or bad. Catherine was of the opinion that Matron had misgivings about the level of commitment of volunteers, often from well-to-do families. She desperately hoped that she and her sister had performed adequately. A few of the girls that Catherine had encountered did seem to regard the whole war thing as a bit of a lark. Always at the back of Catherine's mind was the realisation that she and Annie would have to prove themselves to be given any respect. Catherine had been working as hard as she could to prove to Matron that she had every intention of becoming a nurse. She knew what she wanted: the chance to be allowed to travel to the battlefields to nurse the wounded.

The happy bubbly feelings that she was moving towards this goal, day by day, and that Ben Trueman was not far away, were soured by the irritating fact that Annie was not as committed as she was and that this might affect Catherine's chances of achieving her dream. The smile vanished from her face and she ran her fingers through her red curls making a veritable bird's nest of them. *What could she do about Annie whose enthusiasm was waning by the day?* Catherine marched up and down the room with frustration. She hoped Matron was not going to scold them.

There must be a way to overcome the problem. Catherine could not let all her plans be foiled by Annie's attitude. This was her chance to escape the tedium of an idle life with endless days of shopping, visiting and leaving their calling cards. It was the opportunity to prove that girls, when properly educated, were just as capable in all roles in life as boys. Catherine had always felt that she was every bit as clever as her male relatives, yet nobody would ever take her seriously. Gradually she came to the conclusion that the best way forward was to follow her own path, be the best she could and leave Annie to follow her chosen path.

'I have called you in to say that you have been working very hard and I am extremely pleased with the effort you have put in.' Matron always believed in the carrot and not the stick. 'Also, I have here an invitation for both of you.' She handed a thick cream envelope to Annie as she was the older sister.

'Many of the local landowners want to support the war effort by providing comforts for the young officers when they are sent home on leave. One of these is Major Bowmaker. He keeps hunters in the stables so that they can go out with the hounds. His wife, Arabella, holds tea parties to which she invites friends in the area to come and converse with these brave boys before they have to return to their duties at the Front. You have been invited because you seem to be suitable young ladies for this task.'

*

The old grey mare took up a fast pace as she pulled the carriage on a circular driveway towards the farmhouse. No doubt she was looking forward to the warm stable and bulging hay net.

'What a beautiful house,' Catherine exclaimed, 'we must mind our manners here.'

'How grand it is,' Annie sighed. 'It makes a pleasing change from the grim old workhouse and those endless fields full of cabbages.'

As the mare came to a halt alongside the front door, it was pulled open and a figure clad in tweeds filled the doorway.

'Welcome, welcome, let me help you down, ladies. Don't want to get those pretty outfits torn!' bellowed a stern looking military figure, 'So you are the nurses who are coming to help Matron set up the hospital.'

'That must be the Major,' whispered Catherine. 'He looks a bit like Father, but much stricter.'

The Major did appear to be very similar to their father in terms of hospitality and attitudes to life in general. Ladies were delicate and needed looking after. Men should be bluff and hearty, and appear totally in charge of the situation, no matter what chaos the world was in. A British gentleman was always in charge.

The two sisters were ushered into a long stone-flagged passageway, as wide as a room that stretched from front door to back door. The walls were festooned with a variety of hooks for coats for all weathers, whilst the floor was crowded with boots of all sizes and descriptions.

'Typical Somerset farmhouse!' the Major bellowed as if he was addressing the soldiers on the battlefield. 'Fellow can go from back to front without taking mud into the house. Come through into the warm.' He threw open a door to the right and ushered them into a very comfortable room with a blazing log fire. The girls surveyed the room and walked forward. Annie grasped Catherine's hand, whispering:

'Look, Catherine, it seems very genteel. I am so glad that I brought some decent clothes with me. Who knows what kind of people we will meet today?' Annie turned away in order to pinch her cheeks into a becoming blush, then shaking her curls into place put on her most winning smile for the company who would soon arrive. Catherine could see Annie had already perked up from her low mood and was flirting with Major Bowmaker in her usual way.

Annie is so different to me, Catherine thought; *she likes her home comforts too much. She's far too interested in homely occupations to be a nurse. The vogue for making knitted comforts for the troops has captured her imagination.* Catherine recalled all the pictures her sister had shown her of famous figures wielding their knitting needles. The women's magazines were full of them: stars of the silver screen knitting whilst waiting to be called on set; royal princesses knitting socks on four needles;

elegant ladies in cocktail dresses carrying exotic needle cases and wool bags. Piles of knitted comforts for the boys were being produced all over the country. It was quite the done thing to be seen at any social event with a glamorous knitting bag on an arm and a half-finished sock in your hands.

I'm not going back home to all that stifling femininity, Catherine thought, *I intend to go to the Front to nurse wounded soldiers. Then when the war is over, I am going to do something sensible with my life.* Comforted by this assertion of her intentions, she smoothed down her skirts and stepped forward to enter into this new world.

An elegant well-dressed lady rose from one of the flowery sofas and introduced herself as Arabella, the wife of Major Bowmaker.

'So lovely to meet you, my dears, and how charming you look. We are very pleased to have your company today to help us entertain our courageous boys, back home from the battle preparations. They will be arriving shortly, but we thought it would be nice to get to know you first before they come. It can be a little awkward as it is only a short time since they were living in the barracks and sometimes it takes a little while for them to adjust to polite society.'

'Thank you for inviting us. It is so marvellous to be in your beautiful drawing room after staying in Matron's cottage, which is very nice but very small and right next to that gloomy workhouse.' Catherine was taken aback at this bold and rather impolite statement by Annie who was wide eyed with admiration for the quality of decoration in the room and the elegant way in which Arabella was dressed.

'The Major and I feel that it is the very least we can do for King and Country. Dear Monty wanted so much to go himself but he sustained a very bad leg injury in the Boer War. Now we have to content ourselves with providing events like this afternoon to cheer up the boys on leave. We were delighted when you arrived to help in our hospital for the wounded men.' Arabella beamed at the two sisters.

'Please forget my sister's impulsive speech.' Catherine frowned at Annie and tried to convey an unspoken message. 'Matron has been most solicitous of our comfort but after all we have volunteered for VAD service so we have to live like proper nurses would. Working in the new premises is very exciting, a real chance to make a contribution to the war effort.'

'Oh no, I didn't mean to imply that Matron had not looked after us well.' Annie was blushing. It was clear to Catherine that Annie was overcome with mortification at her thoughtless words, she was the epitome of kindness but rarely thought before she spoke, and she was obviously missing her Cardiff home more and more.

Annie continued with her embarrassed explanation. 'It's just that we are so used to living in a nice big house with lots of home comforts and I do so miss our dear Mama and all the tea parties she would throw, and all the shopping trips and the pretty dresses. I fear you will think me very frivolous and I do want to help, but I am not the same as Catherine. When she puts her mind to a task, she always seems to succeed. I have followed her into this without much thought as usual.' Annie was becoming quite distressed; her big blue eyes were brimming with tears.

Arabella patted her arm gently and offered a lacy handkerchief. 'There, there, my dear. I understand. You are just a little homesick and it is a compliment to your mother that she has made such a comfortable home for you. Whatever you say here will remain between us. We are all made in different moulds and God may have a different task for you in this conflict. There is no disgrace in wanting to be a homemaker, with a husband and children, providing comfort and support for those soldier husbands.

'Sometimes I think that too many women are being encouraged to be modern and bold, abandoning their mother's ways. By the look of you, I would say that your mother has made a very good job of bringing you up, both of you, my dears.' Arabella took Annie's hands in hers and squeezed them for encouragement.

Annie replied in a wobbly tearful voice: 'I think that I have followed Catherine blindly for too long. This separation from our parents and their home has taught me that I have to make my own decisions and that does not mean, Catherine, leaving home but instead staying at home with Mother and Father with the hope that one day I will have a home with a husband and a life as good as theirs.'

Catherine, for once, was lost for words. Here was her sister, not following in her turbulent wake, but standing her ground and expressing her own opinions. What she said made a lot of sense too.

Catherine could not really imagine Annie in any sort of hospital, dealing with wounds and dying men.

'Sit down, my dears, and compose yourselves. Let me ring for the maid and ask her to fetch us some tea before our special guests arrive. We wouldn't want them to see us all in tears, would we?'

Catherine watched with trepidation as a very small maid staggered in with a heavily laden tea tray.

'I'm training her to be a parlour maid,' Arabella lowered her voice, 'but it's proving to be a very difficult task with this one. She is all fingers and thumbs; she keeps chipping my best china. She's come over from Ireland and is very sweet and willing, but I think she would rather be outside helping the Major with his horses than here in my parlour.'

'I thought all the horses had been requisitioned?' Catherine replied. 'The carter was saying that most of the good ones had been taken away to go to France for the troops. Unless they had vital duties to fulfil, of course.'

'The Major has been allowed to keep his hunters so that our boys can ride out with the hounds. And the little grey mare that brought you here is kept for social occasions such as this one. It is important to keep up the morale of the officers and it is felt by those in authority that the kind of rest and recreation that we can offer here is a worthy cause. Our own son always says that it is the thought of coming home to his hunter Nimrod that takes him through his darkest moments. You will be meeting him soon.'

A thought flashed briefly across Catherine's mind of Daisy's brothers who had apparently been signed up and shipped off to France. This aspect of war seemed totally removed from the concept of visits home for hunting and afternoon tea, but surely it would all be the same when they were together in the trenches. The war seemed to be very different in practice to what she had been expecting. There still seemed to be the concept of the class system and people knowing their place in life even when they were fighting side by side. Her thoughts were interrupted by the arrival of a group of young men who edged rather sheepishly into the room, clutching their headgear in both hands. The Major was chatting and laughing with them obviously trying to make them feel at home.

'Where's the maid, what's she up to now? Nelly, Nelly where are you? Come and take these gentlemen's caps and put them on the hall table.'

The tiny maid scuttled in and seized their caps. Catherine wondered if they would ever get the right ones back again.

'I thought she was Irish? Nelly doesn't sound like an Irish name,' Catherine asked Arabella.

'I found her real name too difficult to pronounce so I have rechristened her, Nelly. We can manage better with that one.'

Catherine thought that this must have caused a great deal of confusion for the little waif and would probably account for her baffled behaviour.

'They come and go with such regularity, these Irish maids, always off to somewhere better, that I christen them all Nelly, it saves me having to remember their real names. Never mind about that, my dear, there are more important matters to attend to. Let me introduce you to one of our boys from overseas, a Canadian whose grandparents came from Wales originally. He will adore your Welsh accent.'

Catherine was not listening. She was worried about a frill on her dress, which had become entangled with a metal fastener on her dimity bag. It could cause great damage – pulling the entire frill off. How her mother would scold her if this happened. She looked up and gasped, for there were the two soldiers she had met on her walk. They must have been the last men to enter the room. This was the third time she was gazing into those melted chocolate brown eyes. Her cheeks grew so hot that she imagined people would think she had been at the rouge pot.

'Hello again, I hardly recognised you in your uniforms.' Looking very flustered, she turned to her hostess. 'Arabella, I met these two gentlemen during a walk I took exploring on my first day here in Kingcharlton. I don't expect they will recognise me for I had lost my hat in the brambles and I must have looked like a scarecrow.' Catherine suddenly realised that she was talking too much, gabbling like a silly goose. It was the pleasure of meeting Ben again so soon.

Ben's handsome face broke into a grin. 'Why, it's lovely to see you again. I enjoyed our little trip to the mule field. Being in England is so strange: both familiar and unfamiliar. And this must be your sister, Annie. How do you do, Annie?'

As Ben leant forward to grasp Annie's hand, Catherine realised that the two of them had broken the etiquette of introductions, as the others had been left standing whilst she conversed with Ben. She looked round to see Arabella smiling at her, and Ben's companion had a huge silly grin spread all over his face. Catherine's instant attraction to Ben had not gone unnoticed.

'Would you like a cup of tea?' Arabella returned to her hostess duties, handing Ben a fragile eggshell cup that looked as if it might be crushed in his sturdy soldier's hands. He whispered to Catherine as Arabella moved away to speak to the other men. 'Is this how you all take tea in the afternoon? I come from a farm – my parents' place outside of Vancouver is very plain compared to this. My mom would surely love all these pretty little cups, she doesn't get to do much entertaining like this.'

Catherine could see him struggling with the silver tongs. The sugar lumps kept slipping away. 'May I help you? They are difficult to manage.'

Ben handed the implement to Catherine as if it were burning his fingers, like a hot iron poker emerging from the furnace.

'Will this be sufficient for you?' she murmured as she popped two sugar lumps into his tea without any splash at all. 'They don't take tea like this every afternoon. This is all for your benefit, to thank you for coming to fight our war with us. It's meant to cheer you up and send you back to the Front refreshed.' Catherine found herself trembling at the closeness of this handsome stranger.

'It's a bit overwhelming for me.' Ben breathed a sigh of relief now the sugar bowl and tongs had been taken away 'Hey, you know what? The Major has hunters in his stables. We were exercising them the other day when we met you. Would you like to take a look at them? I wish I could show you my own horse. I've left a beauty back at home. Not a hunter, but I ride her all the time on the farm. Many, many miles to cover, only way it can be managed is on horseback.'

Ben seemed to be less nervous now the subject had turned to horses and he became quite animated, telling Catherine all about the mare he had left behind. It was a world that Catherine was not acquainted with but she realised that if she just listened to Ben's tales, it would give some comfort to this soldier, far away from home and all familiar objects.

It was not long before they found themselves walking towards the stables, wrapped up warmly: Catherine in an extra borrowed shawl and Ben in his sturdy soldier's coat for it was chilly outside. The temperature inside the stables was better, as the fragrant hay bales stacked in one corner and the heat from the horses' bodies provided some warmth. Catherine found the smell of mown hay mingled with a strong smell of horse was strangely comforting.

'Why, it's quite cosy in here,' she said at which Ben chuckled and pronounced: 'Best place in the world – a well-run stable.' At the sound of their voices, velvet noses popped out of their stalls inquisitive to see who their visitors were. White doves overhead cooed on the rafters and there was a feeling of calm away from the formal activity of the drawing room.

The Major appeared at their sides, his face beaming with pleasure to see a fellow rider admiring his horses. 'Would you like to take one out again for some cross-country one day, Ben? I understand that you are not used to hunting. What about you, young lady? We could find a gentle one for you if you wanted to show this young man some of our Somerset countryside.'

Catherine smiled warily. She had very little experience of horses and found them rather daunting. But if spending time on horseback meant she could see Ben again, she would have to learn to ride pretty quickly.

Chapter Eleven - 2016

Lizzy had always enjoyed the journey to her mother's care home – the pleasure came from driving through some of the prettiest countryside in Somerset. But this day was different, her mother's erratic behaviour was increasing – it was so difficult to have a simple conversation. A feeling of doom filled the car – even the mystery of the tin could not displace the battle going on in her head. She needed to find a diversion.

'What about some music, Wellington, something soothing to prepare us for what might be a trying afternoon?' Wellington said nothing; his eyes had closed before they had reached the end of their road.

Lizzy pulled into a lay-by and sorted through her limited stock of discs. Every time she did this, she could hear her daughters' voices listing the merits of "bluetoothing their iPods" before launching into a highly technical explanation about how simple the process was. It sounded far too complicated for her to bother with. There must be a gentle soothing ballad-themed disc amidst her stash, one that would lull her into a detached and relaxed mood – nothing heavy would suit today.

'We like the old discs, don't we, Wellington? I'm not changing anything till it becomes obsolete,' she muttered as she rummaged through all the possible places in her overflowing car for a missing disc – her favourite.

'Aha, here we are – this'll do fine.'

Soon music was filling the car and Lizzy began to unwind. The countryside sprang into focus – passing through villages that were centuries old, marvelling at the batches of cottages lining the road, her mind became diverted from the worrying fact that her mother might be in one of her temperamental moods and hurl rice pudding at her like last time.

'Next left, Wellington, we're nearly there.' A lot of heavy panting ensued as Wellington hauled himself upright to look out of the window, checking the location out. His arthritis was really bad. 'We'll have to pop to the vet soon for some more tablets.'

The nursing home stood alone down a leafy country lane. It had once been the dwelling place of monied gentry and had retained the appearance of an aristocratic home – an enchanting building with beautiful grounds. Wellington made small squeaking noises of pleasure; he recognised the place and he knew what was coming.

When the car was parked, he attempted to spring out but became stuck and needed a hand. He waited patiently for the lead to be clipped to his collar before he was off, heading towards the front door and the source of biscuits – nothing wrong with his appetite.

Lizzy found it disturbing that her mother could not or would not recognise her. That was why she always brought Wellington with her. His happy presence soothed her troubled mind; stroking his coat so comforting at difficult moments when she had to count to ten slowly. At such times she tried to recall the kindness of her mother in former days. There were so many recollections of her mother's tenderness in Lizzy's childhood. The memory of those happy times compelled her to come visiting despite the pain it caused her. Her mother had loved her once but that was in another lifetime.

Inside the front door, walking over the highly coloured patterned tiles that graced many a Victorian hallway, Lizzy smiled at Wellington's eagerness to enter the day room. He knew that he was going to visit the residents and be made a fuss of – biscuits would appear at some stage – it would be doggy heaven. He pulled Lizzy towards the open door.

Lizzy's mother Harriet was sitting in her favourite armchair, gazing out at the swaying trees, apparently hypnotised by the movement of the branches and leaves interacting with the sunlight.

'Hello, Mum. How are you today? I've brought Wellington to see you.' Lizzy was relieved to see that the face turning in her direction was smiling and appeared to be untroubled. But when Lizzy went to sit in the adjacent armchair she was halted by: 'Don't sit there, dear. I'm keeping that for my daughter, in case she pops in. You can sit over there,' pointing as she spoke to a chair at the other side of the room. What a welcome – it was not looking good. Lizzy felt the familiar twitches of irritation and rejection. As her mother was now kicking her slippered feet into Wellington's flanks, she took a deep breath.

'Come on Welly boy, let's have a little walk round the lake and see if there are any hungry ducks.' Maybe her mother's memory and temper would be improved later in the day.

The door to the garden was heavy and needed a code number. But the air outside was fresh and invigorating after the stuffy warmth of the nursing home. Wellington would have to stay on the lead according to the rules, but he wouldn't mind. He enjoyed watching the ducks feeding and hoping a stray morsel would come his way.

Halting at the gazebo by the lake she sat on the cold stone seat, watching the moorhens scuttle away from this scary visitor. Vivid pictures of the past streamed through her mind like a looped film. She would have to deal with them, push them back into the dark caverns of her memories, before she spoke to her mother. There was never a resolution to these sessions – it just ended with one or other party leaving it hanging in the air until next time. Lizzy could never work out whether not recognising her was a ploy on her mother's part – at other times she seemed so sharp, especially about the past and her childhood.

A group of ducks wandered up the grassy banks looking for titbits. Wellington regarded them with elderly indulgence when the bag of duck food emerged from Lizzy's pocket. The care home was most protective of their wildlife and insisted on proper food. Wellington's languor kicked in and he sank down to watch the scrabbling ducks joust for a titbit. Lizzy's thoughts unfolded in a familiar pattern:

when and why had it all gone wrong? As usual she started to tell Wellington all her woes; now that Gerry was no longer with her, the dog had become her confidante.

'What has happened between Mum and me? We used to be so close or at least I thought so. I wonder if it has been there since the start of my life. She lives in the past. She and her mother would talk about the old days when Granddad was alive. I never met my granddads – both died before I was born. Now she doesn't even know who I am. If only I had brothers or sisters to help me with this awful situation.' Lizzy bent to stroke Wellington, his plump flanks giving her comfort. He grunted contentedly, unaware of the important role he played in his owner's life.

Lizzy's father had always appeared as a shadowy figure, putting the brakes on his wife's erratic temper, but not often there, having important business elsewhere. Being an only child had given him a rather self-centred character. He knew no different than to expect maximum attention when he was about and to have his wishes dealt with first. He was a handsome charming man who appealed to both men and women. He didn't even have to try; he was a natural manipulator of all around him – a charismatic personality, at ease with people from all walks of life. Lizzy had not worked all of this out in her childhood, but with the wisdom of experience she could see the patterns of her life more clearly. She began to feel sorry for her mother, as some of her life had been quite difficult.

'Come on, old boy, we'll go and see if Mother is feeling more chatty.'

As the glass door closed behind her to shut out the freedom of the garden, the claustrophobic atmosphere of the room enveloped Lizzy once more. Her mother was fast asleep in her chair, showing no sign of waking up soon. Should she abandon her efforts and set off for home? Was this not the right time? Lizzy was getting agitated when she heard a voice on the other side of the room calling out: 'Come and sit here by me.'

She turned to see a woman waving at her whilst pointing to the chair beside her. Her bright cheery face topped by an elaborate hairdo of tightly coiled curls reassured Lizzy in her moment of despondency. She walked over and sat down.

'Don't upset yourself, dear. They get like that some days. My old mum was the same.' She leaned over and patted Lizzy's knee with fingers festooned with rings. It was a little uncomfortable due to the surfeit of jewellery, but obviously meant kindly, so Lizzy endured it without comment.

The arrival of the tea trolley brought the patting to an end so that Lizzy was able to observe her comforter more closely. She appeared to be younger than the other people in the room who were unmoved by the advent of refreshments. Wearing a smart outfit, glowing coral lipstick and fingernails to match, her new friend resembled an exotic Californian poppy in a field of moon-daisies.

'I'm not as old as the others, dear. I can see you are wondering how I come to be here.' Lizzy was aware of a pair of sharp eyes making a judgement. 'What it is, I get these dizzy spells. They can't seem to sort them out and I keep taking a tumble and ending up in hospital. That's why the kids clubbed together so that I could stay here for a couple of weeks whilst they all shoot off to Benidorm for a family holiday. They go every year and I usually go with them but I'm not well enough this year.' She sighed and the grin disappeared for a moment.

'But it suits me very well – it's like a five-star hotel – the food is marvellous – one of my grandsons is the chef here. Besides, I am the only one who knows how to operate the television remote control,' she giggled, her face wreathed in smiles. She patted her tight curls with a sparkling hand.

'You sit and chat to me a bit – love a chat I do. I'm Mavis Padfield, formerly Hollis. And who are you? It's nice to have someone awake enough to have a decent conversation.' Another rumble of laughter shook her neat little body.

'I'm Lizzy Redland. That's my mum over there' She sipped her tea whilst Wellington wandered off to seek out other residents willing to part with a portion of biscuit. 'I've driven over from Kingcharlton to visit but it looks like it's been in vain.'

'What a coincidence, I live in Kingcharlton too, with all my relatives spread around me. We're a big clan. Our family have lived there since it was a little hamlet. Of course it's not like that now, grown up into a proper town now. But we do still call it a village amongst ourselves. My grandson, Jordan has been researching our family history for a project at school. Taken us right back a long way, so he has.' Mavis preened her hair with pride at Jordan's progress.

Lizzy began to pay careful attention to what seemed like casual chit-chat. There, sitting right next to her was the sort of person who would know all about the workhouse and its secrets – an unconscious keeper of oral history. Maybe Mavis had a tale to tell about the Welsh nurse and Canadian soldier. Her older relatives might have known the situation. People didn't move about so much in those days – visitors with strange accents would be noticed. But Lizzy would have to be careful how she asked her questions. She knew from experience that Kingcharlton still operated on a small-village policy of keeping themselves to themselves and that any obvious attempts to delve into this archive of knowledge would be deflected with agility. She must be circumspect or the iron gates of enlightenment would be closed with a clang.

'That's very interesting. Isn't it funny how you meet someone from Kingcharlton wherever you go? It happens to me all the time. But I don't think I have bumped into you before. Your grandson sounds like a very clever boy. There used to be a workhouse, didn't there? I see they are pulling it down now. Has your grandson found out anything interesting about that?'

'Oh, he don't need to investigate much about that. My nan used to work there, went there when she was twelve, Matron's little helper. Daisy Hollis she were then. She could tell some tales, keep everyone entranced she would. Wonderful storyteller she was as she grew older. All of our family has heard them over and over again. But she would only tell them to people she knew.'

Lizzy feigned indifference, even slight boredom whilst excitement ran up and down her spine. Mavis went on to be more expansive. 'They used to train nurses in the war, the First World War in the memorial hospital what used to be the isolation section. VADs they called them.'

Bingo, Lizzy thought, *she thinks she's losing a captive audience. She wants me to listen to her tales.* 'VADs' she replied casually, 'what's that?'

'Voluntary Aid Detachment – like the Red Cross today. My Jordan looked it up. Very keen they were in Kingcharlton on the Red Cross. Had a big headquarters on Charlton Road by the old cinema.' Mavis was watching her intently to make sure she was listening properly.

Lizzy wriggled on her chair and screwed up her courage to try something more intrusive. 'I think I know what you mean. Somebody was telling me all about a nurse they once knew, a distant relative, called Catherine. I don't suppose you've heard of her. She was stationed at the hospital in the workhouse grounds for a while – at least I think she was.' Lizzy raised her head to look at Mavis. 'She came from Cardiff, I think.'

The question was a step too far. A veiled look came over Mavis's face and she talked animatedly about the farmers' market and what a pity it was that the local traders had banned it. Lizzy realised that no more information would be forthcoming. But she had learnt some useful things. Mavis would be a good source of local gossip if handled with care – Catherine had been at the hospital for a while. Mavis had recognised the name, she was sure of that, and there was a secret hidden away. How intriguing. As she stood up stray biscuit crumbs tumbled off her jeans. Wellington uncurled and wobbled into action, hoovering up the fragments.

'It's been lovely chatting to you, Mavis. So interesting to hear all about old Kingcharlton and your clever grandson.'

Mavis almost purred with pleasure at these words. She patted her immaculate curls. 'I'll see you again, won't I? You'll come to visit your mum before I leave? I'll keep an eye on her for you.'

Lizzy felt accepted into the Kingcharlton community though only with "incomer" status. But that was good going; her family had only lived there for fifty years whilst there were people who could trace their ancestors back to the Domesday Book, at a time when the village could boast three mills and an abbey full of monks.

'Bye, Mavis. See you soon.' She waved goodbye to her mother as she passed her chair but there was no response. Why did it hurt so much when she knew there was a logical explanation?

Chapter Twelve - 1916

'Miss Catherine, can you help me with something? I ain't got nobody to ask.'

Daisy held out a crumpled piece of card, which she must have been carrying about in her pocket for some time, as it was rather grubby.

Catherine smoothed it out with her slender fingers, trying to read the words. It was a very thin cardboard postcard, beige in colour with a list of possible messages to tick in black print. *They must hand these out to soldiers at the front to send home to loved ones,* she thought as she turned it over. The postcard was already embellished with a red stamp bearing the head of George the Fifth. She beckoned Daisy over to look at the postcard over her shoulder.

'This is nothing to worry about, Daisy. They give all the soldiers these postcards. Look there is your address on the front with the King's stamp to show the postman that the delivery has been paid for. All the soldiers have to do, is to tick the boxes, sign their names, write their family's address on the front and post it in the army pillar box.' Catherine turned the card over. 'Look, see here where your brothers have ticked things like *Arrived safely*.' She pointed with a long slender finger.

'But my brothers can't read or write. Never had much time for schooling what with the farm work, keeping hungry birds off the crops, the crows from the new-born lambs, stone-gathering, harvesting in the summer and ploughing in the winter. Mother needed their wages. Don't know how they came to write this postcard out, but it arrived at our cottage a few days ago. We didn't know what to do with it, but I told Mother I would ask you because you have allus been so kind to me.'

Catherine could not remember all this kindness. She had seen the girl on the staircase from time to time, performing the housework at Matron's cottage. Catherine had always said hello and sometimes engaged her in conversation about how she was getting on – just good manners really. But obviously it had made a huge impact on Daisy. Catherine could feel it in the big brown eyes that peered up at her trustingly. The girl was looking much healthier; her cheeks had colour and she seemed to have grown a little taller and more padding was on her bones. She no longer looked feral and she seemed in good spirits apart from this worrying postcard.

'It seems the padre has written the address and ticked the boxes for your brothers. He has written you a little note concerning further communications. Look here – this writing.' Catherine pointed to the spidery words squeezed into a corner of the card.

'Do you know what a padre is, Daisy?'

'No, miss, I know very little about anything.'

'I expect you know what a vicar is. A padre is a sort of soldiers' vicar, he goes with them wherever they go and helps them say their prayers and worship

God. There are no churches out where they are, you see. Most of them have been bombed. He also helps soldiers keep in touch. There are lots of soldiers out there like your brothers with little schooling. Don't let that trouble you, Daisy. They are very brave, volunteering to fight for King and Country.'

Daisy's eyes filled with tears. 'I misses them, Miss Catherine. I don't want them to be killed. They used to tease me something rotten, but I misses them so much.'

'Why were they allowed to enlist, Daisy? Surely they were not old enough to volunteer. They are not much older than you, are they? I thought you had to be eighteen to volunteer?'

'They lied about their ages, Miss Catherine. They are big sturdy boys, not little like me, and the soldier man let them sign up, taking the King's shilling. That's what my brothers called it. They were strutting about like anything after making their mark on the paper. Thought they was proper men, so they did. Didn't think about getting killed till later on and it was too late then.'

'Your mother must miss them a lot.'

'Oh, she do miss them. She cried for a whole week when they went. They used to help her a lot with men's work – our dad being pretty helpless with that sort of thing since the trouble with his legs.'

'Well, Daisy my dear, the padre has written on here that if you can get somebody to write a letter for you, he will read it to your brothers. Then he can send news to you so your mother will know what is happening.'

Daisy thought how clever Catherine was to know all that from those little squiggles. People who could read and write could understand the shapes, write them down and read what they said, then they would know what was happening. She wished she could have learnt more at school, but she was often absent: it was helping Mother with her washing job, and the babies whilst she went out charring, that had kept her tied to the home. She was the eldest girl and that much was expected of her. Her younger sisters were doing much better, not reading and writing fancy stuff like on that postcard but some writing they could make out.

'Daisy, you look so sad. Don't worry. I am sure your brothers will soon be home on leave.'

'It's not that, miss. I wish I were clever like you and could read and write words. I hate being ignorant. I want to be like you.'

Catherine patted the sobbing child on the back. She felt a little ashamed – she had never thought of maids as having aspirations. She had just assumed they were happy doing housework all day long. That thought made her feel even worse. Why shouldn't servants want to read and write, all of them, not just those at the top of the pile?

'Listen, Daisy, I will teach you your letters if you promise to stop crying. We will find some time each day and practise. Then you could write your own postcards to your brothers. Here, take my handkerchief, wipe your eyes now and cheer up.'

Daisy did as she was told and managed a watery smile. She went to give the handkerchief back, but Miss Catherine said, 'No, put it in your apron pocket.

All ladies need a handkerchief, and I am sure you will grow up to be a lady and read and write. So run along now and give that grubby little face a good wash – and those nails could do with a scrub too.'

It was at that moment that Daisy felt undying love for Miss Catherine. Nobody had ever been so kind to her in her whole life, apart from her mother and Matron, but theirs was a gruff stern kind of love, which you knew as kindness but was not so overwhelming as Miss Catherine's who looked good and smelt of lilies-of-the-valley.

Nobody had ever given her a present like this; a lady's lacy pocket handkerchief with the letter "C" embroidered in violet in one corner plus forget-me-knots and daisies all over. There was no room to blow your nose really, that's what made it so special.

'Thank you, miss – you are ever so kind. Will you keep hold of the postcard for me as I got nowhere to keep it safe?'

Catherine put the card in her capacious pocket and swept off to talk to Matron about supplies.

Daisy stood in wonder, gazing at the delicate handkerchief in her hand. She had never owned such a beautiful thing before. She was going to put it somewhere special and treasure it all her life. And she was going to learn to read and write too. Miss Catherine had achieved saintly status in her eyes.

*

Meanwhile, Daisy's brothers were waiting to move up to the trenches. They stood, leaning against a bank in a ditch called "Sunken Lane", clutching their rifles, listening avidly to the wisdom of the older men.

'Bleeding waste of time, this,' spat out one lounging figure. Lofty Livingstone, a London lad, had no difficulty in voicing his feelings. Even the presence of the man with his bulky camera taking photographs and moving pictures did not deter him from expressing himself. After all, these were silent films, no speech was recorded to be played in electric theatres, so the soldiers could say what they liked as long as they remembered to smile and look patriotic and enthusiastic at the prospect of going into action.

'Much more of this and I'm going to scarper. It's a mug's game. We're like bleeding sitting ducks – we haven't got a chance. There's a farm over there. Bet they'd help us for a few fags. I could go back to the Smoke and disappear for a while. Done it loads of times before when things got a bit hot with the coppers.'

'Don't be silly, Lofty,' his companion muttered, defeated by the whole process of war. 'They'll catch you straight away and you know what they'll do to you then – they'll shoot you – have a court martial, stitch you up and shoot you.'

'What's the difference, between them shooting me, or the Huns doing it? At least they'd do it quickly and cleanly. I won't be left screaming in agony in No Man's Land, my guts hanging out, sprayed in bits of other men's bodies, listening to the horses scream. Does my head in, that does.'

Lofty had been in charge of the horses in a big London dairy and while being no sentimentalist over the position of animals in the scheme of things, he had come to have an affection for his charges. Deep in his heart was the fear that much more of the horses screaming would send him barking mad. You could put up with the suffering of men, citing their bad points, their petty squabbles, their foibles and so on, but the horses were different. They deserved better, than this: no fodder no decent water to drink, their hooves covered in mud. Lofty sighed.

The men were silent, glumly listening to the shells thudding to earth beyond the front line. This bombardment would create huge craters making a safe place for the advancing troops to shelter in before they moved forward again. The bottom would be full of gas, carbon monoxide they called it, so they would have to keep to the rim or perish. That was the generals' plan written down in their diaries, immutable. Useless of course, it wouldn't work. Lofty was sure of that. Nothing the generals planned ever seemed to work.

Beside him, Dick Farthing wondered if it was a sin to wish he could be far away from this conflict – to be at home. Where was that glorious feeling of being patriotic that had caused him to volunteer along with his mates, his cousins and his brothers? This was not a well-trained army but a body of honest men with good intentions. Now, it was becoming obvious that many of them would never leave the fields of Flanders. He thought of his wife Jenny humming to herself as she pummelled the dough before setting it to rise. A tear rolled down his cheek, which he wiped away with a grimy hand. The dirt out here was incredible; he had never been overly fussy, but they all seemed to be coated in mud and crawling with lice.

Jenny was so pretty. He recalled the first time that they had made love. There was nowhere for them to be alone; for privacy they had coupled in a dark alley where no lamplight shone. Jenny was a good girl but a primeval memory overcame them, sweeping aside all caution and moral sentiments. Of course when Jenny's condition had become known, he had to marry her. No question of that. That was the way it was done in his world. You did the deed as much as you dared, but if there was a baby coming you had to step up to the mark and make her an honest woman. Her male relatives would see to that. Not that he needed any coercion, he loved Jenny – her beautiful honest face and shiny dark hair – the little dimples in her cheeks when she smiled. How he wished she were here now smiling at him, holding out her warm arms for his embrace. He closed his eyes and imagined it.

'Wotcha, Dick, I think you've had a drop too much rum, my son.'

Visions of Jenny with her floury arms and swelling belly were cut short by Lofty's rasping twang. The faces of the men in "Sunken Lane" snapped back into focus.

'Not long now, lads,' a sharp cultured voice rang out and a smart business-like figure moved along the line. Pipe in mouth, cane in hand, he looked the very picture of an officer. The irony that he was only twenty-one with barely the ability to grow a beard was not lost on the men, most of whom had a greater experience of life than him. But the nature of their upbringing had trained them not to question his right to lead them into battle.

Chapter Thirteen

Catherine's life changed now Ben and Charley were part of it. They had taken to spending any spare weekends at the Major's house instead of delving into the dubious delights of London. Ben, Charley and Catherine formed a trio of friends escaping from the horrors of the war. There were walks in the countryside, fresh winds stinging their faces, tea in the parlour, Gentlemen's Relish sandwiches and china cups, sneaky forays into the kitchen to beg warm jam tartlets from Cook who had adored Charley from the moment he was born.

Life became even more fun when Charley took up a new hobby; he returned home one day staggering under the weighty equipment needed to produce photographs. One of the spare bedrooms was turned into a darkroom. Soon there were numerous photos of the trio hung on the walls. Charley found an old trunk in one of the attics, full of clothes for charades. They had dived in, dressed themselves in feathery boas, silken garments and fancy dress, and then took photos of themselves looking like actors at the end of the pier. The staff all had their photos taken and there were squeaks of delight as Charley handed them out.

He was a very generous person, though rather wild and given to thoughtless action.

One day a minor incident changed the dynamics of the group. They were sitting round the big oak table in the dining room, poring over Charley's latest efforts, making cheeky comments about his progress as a master photographer. As they leant forward to peer closer, a stray curly ringlet of Catherine's abundant titian hair fell forward over her face. It happened all the time, she could never control that particular lock of hair, even with the most severe clips. Most people found it irritating but Ben seemed fascinated by it. Before Catherine had time to follow her usual habit of tucking the strand back behind her ear, Ben unthinkingly leant forward and pushed the tress of hair into place. The feel of his fingers on her face, the shock of his skin touching hers stopped Catherine's light-hearted chatter midstream. His fingers on her cheek sent shivers down her spine.

Suddenly aware of his action, Ben quickly drew back, self-conscious of being too forward. Catherine gazed at him, searching his face with her gold speckled eyes, lost in a daze. They both looked bewildered, but Charley smirked in the background. *Ben is falling for that girl,* he thought – *I'll have to do something about that. Help him along a bit. He's only a simple country boy from the colonies*. An idea flicked into his mind, usually confined to thoughts of horses, girls and military matters – he grinned.

'Here Catherine, keep this jolly good one of Ben and here's one of you and Ben together. A memory for when we all go our separate ways. And Ben, here's a couple for you too. Don't expect anyone wants one of my ugly mug?'

Now to carry out my plan, he thought, *I must write a few letters.*

On a crisp frosty morning, a small procession walked along the bridle path leading from the farmhouse, winding through the fields to the Five Acre Meadow. Two splendid bay horses with fit sturdy young men in the saddles and one small, dappled pony with a body like a barrel bouncing along with a rather nervous Catherine holding on as best she could. Ben had been giving her riding lessons on his weekend leaves, but Catherine felt more confident handling her father's automobile than a pony that refused to obey any commands. She liked the expeditions, the three friends laughing and sharing light-hearted conversations but most of all she loved being with Ben and this was one way of spending a whole morning with him.

When they reached the first field, Charley leant over like an acrobat and unhooked the five-barred gate so that Catherine and Ben could trot through, then brought up the rear and fastened the gate behind them. The two hunter horses stamped their hooves and shook their manes, excited by the vast green field spread out before them. They knew what was coming; the freedom to gallop to the other side. Their whinnies cut through the clear air across the valley. How they pranced and pirouetted, eager to be off like equine dancers, graceful and powerful at the same time. The men whooped and urged them on, racing away into the distance. Catherine meanwhile sat nervously on the plump little pony that showed no sign of motion but grazed contentedly on the grass at her feet.

'Pull her head up, trot after us,' Charley shouted, 'show her who is the sergeant major!'

Catherine pulled hard on the reins, an action which had no effect on the pony at all. Catherine sighed – she just could not get the knack of controlling a horse. Her companions had been brought up with horses all their lives, starting as soon as they could toddle away from their mother's knees. The gentle nuzzling creatures with soft velvety noses seemed to change into stubborn mules or intractable monsters as soon as Catherine climbed into the saddle. They had tried out all the smaller ponies in the area and this one was the only one that Catherine felt vaguely safe on. Not so far to fall to the ground either on this fat little pony, usually ridden by children. Small did not mean obedient though; the little pony had an insatiable appetite and refused to move when something tasty was in close proximity. Her owner had named her "Sparky" which seemed the very opposite of her temperament.

The men had reached the other side of the field and were waving, looking back to see if she was following. Whilst she endeavoured to persuade Sparky to move, the men raced back and forth, the horses panting, flanks glistening with sweat, muscles on their backs rippling as legs pounded the turf. Suddenly Sparky moved forward to sample a tempting clump of grass and stumbled into a hidden rabbit hole. Catherine lost her balance and slid clumsily off Sparky's fat little body onto the frost-spiked grass. Ben rushed over to help her, laughing to start with, but then his face looked concerned as Catherine tried to stand up. It was obvious that her ankle was injured in some way.

'Here, let me help you.' Catherine felt herself encompassed by strong arms, lifted upright. Her ankle hurt really badly but the pain was overcome by the sensation of being held closely by Ben. She was enveloped by the mixed scents of tobacco and shaving soap, his warm breath on her face as he asked her where it hurt. She was so close she could see the long eyelashes framing his deep brown eyes, his firm mouth moving to show sturdy teeth as he tried to reassure her. She felt faint, not with the pain but with the effect Ben was having on her body. They were in a little world of their own.

'Hey, what's wrong?' Charley, racing around the field on his mount in his usual madcap manner, suddenly realised that Catherine was in trouble, and had reined in his steed to help. 'You'll have to give her a ride home, Ben, she can't hobble along or get that lazy pony to move.' Charley grinned, more convinced than ever that Ben needed a push forward in this romance.

'Is that alright, Catherine?' There was the weird sensation of being swept up by Ben's arms to be deposited on his horse's saddle, a position that felt alarmingly far away from solid ground. 'Just hold his mane if you feel insecure. I will take charge of the reins to lead him back.'

The horse's mane felt coarse and strong as Catherine wound her fingers round clumps of black wiry hair. Whatever would her parents say if they saw her now? They would order her home for sure if they knew she was here in the middle of a field in Somerset, all ruffled from falling off a pony, astride the horse of a man she had only known for a short time.

'Ready to go now, Catherine?' She nodded and the horse started to move. What a weird sensation. Sitting on top of Sparky had been like sitting on top of an overstuffed sofa but this was like nothing she had experienced before. Powerful muscles moved in sequence, a constantly changing platform that was rather alarming. She felt out of control, which was not what she wanted; she had to put her trust in Ben to keep her safe. Her emotions were in conflict. *I want to be emancipated,* she thought, *but I want to be with Ben all the time. Is this what falling in love feels like?* Catherine kept silent hoping this ordeal would soon be over.

They formed a strange procession back to the workhouse grounds: Charley leading a reluctant pony whilst riding Nimrod, Ben walking while Catherine sat astride his horse. What would Matron think? Would it spoil Catherine's plans because Matron thought her too wild and frivolous to be a sensible nurse?

Reclining on her bed, resting her swollen ankle, it occurred to Catherine that it might be a good idea, to conceal her photos and correspondence from prying eyes – if possible, to keep it with her all the time. Her relationship with Ben seemed to have reached a different level. It might be wise to be discreet with photos and letters. But what could she use?

Searching her meagre belongings for something small that would keep them safe, she came across the tin of cough pastilles, discarded in a drawer. She had not been able to bring herself to throw them away because Cook had been so kind on her first day. An empty tin would make a handy container to store precious items and if anyone saw it, they would think it was still full of cough sweets. It would fit in her pocket too.

First, she must get rid of the contents; they were too horrid for words. Tipping them all into a twist of brown paper, she stuffed the offending items into her coat pocket. They could not go in any household bins as Cook might see them and be upset by her behaviour. The bedroom window was so stiff she could not open it to put the offending objects out on a ledge, her first solution. She would have to hide them in a hedgerow on her morning walk and hope that they would not kill off any small creatures. She cleaned out all the sugary crystals littering the tin and lined the inside with tissue paper to protect her treasures. The photos fitted inside well, so did a letter from Ben, written whilst he was away training, with news of his next leave. She then put a page of the letter from her mother in an envelope so that if anyone did open the tin, they would think it was merely family correspondence. Finally, she scratched her initials: C.W. on the tin to distinguish it from the myriad tins in the workhouse kitchen given out by Cook. She popped the tin in her pocket; it fitted perfectly, especially if she added a couple of handkerchiefs on top to stop anything dropping out.

Now that she was assured of the security of her precious memory tin, she felt carefree as if a worry had been obliterated. Her feelings for Ben were hidden away from the world. When she looked in the age-mottled mirror in their bedroom, her cheeks were glowing, her eyes were shining and her hair stood up around her face like a fiery halo, hairpins ready to drop out at any moment.

Chapter Fourteen - 2016

'Mum's looking happier these days.' Nicola was sipping a latte in The Coffee House, eyeing up the tall dark barista with his elaborate flourishes and flounces, twirling knobs, swishing steaming hot milk into dark brown coffee with all the panache of a matador fighting a bull. It was worth the extortionate price of a coffee to watch the performance.

'Stop ogling that young man. He's far too young for you. You've got a husband and two kids at home. Nice bum though.' Claire smiled at the sight of her sister in a trance, spilling crumbs of caramel salted flapjack everywhere. 'What's this Tom like? He sounds very kind. He's certainly woken Mum up. She has seemed a bit out of it since she lost Dad.'

Nicola dragged her eyes away from the brooding barista and laughed, 'Only looking! Yes, Tom seems like a really nice guy. He's interesting to talk to; he knows lots of stuff about the old days. He's taking Mum to a local history meeting at the Fry Institute to see if she can find out anything about this mysterious tin of hers. He's not like a "special" friend; it's not that sort of relationship, I don't think. However, he is encouraging her to join things so she is getting out a bit more.' She took a sip of latte and ended up with a frothy moustache. Nicola wiped her mouth with a napkin and continued.

'That little silver match-case could be quite valuable. I've looked them up on my laptop. They sell for about £50 to £100 depending on their condition. The one Mum has is a bit dull, hidden away for years and not polished, but the way it was found would make a good story for the Antiques Roadshow, especially with the letters and photos. It's a piece of history. There's a lot of interest in items about the First World War at the moment. Maybe Mum and Tom will end up on the telly.' She pushed her plate away. 'Let's hope this search for the people in the photos keeps her interested. Like you, I was becoming a bit worried about her before this mystery tin sparked her interest.'

Claire gathered up her belongings and stood up. 'Sorry – must go I can't stay too long today – this week has been madly busy. Is she going to the local history meeting tonight in that funny little village hall? I'm surprised it's still standing. Remember going to Brownies and Guides there?' Claire giggled at the thought of herself in uniform. 'I expect that'll be knocked down soon for something more modern.'

'Yes, it's tonight. Tom's picking her up in his Morris Minor Estate.' Nicola took a last lingering look at the barista. 'Apparently, he belongs to some sort of club for rescuing old Morris Minor cars and restoring them to their former state. They have rallies and things. Perhaps he will be taking Mum to some of those. Same time next week?'

The girls left the quiet peace of the coffee shop with its dark wood furniture to join the hustle and bustle of the crowded street outside, chuckling at the thought of their mother off on a new adventure in a Morris Minor. That was more like their old mum, full of life and spirit. Maybe this would be a good year for them all.

*

The tinny melodies of the doorbell chimed, heralding the arrival of Tom. Lizzy shivered with a mixture of happiness and apprehension. She was looking forward to her evening out, however mundane it might seem to others. Her nerves were tingling as usual but she was determined to go. Many years had passed since she had been to a dance in the village hall. Not since local groups with badly tuned guitars mangled the latest pop hits, while grown-ups supervised, selling bottles of fizzy lemonade and packets of crisps at half time. She and her friends would make eyes at teenage boys who were too anxious to approach them to ask for a dance. Those were the days – when everything was yet to come, and she was still innocent and expecting the best.

'All ready, Lizzy? It's a bit nippy out here. You might want a warm cardigan for the hall, which is draughty to say the least. One of our members brought a hot water bottle last week.' Tom's face was cheerful as always and he looked very dapper, separated from his gardening clothes.

Lizzy had spent hours deciding what to wear. She wanted to look serious, but not too dressed up. Did she have the right sort of notebook and pen? Not one that would leak and spoil the lining of her handbag. Tom's prompt arrival meant that she could stop fussing and just go as she was, leaving behind her stress.

Tom was right about the temperature of the village hall, a relic of nineteen thirties' architecture: quaint but sparse in modern amenities. Lizzy didn't feel the cold however – as soon as they entered a room full of people, she felt her cheeks flush and her body firing up like a furnace. *I hope they like me,* she thought, *will they think I am too ignorant to join?* They looked very pleasant, no high-pitched voices shrieking, no gushing. They huddled in little groups absorbed in animated conversation. A lone lanky figure stood at the front of the room near the drop-down screen, fiddling with a tangled knot of wires and digital connections.

'That's Peter Catchpole,' Tom whispered, 'he's the one giving the talk this evening – he's very keen on anything historical and absolutely mad about railways.' Lizzy could not see his face, only his back stooped over many tangled wires. When he eventually stood up and walked forward to face his audience, she was amazed to see how handsome he was. When Tom had mentioned railways, she had imagined an old buffer in a tweed jacket, or a spotty adolescent in an anorak.

Once he began his talk, his enthusiasm was electrifying. The subject was the demise of a minor obsolete railway line that had carried goods from Fry's chocolate factory to the local station. His words evoked a vision of a small blue tank engine on its journey across the main road pulling trucks loaded with chocolate treats. He painted a vivid picture of the sturdy little train rattling along the iron rails embedded in the tarmac of the road whilst an assortment of farm drays, horses-drawn wagons, and the very occasional car, waited patiently.

The branch-line, unused for many years, was being dismantled at last. Entrepreneurs had purchased the factory grounds and were building houses on the land originally designated for the well-being of the workers. It had never been intended for concentrated housing schemes. A wave of sadness swept over Lizzy at the thought of the ploughed-up sports-fields. Then there was the wanton destruction of the thriving community hall, which had held so many happy memories of family occasions. But at least the magnificent driveway with its borders of ancient, glorious chestnut trees was still in place. Generations of children had filled their bags with shiny brown conkers. In Lizzy's childhood in Kingcharlton, the happy hours of dedicated conker fighting were as eagerly anticipated as Bonfire Night.

After the talk, there were refreshments. Lizzy was relaxed now. Tom had spotted a familiar face and wandered over, leaving Lizzy to queue for a drink. She was just about to pick up a cup of coffee when she became aware of someone standing close to her, trying to attract her attention. Turning round to see if Tom had returned, she found herself gazing into the intense eyes of Peter Catchpole. Lizzy could tell he was about to quiz her. Oh no, she was not ready for intense conversations – he looked so clever. But his opening comment took her by surprise: 'I was hoping you might turn up here.'

‘Why? Have we met before?’ Lizzy was intrigued. She was sure they had never met or spoken before.

‘You don’t know me; we have never been introduced. I saw you pick something up that fell off a lorry leaving the workhouse.’ He frowned as if seeking to explain why he had been so familiar. ‘I live opposite the workhouse. I was looking out of the bedroom window to see if the recycling lorry had been and I saw something fall off the lorry. You picked it up and you put in a bag and took it away. That means it must be an item of interest. I was going to come down and help you but I tripped over the cat, I was so excited – sprained my ankle. I wanted to explore the ruins of the workhouse looking for ancient unwanted relics, but it wasn’t allowed. The developers wanted all the rubble disposed of as quickly as possible.’

He scrutinised her with a hypnotic glare waiting for her reply, as if to draw the information out of her. Lizzy was flummoxed. The nerves were tingling again. Was her action illegal; she knew there were laws against raiding building sites for items of value but a rusty tin hurled at her? It was going to landfill anyway. But it was a shock to realise a stranger knew about it. In her mind the tin was a private connection to the people from the past.

‘It was only a rusty old tin. I almost threw it away. The lid was stuck tightly; Tom had to ease it off. He brought me here this evening. He has been very helpful.’ She half turned and gestured towards Tom, deep in conversation with a lady she had recognised, one of the familiar faces of Kingcharlton.

‘Who’s that woman speaking to Tom?’ Lizzy asked her inquisitor. ‘I know her by sight, but not to speak to.’ Peter, standing in front of her, swivelled round to peer impatiently at Tom as if he were irrelevant to this conversation. He leaned forward, his cold coffee slopping out of his cup down his jumper. The mother in Lizzy wanted to lean over and take the cup away but she was too nervous, unhinged by this strange man. Mesmerised by the dripping coffee, she could not follow what he was saying. She grew anxious at his fervour, her face flushed.

‘But what was in the box, what type of tin was it?’ Questions flew out of his mouth like a swarm of angry bees.

Lizzy felt intimidated by Peter but realised he might hold answers to her questions. He was obviously clever and dedicated. She must get a grip on her feelings. ‘We know it is a cough-sweet tin, pastilles they called them. We think it was being used to keep safe mementos of a romance between a Welsh nurse and a Canadian soldier during the First World War. How it got lost or was discarded we do not know. There are some photos, letters, and other items.’ She did not mention the silver matchbox – caution held her back. She would find out from Tom how reliable Peter was. Could he be trusted?

‘Can I see the tin and its contents? I would love to explore it. I could help you find out more. I know lots of websites. I’m good at searching and you must be interested in finding out where it comes from?’

Lizzy was floundering as to how to answer. She was reluctant to show her precious find to a complete stranger. It was her secret. At that moment, Tom tapped on her shoulder. 'I see you've met Peter. A good solid fellow.' Lizzy thought that Tom had seen her discomfort and come to rescue her, with his usual thoughtfulness.

'Peter's your man when it comes to research, Lizzy! If anyone could solve the puzzle of the tin, he can.' He turned to face Peter, 'But don't say anything about the tin to anyone else yet, my friend, as Lizzy wants to keep it quiet until she decides how to proceed.' Peter nodded but still looked eagerly at Lizzy, as if he expected an answer to his question.

Lizzy studied both men for a moment or two and came to a decision. 'Would you both like to come to my house for coffee and cake and we will study the contents of the tin together. See where we could go from there. But yes, please do keep it a secret for now. I don't want to be whisked off to prison.'

A time was arranged, and Peter went to pack away his equipment. He accosted her again as she left. 'Don't forget. I'll bring my special camera and we can start documenting.'

'A nice man but a bit intense,' Lizzy remarked to Tom as they travelled homewards. 'He made my head ache after a while. Please can you come too and help me out.' Lizzy was glad that Tom would be there at the inspection of the tin and its contents as Peter was rather alarming in his fervour. Her life was changing – two new friends in the space of a week.

Chapter Fifteen

Lizzy checked her display: the battered tin, the photos of the young couple staring out at a promising world, the soldier ready to fight, the nurse with her voluminous outfit, and the faded crumpled letters covered with sepia words. The silver matchbox was open, displaying the tiny red heads of its matches.

There was a knock on the door. Lizzy peered through the security-eye. Tom stood there smiling with a packet of chocolate biscuits. 'My contribution to the ceremony of the tin,' he said, grinning, as she opened the door. 'After all, I was there at the start of this adventure.'

Lizzy beamed with relief at Tom's friendly face. 'Thanks for coming a bit earlier, I still feel uncomfortable about sharing the tin with other people. You know Peter – you can take control of the situation.'

Tom smiled. 'He's not so bad when you get to know him – just over-enthusiastic, that's all. Don't worry, there's really no need.'

Tom's got a lovely smile, Lizzy thought, *very comforting without being overbearing. Though he looks wistful at times.* She had invited him to this meeting, not only for her benefit but because she thought he might like the company. In the short time of their acquaintance, Lizzy had already realised how much he missed his wife.

Peter arrived promptly, as the grandfather cloak chimed out ten sonorous notes. Earlier, Lizzy had spotted him pacing up and down the pavement checking his watch constantly. He was carrying a battered old leather briefcase that looked like a prop from a BBC television play set in the fifties.

Peter refused the offer of coffee. 'Let's get on with it, shall we? I'm dying to see this tin and what's inside.' He glanced over at the display on the table, 'Can I touch these treasures, look at them closely? I carry an eyeglass with me at all times.'

There followed an interlude of solemn silence as Peter studied each item. He scrutinised the photos and read the inscriptions on the back. Lizzy need not have worried; he handled each item with reverence. He picked up the silver *Vesta* case and tried opening and closing the lid, looking for a hallmark and taking note of the initials etched on the front. The folded letters were carefully laid out flat so the messages could be read. Finally, he drew a very complicated camera out of his leather bag and took a great many photos from different angles, even ones of the scruffy tin, muttering comments to himself as he did so. 'Fascinating' he murmured, 'it's like a time capsule buried for so long. Full of primary sources and comments. Well done for picking it up and bringing it home.'

Eventually, he turned to Lizzy and spoke his mind. 'We really need to share this find with the local history group. They would love it. I could use all my photos and help you with the presentation.'

'Oh,' gasped Lizzy. 'I never wanted to tell other people. I thought we were keeping it to ourselves. I'm not sure I'm ready for contact with large numbers of people. Since my husband died a year ago, I've lived very quietly.'

Peter's face lost its elated grin. He shuffled from one foot to another. 'At the moment, the general population are interested in everything about the First World War, even those who never took any notice before, because of the many centenary celebrations. There will be a lot of interest locally at the group and at the British Legion, to mention just two organisations. I have not mentioned your find to anyone else yet, mainly because I wanted to have first dibs at it. A bit selfish I suppose. But some of them can be so pushy, you know.'

Tom and Lizzy exchanged glances. This was something neither had envisaged – this enthusiastic man with so many plans for what they thought of as their tin. Peter was planning and plotting. He gazed intently at both of them, like a dog with his eye on his bone. Lizzy hated having to spoil his joy at her find but there must be a compromise to suit them all.

'Give me some time, Peter, to think this over. We ought to gather more information before we think about giving talks at the local history group. It's not much of a tale so far. If we could find out more about what happened to these people, I might be persuaded to share the story with the group.'

Peter's face beamed with excitement; he ran long bony fingers through his curly hair so that it stood up all around his head like an ebony halo. 'We shall be like the three musketeers battling through.'

It seemed that Peter now considered himself as one of the team. 'I want to go back now to print out the photos, if that's okay with you. Can I come back tomorrow to share my progress? Same time all right with you chaps?'

'I suppose so,' Lizzy said, not really sure she wanted another visit so soon. But he looked so keen like a puppy ready to play; she could not say no. 'What about you, Tom?'

'Okay by me.' Tom nodded.

'That's it then, chums. See you tomorrow.' Peter looked blissfully happy.

As the front door closed, Tom and Lizzy let out a deep sigh. Lizzy could no longer contain her feelings. The words tumbled haphazardly out of her mouth.

'I don't know what to think, Tom. When the tin landed at my feet, I was curious. When we prised it open and saw the photos, I thought I would like to discover more about these people, but in a private slow-moving type of way. It seems as though I might have to adjust my thinking if we want Peter's help.'

*

Next morning Peter rushed through the front door and dived into his brown bag, without any ceremony of "hello and how are you".

'Here are the photos I took yesterday. They seem to have come out quite well. There are copies for each of you.' He placed two plastic envelopes on the table – one for Lizzy and one for Tom, presumably keeping a third for himself. Then he delved into his old brown bag once more, bringing out a handful of vividly coloured brochures that he fanned out like a hand of cards, pointing at the most prominent one. 'Look what I've found; a firm which provides tours around the battlefields and cemeteries of the First World War in "luxury coaches", with "experienced guides". We could all go on a field trip: The Three Musketeers solve a mystery.'

'My, you have been busy.' Lizzy was amazed, not at all used to moving at this sort of speed. It was mind-bending. She hoped she was not heading for a migraine. 'How would it help us to go on a "battlefields tour"? We don't know where our soldier fought or whether our nurse even left Britain. A lot didn't; they stayed nursing in this country. I have been doing a little research on Wikipedia myself. I know it's not always reliable, but it does give some idea of what was going on. I've also ordered a book from Amazon about wartime nurses and their roles. It looks really interesting.'

'And I've done nowt,' said Tom, 'except for wrestling with a tin and an oil can.' He grinned and looked suitably humble. Lizzy immediately leapt to his defence, annoyed with Peter for trying to take over.

'Don't be daft, Tom,' Lizzy smiled, 'you prised the lid off the tin of secrets. You were there at the beginning. You persuaded me to join the local history group and introduced me to Peter here. You are a valued founder member of the Three Musketeers, if that's what we are going to call ourselves.' Lizzy thought this title was rather immature like the Famous Five but kept quiet for the moment. She wanted to see what Peter had discovered.

Despite his intense enthusiasm, Peter managed to sit down and consume a cup of coffee and a digestive. It was as if he had expended all his nervous energy and could relax a little. He seemed almost normal as he dunked his biscuit in his coffee and chunks fell off as they always do. His eager words tumbled out of his mouth as he shared his findings. 'I've identified the uniform as Canadian, not quite sure of the unit as yet but I'm working on it. Apparently, the Canadian troops had a significant victory at a place called Vimy Ridge. The dates on your letter would seem to fit this action. What we need now is to know whether he survived the battle. I have emailed a site, which might be able to provide that information.'

Lizzy was writing notes in her diary. She wanted to do some of her own investigations later on but knowing the right sites to search would be useful. Peter continued his lecture.

'After the war, the Canadian Government erected an enormous white monument, not far from the battle site, which can be seen for miles around. We could visit it and search for the name of the soldier. There are records of all the men known to have been killed in this battle, even if their bodies had not been found to bury. If his name is not listed there, we will look elsewhere. There might be a book to be written about your discovery if we could follow the progress of the couple to the end of the war and beyond.'

'Well done,' said Tom. He looked overwhelmed, lost for the words to express his feelings; what had begun, as a gentle exploration of the past, had turned overnight into a super charged whirlwind of activities.

'Oh, to be young again and have all that energy,' he said, winking at Lizzy. 'We can't go until next year anyway. Look at the brochure, they stop after November and don't start again till April. Let's see how we feel about it when the time comes. We might have a lot more information by then.'

Lizzy was not sure whether Peter was rushing ahead too fast. She didn't want gentle reassuring Tom to be pushed aside by Peter, who had all the facts and figures at his fingertips. Nor was she sure she wanted to spend a week with him on a pilgrimage to the war cemeteries. It was her tin and her mystery. What Mavis had told her was very interesting but was it enough to go charging off to France?

She resolved that when Peter left to plunder the Internet once more, she would tell Tom all about her conversation with Mavis at the nursing home. Lizzy trusted him to be discreet. She had a very strong suspicion that Mavis would shut up as tightly as a clamshell if she suspected that Lizzy was sharing that information with other people. So far Mavis had only spoken in general terms, sharing information anyone could find out. But Lizzy had a feeling that Mavis held the key to her mystery nurse and her soldier friend and that she might be persuaded to reveal all.

There was an old saying for moving cautiously, now what was it? Softly – softly - catchee monkee. That was it, move slowly and quietly to achieve the goal.

Tom was her oak, solid and reliable… and Peter? What was Peter exactly? A loose cannon, maybe?

Later on, lying in bed gazing at the stars and a lemon-wedge moon framed by the open curtains, Lizzy had second thoughts about a battlefields tour. It might provide some clues – they could look for Ben Trueman's name on the Vimy Ridge memorial. If they found it there, it could lead to other connections and maybe even to Catherine Waterman's story. The tin contained a small fraction of the lives of two people at a time of peril; Lizzy would dearly love to know how the story ended.

What clothes would she take on a trip like that? Would they need overalls for muddy trenches? Would there be social time in the evening? Had Peter left that brochure for her in the pile of information on the kitchen table?

'I'll hunt for it in the morning, Wellington.'

Wellington grunted, changed his position and returned to his dream of chasing rabbits

Chapter Sixteen

'Mum, how do you feel about Christmas this year? We'll go along with anything you say. We don't want you to be upset.' The Festive Season was approaching fast – shops were clad in tinsel and the television was nothing but adverts for massive overspending.

Lizzy was silent. Memories of past Christmases when Gerry was alive filled her mind, blocking out everything else. He had adored all the hustle and bustle – making all the preparations. This year she had remained immune to the gathering excitement all around her. Eventually she realised she must say something because Nicola and Claire would be impatient to start shopping and planning the festive season.

'I don't really know what I want. But I do know I don't want to organise anything. Why don't you take over the family Christmas this year, Nicola? You're really good at that sort of thing, just like your father was. You and Claire arrange everything, and I will be a guest. It'll be a change for me to be waited on hand and foot.' She laughed to disguise her wish to forget Christmas altogether as she had last year. She felt obliged to pull herself together and make everyone else happy.

'It's a shame that we've already missed *Stir-up Sunday*. I used to enjoy making the cake and the puddings, all together as a family.' The thought of the familiar ritual sent her into a trance, taking her back to a happy place. First came the shopping: choosing the ingredients at the supermarket: exotic spices, flour, free-range eggs, brown-shelled and healthy nestling in cardboard boxes, shiny glace cherries sticky to the touch, bags of mixed dried fruit bursting at the seams, a tin of heavy black treacle, and moist dark brown sugar. Greaseproof paper, brown paper and string were needed for the inside and outside lining of the cake tin to prevent the danger of overcooking. Last items were the icing sugar and marzipan to decorate the cake reeking of the brandy. The grandchildren were in charge of the cake decorations: plastic snowmen and Father Christmases, cheery messages and wobbly reindeer, fringed gaudy wraps with festive greetings and a silver cake board so that it could be presented with due ceremony at teatime. What fun it had been. Surely, they could recapture that happy feeling.

Nicola watched her mother's face anxiously. From her expression, she seemed to be reliving past Christmases. What if she burst into tears? A family meeting had been convened to decide what would happen over Christmas. It had been decided that Nicola would be the most suitable person to tackle this sensitive task of seeing what Lizzy wanted. *Best thing to do was to sit and wait,* Nicola thought, *there was no point in rushing the decision-making if later it turned out to be the wrong choice.* She sipped her coffee and waited for her mother to come back to her.

Lizzy was still deep in her memories. *Stir-up Sunday* in November was when the baking began. All the ingredients ended up in a brown and white bowl to be stirred by each member of the family in the turn, hence the name. The preparation of the ingredients came first. Ruby-coloured glace cherries were quartered and rolled in flour to stop them sinking to the bottom of the cake, mixed fruit was steeped in brandy to swell, eggs were beaten with vigour, flour sieved, butter softened, soft brown sugar weighed and dark black treacle spooned out. The tin was carefully prepared so that the mixture inside would bake very slowly – that was the secret of a good moist cake. First it was lined inside with greaseproof paper. Then a cummerbund of brown paper was wrapped round the outside and secured with string. It towered over the rim of the baking tin looking like a chef's hat with the top missing.

All the preparations were completed before Lizzy brought out the old-fashioned cream and brown china bowl and placed it with due ceremony on the table among the smaller bowls of the various ingredients. The children were restless with excitement as flour, butter and eggs were beaten together by Lizzy, who then stood back to supervise as they took turns to add an ingredient and drop it in. When all the surrounding dishes were empty and there was no more to add; the proper stirring ceremony began. The grown-ups went first as the mixture was still rather stiff and heavy to handle. But when the dried fruit, plumped-up to twice the size by soaking in brandy, were added the mixture became sloppy and gooey. Then the little ones took over, kneeling on stools or held by their parents according to size. You made a wish as you stirred: that was the most fun part of the ceremony, apart from being allowed to lick out the bowl. Lizzy took over when the mixture was deemed well stirred, tipping the delicious-smelling mixture carefully into the tin. Then the cake was ready for the oven where it would stay for most of the afternoon, pricked at intervals with a slender knitting needle to see if it was firm enough to be lifted out of the oven.

When all was finished, a bottle of red wine was opened to help with the washing up whilst the children had fizzy pop as a treat and ran riot round the house. *It was always such a lovely family day,* Lizzy thought. She suddenly snapped out of her reverie.

'I think you should do whatever you think best, Nicola. I am happy to go along with any of your plans and give you all the help I can. Thank you for offering.'

'Right, Mum, Claire and I will organise the Christmas festivities and your birthday. Are we going to put up your Christmas tree then as usual – letting the children finish it all off? They've been badgering me non-stop as they've been making decorations at school and they want you to have them this year. Claire and I have kept them quiet so far about it but then we thought perhaps you might like it this year. We can keep it simple.' Nicola stared at her mother intently, hoping that she was focussed on the subject in hand and not away in another daydream about making Christmas puddings.

'So, you are happy with us, coming on your birthday, putting your tree together and dressing it with some decorations, mainly for the children to enjoy? I will bring the birthday cake and a few bits and bobs for a party tea. Keep it simple, like I said.'

Lizzy smiled and gave her daughter a hug. 'Thank you so much for all your kindness, you and Claire. I hope you realise how much it is appreciated.'

*

It was not until Christmas was over and all the decorations had been safely stored for the next time, that Lizzy remembered Tom who had been so kind helping with the allotment and her tin. How had he spent the Christmas period? She was horrified that she had forgotten all about him whilst she was dealing with her own emotions and problems. When she finally plucked up courage to ask him, he replied that he had spent a quiet day all on his own.

'Don't worry about me, lass. I had a lovely day watching old films and eating what I wanted. No extra shopping needed.' Lizzy could not summon up a good answer to this. For once words failed her. *You are a really bad person,* she thought, *all that help he gave you and you left him alone on Christmas Day. Not good enough, Lizzy – could do better.* Number one New Year's resolution would be that she would invite him to share next Christmas with her and her family.

It seemed a bit insensitive after this conversation to ask him what he thought about Peter's suggestion of visiting the battlefields and cemeteries of the First World War, particularly as he had clearly not wished to come with them. She could not quite get his measure; he was very kind but reticent on certain subjects. But then he had said, 'Don't worry about Wellington, I will look after him if you decide to go. He can help me with the allotment.'

Did that mean that he thought travelling to the cemeteries and battlefields was a wise move? Now that the Christmas furore was over, she thought she would like to visit France where the mystery couple had fought for freedom. She could soak up the atmosphere of the terrain – try to visualise what the lovers had experienced by visiting restored trenches, looking at the piles of golden brass shells and recovered items from the trenches and tunnels, according to the glossy brochure. Apparently, an underground tunnel had been rendered safe enough for visitors to descend and experience what life had been like for the soldiers living down there. She must contact Peter and give him the go-ahead to book a visit in the spring.

Chapter Seventeen - 1916/17

Ben arrived for an evening walk with Catherine in a great state of agitation. He burst into speech as soon as they were alone together.

'I'll be going "over-there" soon. They've given us forty-eight hours embarkation leave. Then we have to return to our camps to depart at any moment.'

Catherine was stunned by the news. Although she knew it would be coming, it had seemed to be a far-off event. She could not imagine what it would be like not seeing Ben at regular intervals. How would she manage? She muttered to herself:

'Pull yourself together, you silly girl. A great many women are in the same position as you and they just carry on in a loyal dignified manner.' She put on a brave smile to support Ben as best she could.

'We will have to make the most of these last few days.' Ben looked troubled – he appeared to be devastated by the thought of leaving Catherine.

'Charley has been chatting to me. He reckons he can get us an invitation to a New Year's Eve house party this weekend, in the Cotswolds. Beautiful countryside. We would have two whole days to spend together with evening entertainment, dancing and whatnot. We could make the most of the time left to us. What do you say, are you up for it?'

'Yes,' said Catherine. She was not sure that this was the right thing to do – what would her parents and Matron think? But then Ben would be gone soon, and she might never see him again. She must seize every opportunity to be with him that came her way. She pushed all disapproving doubts to the back of her mind, mindful of Shakespeare's words about opportunities taken at the flood that never come again.

The weather was disappointing as they set off. A misty grey day did nothing to raise their spirits. Both of them were nervous for different reasons. Catherine because she had never been in this situation before and Ben because he had a secret, he was not sure Catherine would approve of. Charley had lent them his automobile, a real bone-rattler. Its roof was no more than a scanty canopy, which kept some of the bad weather off. There was no source of heat either. The rugs over their knees and shoulders did little to ward off the bitter cold.

'Be sure to wear a suitable hat. Bring a scarf to tie it on tightly, otherwise the wind will whip it away,' Ben was insistent. He was staring at Catherine fiddling with her bonnet and it seemed as if he was about to say something but then changed his mind.

Catherine's fingers were stiff with cold; she was trying to tie her scarf, but the folds kept slipping from her hands. At last, she managed to pull the gauzy material over her cheeks to protect her complexion already pale with anxiety. Would her parents approve of her going to a house party in the Cotswolds? They would not. It was fortunate that Annie was away in Cardiff and had no idea what Catherine's plans were. If her parents found out, would they order her home, so that she would have to forfeit the nursing and the chance to go abroad to the Front? She had worked so hard to become a VAD nurse, that it would break her heart if she had to give it all up. And yet it would also break her heart to say no to Ben's invitation to a house party in the Cotswolds with a group of friends. Especially as this was his last leave before embarking with the Canadian troops. This was what they had been training for on Salisbury Plain – the big push forward that he could not discuss with her, only hint at the amount of planning that had gone into it. Catherine had the strangest feeling that he was telling her that she might never see him again and that this weekend would be their last chance for a time of light-hearted happiness together.

It was lucky that he had not suggested a weekend alone together in a guest house in Weston-super-Mare. She would have had to say "no" to this. That would have been quite scandalous. Arabella's advice had been sought and she seemed to have no problems with the weekend. Apparently, she knew of the family who seemed to be very respectable and if there were lots of guests there, there should be no problem with maintaining propriety.

Ben chatted away as he drove, as if to break the silence that the strangeness of being alone had evoked.

'Charley and I had a trial run, last time I was down. We were testing out his automobile. He was not sure how reliable it would be. It's rather old, second-hand. He wanted to get a new one, but they have not produced any new models since war was declared. The automobile factories have been converted for wartime vehicles. All the time I was motoring, I was thinking how nice it would be to have you beside me and be on our own for once.'

Catherine shivered and drew her rug closer around her. 'We'd better make the most of it then, for we will soon be in the midst of many people. How many miles still to go? Are you sure of the way?'

Ben negotiated a tricky corner, cursing quietly under his breath. 'Charley has given me an excellent map and I am good at finding my way around navigating by the sun usually. My soldier's training has improved my skills of navigation.'

Catherine blushed at her stupidity. Of course, a soldier would know the way, especially one as capable as Ben. Her nerves were making her gabble out a string of nonsense. Secretly she wondered if she could cope with a house party of strange guests. She was used to socialising quite a lot at home, but they were mostly people she knew. This was a great adventure.

The landscape changed; the gentle hills of the Cotswolds rose before them, their slopes covered by large tracts of trees. As they bumped along the country roads, she shivered in the cold frosty air and imagined roaring fires, roasting chestnuts, and toast on pronged forks. Maybe the house would have those new-fangled radiators of wrought iron, boiling to the touch, nice to lean against and warm one's back. Lulled by the rhythm of the car and the creeping dusk, she fell into a half sleep, musing on the delights to come. There might be splendid meals on tables beautifully laid out with white crisp damask tablecloths, ironed to within an inch of their lives, spread with rows of shining silverware and glittering glasses ready for the wine that would glow in the candlelight. In the middle a crystal dish piled high with fruit of all sorts and sizes. Her mouth watered at the thought and her tummy gave a little rumble. She was feeling hungry. After the austerity of the hospital, she was looking forward to a little luxury.

She hoped she would fit in – she had packed a new dress, silk stockings and patent leather dainty shoes. Not usually one to dress up, she had felt the urge to appear feminine for Ben. Annie had devised a new hairstyle, one that would keep Catherine's wayward curls under control. Once ensconced in a civilised bedroom she could recreate the style by herself. Luckily, Annie had not asked why she needed a new hairstyle. Caught up in these thoughts, she did not notice that Ben had become strangely silent. If she thought anything of it at all, it was that he was concentrating on driving an unfamiliar car.

'Here's the turning, I think.' Ben manoeuvred the car round an impossible bend so tight that his mudguards were adorned with greenery from the hedgerow. They passed through an open five-barred gate bearing a faded wooden placard saying, "Dove Cottage", as the wheels crackled along a stony bridle path. Catherine wondered why a country house, big enough to hold a weekend-party would have such a shabby driveway. They eventually reached a clearing enclosed by tall trees and overgrown bushes in the middle of which stood a cottage of Cotswold stone in varying shades of gold and cream.

'Not quite what I was expecting,' muttered Ben.

Catherine gasped – the dwelling looked more like a charcoal burner's cottage, pretty but not the stately home she had been expecting, and not a suitable place to accommodate a large number of houseguests.

'It doesn't seem like a place to hold a party,' said Catherine. 'Where would all the guests sleep? Have we come down the wrong turning?'

Catherine's heart jolted and she turned to look at Ben who had gone strangely quiet.

'What's this, Ben? This cottage is not big enough to hold a house party.'

Ben did not answer. He was staring ahead of him at the building. When he did speak, it was all he could do to get the words out. She had never heard him stutter before.

'I think I've made a mistake. It's all a ghastly mess. What have I done? Charley said it would work. He has tried it a couple of times now and it has always turned out okay. But you're not that kind of girl, not like one from Charley's fast set.'

He dropped his head encased in a big leather driving cap onto the steering wheel and let it stay there, hidden from Catherine who sat frozen in stunned amazement.

*

After what seemed like hours of utter silence, Catherine whispered, 'you've deceived me, Ben. I've been so stupid. There was no house party, was there? I put all my trust in you. Did you really think I was willing to be tricked into this? Take me home. Take me to the nearest station and I'll make my own way home.'

Ben raised a stricken face to her. 'You can't get home till tomorrow. We are literally miles from anywhere. It would take as long to get to a station as to get back home. There are no hotels around here or I would take you there, book you into a room and get you home tomorrow. This is a godforsaken piece of the country, which I thought would make it discreet. I realise I have made a huge mistake. I am so sorry.'

'I'm not that sort of a girl,' Catherine whispered in shocked tones. 'I was brought up properly. I thought you were too. What would your mother and sisters say to you if they saw you now?'

'I know, I know. I knew it all along. I've been deceiving myself with Charley's encouragement. I knew I would never have the courage to try to seduce you, but I thought it would be so wonderful to spend a whole weekend alone with no one bothering us. I would never want to hurt you, Catherine.'

'Well, you have.' Tears were rolling slowly down her face and she dabbed at them with an ineffectual lace handkerchief. 'I want to go home.'

'I'm sorry, so very sorry, Catherine. I love you with all my heart. I just wanted to be alone with you and tell you how I feel. I wanted to ask you to wait for me till I can come home and marry you – take you home to meet my mom and sisters. Please, please forgive me.'

'I trusted you. I thought you were an honourable man,' was the only thing Catherine could say.

'You gotta forgive me, Catherine. In a few days' time I'll be in France and may never see you again. I couldn't bear to go, thinking that you hate me. I'll take you home as soon as it is light. We can't go home in the middle of the night. Your reputation would be ruined. But we can go tomorrow, and we will make up some excuse to protect you. But please don't say that you hate me.'

'I don't hate you. I am just astonished and disappointed.' The moon shone down on a tearstained Catherine holding a tear-soaked hanky.

'Let's go inside, the chill is settling. I'll build a fire and get us something to eat and a cup of hot tea. You can have the main bedroom and I'll take the other bedroom; there should be two, according to Charley. I promise to make no advances to you. I love you, Catherine, with all my heart. I could never hurt you.'

He reached over and took her hand, which was cold and limp. She shivered as if to repel him but made no effort to take her hand away.

'We will do as you say.' Catherine sniffed and opened the door of the car to clamber out and stumble over the stones to the front door.

Ben lit a match and set light to the generous pile of logs and twigs so that soon there was a good blaze. He seated Catherine on the sofa, her face still blank with shock, and found some shawls to drape around her shivering body. Gently he untied the gauzy ribbons holding her bonnet secure, removed it from her head and laid it carefully on the sideboard. He was distressed to see how pale she was and set about warming up some broth from the basket of provisions concealed on the car's backseat under a tartan blanket.

Once Catherine was sipping her soup, he explored the cottage properly to find the other bedroom, but all the other rooms were full of old dusty furniture. Clearly the cottage was used for one purpose only. He would have to sleep there in front of the huge open fireplace, where the logs were crackling and sparking like a bonfire. And Catherine could sleep alone in the only bed.

*

Catherine lay awake, staring at the stars twinkling more brightly in the midnight blue sky than they ever did in Cardiff or Kingcharlton, wondering how this had happened to her. It was such a shock. She had always prided herself on being sensible, a modern woman. Yet, she had allowed herself to be almost seduced, despite all her mother's warnings and lectures on the danger of getting too close to any man before she was married. She couldn't fathom out whether it was Ben's deception or Charley's thinking that he was helping a couple to get together. How could she have been so blind? It was obvious now she thought it all through, but she hadn't expected Ben to lie to her; he seemed so straightforward and honest.

Was this how girls carried on, weekends away with men without the sanctity of marriage? But was she being very old-fashioned? What would Annie do? But Annie would never get herself in this situation; she was calm and sensible, not wild and impractical.

Catherine had never imagined it would happen to her: that she would have been forced to make this choice in such circumstances. Before this upset had occurred, she had felt drawn to Ben whenever he appeared. There was an attraction there, and he seemed to feel the same. Strange tremors swept through her body when they walked close together. She had imagined him holding her and even kissing her. She could not deny that she had entertained the thought of marrying him, she had dreamed of how it would be.

It would interfere with her plans to become a nurse but even that did not seem to be so important now she had met him, fallen in love with him over the past few weeks. Sleeping with a man before the formality of a wedding was not something she would have contemplated, but they were living in unfamiliar times.

She thought of all the men going off to war and not returning. She had several friends who had already lost fiancés. The way it was going with the losses; she and Annie might never have husbands. Was she doing the wrong thing? Was she being stuffy and old-fashioned? She didn't like the thought of never having slept with a man, but what about babies? Surely not if you just did it once.

Her bed was comfy, but she tossed and turned, tormented by her feelings and her hot restless body. She knew Ben would never approach her in this way again. And what if he never did come back? She would be filled with regret that she had not allowed herself the experience of being held in his arms. She might live her life heartbroken that she had pushed him away when he wanted her.

*

Catherine threw back her covers and put her bare feet on the floor. The tiles were chilly to the touch – she started to shiver. Gently, she opened the bedroom door and gazed at the firelit scene before her. Ben lay on the sofa, a blanket askew over his body, his handsome face troubled in dreams. She stood in silent contemplation – wondering what to do.

Moonlight lay across the floor between them: a silvery path to guide her to him. She gazed on the unfamiliar body, so far felt only through fabric, a hard lean body from working on the farm. She leaned forward and trailed her fingertips across his shoulders. She stroked the soft tantalising skin with a tentative finger. His eyes opened.

'Catherine, what's the matter. Are you frightened?'

'Ben, come and share my bed. I have decided I was wrong. We are both modern people being kept apart by war. Why should we not show our love for each other? I have not slept with a man so you will have to teach me how to love you.'

She bent towards him. Their mouths brushed as soft as butterfly wings. The kisses became more fervent; they were shivering with the cold and pent-up passion. They looked at each other, taking in the vision of their half-clothed bodies. How to begin? Were they both on unfamiliar ground? Catherine made her decision clear.

'It's cold out here. Come and share my bed, there's room enough for two.'

As they lay like statues side by side, both uncertain as to how to proceed, she whispered: 'I would have waited for you, Ben, until war was over and we could get married but as things are, this might be our only chance to be together as man and wife. I cannot live a whole lifetime regretting that I did not love you properly.'

It felt so strange; who should make the first move? What constrictions lay upon these lovers, controlled by the rules of their families and the judgement of society?

Catherine turned her head and gently kissed Ben's cheek. His lips brushed her mouth. Where their bare skin touched, the sensation of warm yielding flesh soon had them burning with the heat of desire. Tremors ran through their bodies, as they kissed and caressed and explored, growing bolder as their passion increased.

Ben took her in his arms and whispered, although they were alone. His voice had grown husky, its timbre deepening with his growing desire.

'Let you into a secret, honey. I have never done this either. I was waiting for the right girl. Growing up with three sisters and a marvellous mother, I have a great respect for women and their honour. I had plenty of chances, going up to London on leave with the boys and hitting the town but it never appealed to me, that's why I always came home with Charley instead. And when I met you, I was hooked. You were the only girl I wanted.' Silence fell, as words were no longer needed. Their bodies entwined as they discovered the joys of making love in the moonlight.

*

The morning arrived with birdsong and wood smoke drifting through the trees. Catherine awoke and rubbed her eyes, disorientated by her unfamiliar surroundings. Gone were the stark white painted walls of Matron's cottage, to be replaced by stone and beam with thatched straw fringes showing through the windows.

Beside her lay the warm sleeping body of Ben, arms and legs spread-eagled amongst crumpled sheets. His handsome face reposed in sleep meant so much more to her now. They were betrothed, pledged to each other. As he opened sleepy eyes, he took a moment to realise where he was and then reached for her. His stubbly chin grazed her face. The feel of skin on skin was still new to her – the warmth of bare flesh, the shiver of cold hands, the length of a warm body stretched alongside hers.

The contrast between cold air and the heat they produced with their lovemaking was tantalising. The thrill of that moment when his caresses tipped her over into the strongest of sensations – into another world of fluid reality – melting – flying. Her body became a musical instrument attuned to his touch as he played her into pleasure. He stroked her into a state where every contact tingled, and that strange feeling swept over her again.

Their kisses deepened, longer every moment they stayed in bed. The sheets were rumpled, crumpled and strangely damp. They surfaced briefly for tea and toast, and then tumbled back into bed

Sometime later, Ben sat up and seemed to be looking for something on the bedside table. What was he doing? He picked up something and turned to face Catherine. What could it possibly be? There was nothing there last night. He must have gone to fetch it from the other room whilst she was sleeping.

'Catherine, I should have bought you an engagement ring but there has been so little time and I wanted to spend every moment with you. Besides which, I want you to choose a ring that you really like. However, I want you to have a token of my love and a symbol of my commitment for the future. I've been saving up from my pay, I have enough now but that's no use if there are no shops and there's no time left before I leave. I'd like you to have this. It's something very precious to me. It's all that I have to offer you as a token of our engagement. Give me your hand.' Ben watched her face anxiously as he stumbled through a speech which had clearly been carefully thought out.

Into her open palm, he placed a small silver object about an inch square, covered with engravings of leaves and flowers, with the letters B.T. engraved on the front within a small circle.

Catherine turned it over in her palm and saw it had a hinged lid, which opened to reveal something inside. When she looked closely, she saw they were tiny little matches, with white stems and red heads.

'They call this a *Vesta* fob,' said Ben. 'It keeps the matches dry and safe in times of war. It belonged to my granddad – he wore it on his pocket watch chain. His name was Benjamin Trueman too, and when he died, it was handed down to me. My mom has a lovely photo of him wearing it. It takes pride of place at home. It's a family heirloom and I want to give it to you to keep safe for me till I return to replace it with a fancy engagement ring.'

He took the *Vesta* fob from her hand to show her another feature of his gift.

'See this tiny little ring on the side for attaching to a watch chain? I thought you could thread a silver chain through and wear it round your neck. It's very light and would look pretty with a nice dress, or you could conceal it underneath. Either way, I kinda thought that you would think of me whenever you feel it against your skin. You'll have a proper engagement ring when we have gone through the formalities and I have asked your father for permission to marry you. I promise you this faithfully.'

Ben paused to gauge her reaction, hoping so much that this token would assuage some of the pain he had caused her by his naïve deception. With bated breath, he waited for her reaction.

'Oh, Ben, how wonderful. It's so beautiful. I'll keep it with me always. It can go inside my pastille tin for the time being to save losing it, as it is so small. If I sew a little cover for it, it won't rattle at all and there'll be no scratches. I carry that tin with your letters and photos inside everywhere, deep in my pocket.'

She leant over and kissed him.

'I do love you so. I am so pleased I came to my senses and took you to my bed. I would never have forgiven myself if I had let you go without our special time together.'

With this she blushed; she was still not at ease expressing her feelings or having a naked man beside her. He pulled her closer. The hairs on his chest tickled her breasts and made her giggle. They were drawn into their own little world of passion once more.

So, this is what my mother warned me about, Catherine thought, *this deadly peril that I should avoid at all costs. I think it is rather nice, a bit uncomfortable to start with but now giving me all sorts of strange feelings, which are exciting.* She stopped thinking as a swirling sensation swept her away. Ben was stroking her back which was having a distinctly arousing effect. She squirmed as her insides melted and a sort of tornado was released inside her. Goodness, that was a bit different. Together they explored the pleasures of their unfamiliar bodies, riding on the waves of passion or basking in the simple pleasure of lying peacefully together as man and wife.

But much too soon, the day faded, and it was time to pack their bags and leave. About to enter the car, Catherine turned round and took a long lingering glance at the cottage, the scene of such happiness, though nearly a disaster.

It'll be a long time before we will be able to spend another weekend like this one, she thought.

They drove home slowly; stretching out the time they could spend together before they must part to suffer bad times ahead. They reached the bottom of the hill and rumbled up over the cobbles to stop outside the large iron gates.

'Leave me here,' said Catherine. 'If they see us together, they will know we have become lovers.'

She picked up her suitcase containing all the new clothes still as fresh as when they had come from the shop and strode off into the grounds of the workhouse with not one backward glance or even a discreet wave.

'What on earth have you been doing?' Annie asked, back from visiting her parents. 'You look as if you have been cow wrestling. What a state you are in. You reek of the countryside. Were they muckspreading?'

'Funny you should say that. Actually, we saw a sheep on its back and Ben said that it would die if left because they can't get back up by themselves, so we wrestled it to its feet and it seemed to be okay,' replied Catherine, desperately trying to distract her sister from her interrogation. She took herself off to the bedroom. Tonight, she would sleep in her lonely little bed with only Ben's scent on her body to remind her of their passion and love for each other.

Daisy was lurking on the stairs in a dark corner. She looked at Catherine's dreamy expression and thought she recognised that look. Growing up in a crowded cottage, nothing was secret.

'I do hope that Miss Catherine will not get caught, especially if this is her first time,' she whispered to the amber-eyed cat that was standing guard over a promising mouse hole. 'I'll keep my fingers crossed for her.'

Another person in the house had exactly the same thoughts but with a less-forgiving attitude. Matron was watching Catherine return in a state of euphoria.

‘Silly girl,’ she said, ‘silly, silly girl.’

Chapter Eighteen

Ben had been given the wrong information about the embarkation leave: it was a fabrication, part of Charley's misguided plan to help Ben get closer to Catherine. They would be leaving Kingcharlton, but only going as far as Salisbury Plain for one last intensive training session to perfect the new techniques they were going to employ at Vimy Ridge.

Catherine did not see Ben for a couple of months. When he did return, there was no opportunity to be together again as wounded men were arriving at the memorial hospital and Catherine was rushed off her feet with no leave at all. They did snatch a moment's conversation now and then but that was all. Catherine's heart was already aching with the pain of separation.

When the day arrived for the ceremonial departure of the troops it was a poignant experience. Standing on the platform brought back memories of the evening when Catherine had first seen Ben standing on the platform at Temple Meads. His face had smiled at her out of the darkness. Now he was leaving her, travelling to the Front. Here they were – standing together – saying goodbye. She might never see him again, hear his voice, or feel his touch. She shivered and moved closer, feeling his warm breath on her cheek as he whispered in her ear how much he loved her. He had found them a little niche formed by two pillars, sheltered from the buffeting crowd saying their goodbyes. This was the closest they had been for a long time and dormant feelings were awakened.

In front of their cosy nook swirled crowds of soldiers, who in an effort to keep morale up, were exchanging jokes with chums, constantly lighting cigarettes, coughing and spluttering in the early morning mist, hugging wives and sweethearts, and lifting small children onto their shoulders to keep them safe. It seemed as if the whole of Bristol was there to wave goodbye to their loved ones, from lowly shop girls to ladies swathed in furs. Some had been given days off by employers who thought that they were helping the war effort by this act of generosity. Most of the women were wearing their Sunday best apparel to honour their menfolk who were travelling towards the horrors of war.

Ben and Catherine stood close to each other, not saying much, just grateful to be breathing the same air for a little longer. Catherine badly wanted to tell Ben that she thought she might be in a blessed condition. She had missed two monthlies – she who had been as regular as clockwork and could no longer face her porridge laced with golden syrup in the mornings. Her breasts were swelling already, and her nipples tingled in the cold weather – a most curious sensation.

The wind whistled along the platform finding any chink to invade their warm clothes. Fortunately, the sheer bulk of the crowd of soldiers waiting to clamber aboard the train provided a modicum of shelter and warmth. As the numbers increased, Catherine was pushed against Ben. Jammed closer together by the swelling crowd in front of them, Ben put his arms around her to save her from being squashed against the wall. As they cuddled together, her face buried in his great coat, his special scent of tobacco and toothpaste mingled with whiffs of shaving soap enveloped her in a mist. If she closed her eyes, they were back in the cottage, their arms wrapped around each other. She longed to kiss him though that might seem scandalous, but the thought of not seeing him for months made her bold. Her lips brushed his cheeks already beginning to stubble.

Ben's lips sought hers and for a moment she swooned in the maelstrom of emotions that the kiss aroused. Her knees felt wobbly and she leant against him for support. His arms enclosed her even more tightly as if he did not want to let her go. 'My own darling Catherine. You will write to me, won't you?' he whispered, tickling her ear with his words.

'I'll write every day. My thoughts will always be with you, dearest Ben.'

It was at that moment that Catherine made a decision, her feelings intensified with recklessness by the close proximity of Ben's body. 'I'll write to you and what is more, I'll follow you to France as soon as I can persuade Matron to let me go. I can drive an ambulance. I'll come and find you and we'll fight the enemy together.'

'If you do get over to France, make for Arras and Vimy Ridge,' Ben whispered. 'Try to get there before April when the big push will take place. Don't tell that to anyone, sweetheart. Our lives are in your hands.'

Ben noticed the familiar wayward tress of red-gold hair fighting to be free of Catherine's hat. Without thinking, he leant forward, took hold of the rebellious ringlet and tucked it behind her ear, such a familiar gesture that it caused him more grief than the enormity of getting on the train and travelling to France. How would he manage without the anticipation of seeing her, walking with her and talking for hours? 'I have written to my folks back home and told them all about you. I've asked them to look after you if anything happens to me.'

'No, don't say that. It tempts fate.'

'Keep my letters safe. You will find my folks' address there. You can write to my mom. Tell her we are engaged.'

'I have one more thing to tell you.' Catherine took a deep breath. She started the sentence, but it faded into nothingness as she failed to find the right words. Then it was too late as the fiery dragon of an engine wreathed in smoke drew slowly alongside the waiting troops.

'All aboard, lads, we haven't got all day.' Sweethearts were kissed and children were hugged and then the crowds separated into men on the trains and women with their children close on the platform – all trying their hardest to catch a last glimpse of their loved ones. As the train gathered up steam, Catherine felt as if her heart would break. Life would be unbearable without Ben and what would she do if her suspicions proved to be well founded? Her parents would be furious. Already Ben had one foot on the train step.

'Ben, I think I might be with child.' There, the words were out. They hung in the air like bombs waiting to drop. Ben looked bewildered. Then he had to go, the guards were slamming the doors closed. The whistle blew a final time, and the train drew slowly out of the station. Hands were waving, tears were shed, and handkerchiefs were employed as the men rolled off to war. Catherine's last glimpse of Ben was him leaning out of the window, mouthing, 'It'll be alright – don't worry.' Saluting her as he had done before.

*

Ben was flattened against the door with men pushing past trying to find compartments to store their belongings. He managed to catch a glimpse of Catherine's face as the train rumbled away from the crowded platform. His mind was whirling; he could hardly believe what she had just whispered to him. A baby – surely not? They had only made love on that one weekend in the cottage – no other opportunities. He didn't know whether he would tell his mom; she was very religious. This might cause her to think badly of Catherine. He wanted her meet Catherine before the secret was disclosed and see for herself what a perfect lady she was.

*

Catherine remained on the platform watching the train taking her lover away until it rattled round the bend. Following the noisy hustle and bustle of the partings, a communal silence dropped like falling rain as people left the platform, talking in subdued whispers not wanting to share their misery with anyone else but close friends. The air, deprived of human bodies, grew cooler as a wicked wind blew across the platforms. Catherine wrapped her scarf tightly around her neck but still shivered. The cold she felt was internal, a sense of shock and loss.

In the railway restaurant, the lamps glowed in the gloom of the morning, creating an atmosphere of cosiness with all the bottles behind the bar casting twinkling pools of colour. A tray of tea and a currant bun would give her time to calm down and untangle her thoughts. But the tea grew cold and the bun stayed unbitten as she sat deep in contemplation. *Why had she burdened Ben with her fears about a baby? It was early days yet and she could prove to be wrong. Baby matters were such a mystery. There was nobody she could ask. And yet her body felt different and for some mysterious reason, she was sure that she and Ben would become parents.*

Leaving the station, she walked down the long pavement towards the street where an omnibus could be caught on its way to Kingcharlton. Deeply engrossed in her thoughts, the uneven cobbles caused her to stumble. Only the quick action of a passing porter carrying bags to a waiting hansom cab at the bottom of the slope, saved her from falling.

'Watch out for those cobbles, they are very slippery today, miss!' His friendly warning reminded her of the time she had met Ben on his horse and the feeling of loss grew even more powerful as she contemplated a life lived alone. Working through her tangled web of feelings, Ben's instructions to contact his mother surfaced. The large *Craven A* cigarette tin Ben had given her crammed with letters and cards from his family was in her drawer. She would write to his mother, as he had said, but not yet. Tapping her side to make sure that the small pastille tin was safe, she was reassured by its oblong shape deep in her pocket. She would not be telling her own mother about a possible grandchild. Her mother would not approve and would send her father to Kingcharlton to fetch her home.

Catherine sat on an omnibus rattling through the busy streets, watching the people of the city going about their daily routines. She was not interested in what they were doing but rather on her plans to follow Ben to France as soon as she could. *First, she must ask Matron's permission to try for a posting in France, possibly driving an ambulance. There would soon be more women arriving in Kingcharlton to help at the hospital so that Matron might be persuaded to release her. In the meantime, she could start packing her carpetbag.* She was already making a list in her head of useful items.

How would she manage to live without Ben? How did all these other women manage without their menfolk? She had not expected to fall in love with anybody when she planned her move from Cardiff to Kingcharlton. She had never felt such sadness. The anguish of being in love was almost unbearable: sleepless nights, constant agitation, exhilaration when Ben appeared and sorrow when he left. And now he had departed for the Front where unknown perils lurked. Her head was full of horrible imaginings; she had seen the wounds inflicted on returning men. Hopefully nobody would be around when she reached the hospital. If she was lucky, she could slip into Matron's cottage without anyone noticing.

Daisy and the amber-eyed cat noticed, of course, drawing their own conclusions. Daisy was thinking that Miss Catherine would soon be off, she was so restless, and she loved Mr Ben. That was obvious. But would Matron give her permission, she was very strict about certain matters?

Chapter Nineteen

Matron seemed quite happy to release Catherine who appeared to be in turmoil. It was unlikely that she would make a good candidate for hospital nursing. Perhaps her talents were better suited to driving an ambulance over the battlefields of France. Catherine had been a whirlwind of activity, packing and repacking her carpetbag with necessary items. Advice on how to proceed had come from all quarters with dire warnings of the perils she might encounter on alien soil, such as over-amorous soldiers and unsavoury foreigners.

Catherine dealt with this spurious information using the tactics she had learned over the years. She found that saying "yes" to all advice, whilst thanking the giver, made them go away leaving her in peace far quicker than if she argued about it.

Underneath she was wretched with impatience to be away to France. The thought of meeting up with Ben was a shining goal in the distance, a lodestone to which she was pulled no matter what went on around her. Every so often, she would feel for the reassuring shape of the tin in her pocket, keeping her engagement gift, her photos and letters safe. The possibility of losing the tin with her last links to Ben was a constant fear, horrible beyond belief.

Billy the carter was to take her to the station. Matron insisted that he was to see her safely on the train. Climbing onto the rickety old cart, Catherine was reminded of how her life had changed since that stormy night in September when Billy had brought her to the workhouse. It brought back memories of Ben's face lit up on the crowded platform of Temple Meads. Now there was only one more battle to face, one more opponent to overcome.

*

Catherine had a secret – long concealed. It shaped the image she presented to the world and took a great deal of energy to control. It was the one thing that threatened to destroy all her ambitions, much more powerful than her parents' disapproval. Far from being calm, cool and collected, she was constantly assailed by anxiety. An over-abundance of heart-stopping nerves which came into action when faced by life's challenges, had to be conquered on a daily basis. To overcome this curse she sometimes took on tasks most people would dismiss as foolhardy.

Right now, adrenalin arrows were shooting painfully all over her body. She was nearing the point when she would become incapable of any rational thought or action, behaving like a chicken with no head. She tried to remember what her doctor had taught her, way back in Cardiff, when Mother had taken her to his surgery in desperation over these panic attacks. Sit down quietly somewhere and practise deep breathing. *Close your eyes and concentrate, in and out, in and out.* So much more effective than *sal volatile*, which only aggravates the spirits, not soothes them.

Her doctor was very progressive; to the extent that Fred Waterman, her father, became highly suspicious of his methods, declaring that it was a lot of nonsense. But Florence, her mother, driven to distraction by Catherine's nerves, listened very carefully. The doctor had spent some time out in India with the army and had become intrigued by the concept that the mind could rule over matter. The spiritual approach to life fascinated him and he endeavoured to make sense of it all. There were some aspects that were rather extreme and almost preposterous to a western way of thinking, but he could ignore those and take away the things he found useful.

Hence his advice to Catherine which she was finding very useful; he suggested periods of quiet contemplation and deep breathing would help her to deal with her everyday life. If she had not followed his methods, she would never have become a Voluntary Aid nurse, left home or contemplated going overseas. The frustrating part of it was that it was only the anticipation of "things to be done" that almost crippled her. She was capable of attaining so much. Once she had actually started on a procedure that worried her, all fear and apprehension was lost, and she began to enjoy herself. People around her had no concept of her problem and if asked would have described her as overly confident.

She was not going to let her body prevent her following her dreams. She was not going to allow the men to say that women could not achieve what men could, that they were too frail. With these thoughts in mind, she withdrew her precious tin from her pocket and seated herself on the bed. She would look at her photos and her love token, the silver fob, to remind her that all her mementos were still there. One of her great fears was that these possessions would go missing. To calm herself she closed her eyes to meditate, as the doctor called it. Her neatly packed luggage was beside her on the bed. All she had to do now was await the arrival of Billy the carter. All would be well.

A knock on the door interrupted her trance. She blinked, feeling half asleep.

'Are you there, Miss Catherine? The carter has arrived. Matron says to fetch you.' Daisy's voice was faint and forlorn.

Catherine closed her tin, put it down and rushed to open the door, all the nerves tingling again. The last few items went into her bag. She put on her hat and coat and checked her appearance in the mirror.

'Shall I carry your bag down, Miss Catherine?'

'No, it's much too heavy for you. You take my handbag and lead the way.' Catherine dragged the cumbersome carpetbag off the bed, inadvertently side-swiping her precious tin onto the floor where it lay unnoticed, concealed by the fringes of the candlewick bedspread. It was such a rush. The imperative need to catch the solitary train of the day to London took over obliterating all sensible thought. She had already checked her luggage, over and over again. What could go wrong?

Downstairs was a flurry of goodbyes. Annie had already left the day before to return to Cardiff and domesticity. Cook handed over some sandwiches wrapped in crisp white butchers' paper. Daisy offered an apple, all wrinkly and sweet from being stored in the attics. Catherine tucked these presents deep in her handbag, sure that she would be glad of these gifts later on in the day. She thought of her papers, essential for travel, as she made room in the bag. Her mind focussed on her documents, her worries were spent on those and no other thought went to her little tin of treasures. With her thick woollen coat wrapped around her as a protective layer – keeping all inside safe, she was confident that all was well and relaxed. She was on her way to see Ben and she would surely find him.

The train was packed, and she had to fight for a seat. They were passing Reading when she recovered enough to open her coat buttons and feel for the comforting tin in her pocket. Where was it? She stood up to see if it was hidden in the folds of her garments. Panic came thundering in. There was no way she could search properly on the train. She would have to wait until she reached London. She needed to check her carpetbag; maybe she had tossed it in there when Daisy knocked. Catherine tried to remember the sequence of things but her mind was paralysed by fear. There was little room to move, let alone search her bag. She felt as though she was going to faint, her body felt hot and sweaty; she was trembling all over. All she could do was to close her eyes and practise the deep breathing which seemed to help a little. When they reached London, she had some time between changing trains to check through her carpetbag. She managed to find a Ladies' waiting room on the station, with a table where she rummaged in her bag looking for her tin. It was not there. What should she do? It must have been left in the bedroom. She would have to write to Matron who could ask Daisy to search.

*

At the same time that Catherine's train was passing through Reading, Daisy climbed the stairs to what she thought of as Miss Catherine's room in order to strip the beds and place fresh linen on them. The room still held the delicate perfume of lily of the valley. Daisy held the sheets to her face to inhale more deeply the scent of her beloved friend.

Tears were falling unheeded as she wept for the loss of Miss Catherine. Did she feel she would never see her again? France was a million miles away to Daisy who had never left the village of Kingcharlton. Blinded by her tears and hampered by the over-sized hessian apron, she became entangled in the sheets so that she stumbled and fell. Lying flat on the floor, her streaming eyes espied something lying under the bed. It looked like Miss Catherine's tin. Although Catherine thought nobody knew of her secret, Daisy lurking in dark corners had seen her patting her skirt from time to time. She had also seen her putting the tin into her pocket and had come upon her examining the contents. Daisy could not read or write but she was not without common sense and had worked out that the tin contained something precious.

Daisy untangled herself and stretched an arm out to retrieve the treasure Miss Catherine had left behind. It must have fallen accidentally. *Had she missed it already – did she realise it was lying here in her bedroom – was she distraught? How could Daisy help her beloved Catherine?* She opened the tin – saw the photos of Catherine and Ben whom she recognised, sheets of paper with the magic squiggles, and a small shiny object: a mystery until she opened the lid and saw the tiny matches inside.

Letters meant little to Daisy, but they were obviously precious to Catherine. That was what mattered. Daisy scooped up the tin and popped it in her hiding place. Matron had provided her with several pairs of voluminous knickers, which were real bloomers reaching to her knees, made of scratchy unbleached cotton with elastic strong enough to make a catapult. Daisy pulled open the garment at her knee and placed the tin inside. It fitted snugly. There was comfort from having something of Miss Catherine to keep her company. A sturdy uniform dress and everyday wraparound apron concealed all beneath. These heavy clothes gave Daisy a rounded appearance which concealed how skinny she was, though she was filling out under Matron's watchful eye.

Daisy gathered the bedding and staggered downstairs with it to the back kitchen where the copper stood steaming waiting for the sheets and whites of the household. She picked up the wooden tongs and pushed the bed-linen into the soapy suds. The tin would have to wait till she had a quiet moment. But for now, it was safe, knocking gently against her knee as she moved about her tasks. Daisy felt pleased by the thought that she was looking after something of Miss Catherine's. She was happy to help her beloved heroine.

*

Standing alone in the middle of all the hustle and bustle of the busy port of Dover, Catherine watched the weary travellers making their way down the gangplank. How would she manage to get aboard a boat? She had been given permission to travel to France but told she must make her own travel arrangements.

The dockyard was incredibly large and sprawling – the reality of the journey about to be undertaken sank in. Catherine had never acted on her own initiative before. The guidance of her parents had shaped her past life. For once she realised how fortunate she was to have a solid family behind her. Now she missed the guidance of her mother and father with their stern kindness. Her limbs became heavy; thirst and hunger made her weak. The worry of losing her tin hung over her like a bad omen. The small picnic given to her by the cook in Kingcharlton was long gone. Her head was spinning and there was no prospect of eating again for a long time. Amid the crowds rushing past like battleships on the offensive, she was a tiny rudderless boat drifting helplessly.

No longer fired by the rush of adrenaline that had carried her so far, she was assailed by doubts as to whether she could achieve her goal. Travelling to Dover had held few problems, always a spare seat on a train. Friendly soldiers would find a space for her, even letting her sit on their kit bags if necessary. The nurse's uniform helped of course. It broke down barriers of class and fortunes, making her appear more approachable. But away from the cosy comfort and companionship of the railways, she was on her own. There were soldiers on guard at the gangplanks and customs officers checking details and tickets and turning back any suspicious-looking characters. She gathered that it needed a special permit to purchase a ticket. Leaning on a stone bollard for support, a feeling of helplessness overcame her. Oh for a cup of coffee and a hot buttered scone after a visit to the ladies cloakroom. She longed for her mother and Annie to help her out.

Catherine was trying to work out whether she could slip past one of the guards by following close behind a group of nurses when she heard an imperious voice. Startled out of her dazed condition by the strident tones of a lady, she turned to see who the owner of the voice was. Not far from her stone bollard, was a large expensive looking car from which issued a stern voice berating a harassed-looking soldier checking the papers of travellers.

'Don't tell me what I can and cannot do. My husband is Lord Hemsworth, and I am on my way to the war zone to set up a hospital for the wounded soldiers. I have a letter of permission from the Prime Minister himself.' An elegant arm from the gleaming vehicle was waving a piece of paper at the embarrassed guard. The apparent lack of respect for his important position seemed to fluster him even more.

Catherine edged stealthily forward to see what the hold-up was as the lady produced a tortoiseshell holder and inserted a cigarette whilst waiting for the soldier's answer. The owner of the aristocratic voice then swivelled round to survey the scene. Catherine found herself under the intense scrutiny of deep blue eyes in a stern but beautiful face. An imperious hand beckoned her forward.

'Why are you loitering about here, young lady? Have you nothing better to do?'

'I can't find a means of getting on the boat to go to France, your Ladyship.' Catherine assumed that the wife of a Lord should be addressed as a Lady. 'I want to cross the Channel to France to help nurse the soldiers, but I fear they will not let me on the boat. I have no ticket and no authority to buy one.'

'Nonsense, all this red tape! Hop in. I'll take you over. We need all the nurses we can get.' The passenger door of the car was flung open, nearly knocking over the dithering soldier.

Catherine found herself face-to-face with an enormous wolfhound that leant forward and licked her face. He was very hairy and had an intense doggy odour but obviously harmless though he did not like the soldier much – a low menacing growl was rattling in the dog's throat.

'Get in the back, Gelert. Make some space for our new friend.' Gelert unfolded himself and moved to the back seat. To show there were no hard feelings at losing his special place, his wet tongue licked Catherine's neck as she settled herself in.

'Hold tight, my dear, I've had enough of this nonsense. There's a battle waging over the water and they need us.' With these words the gearstick was manhandled into place and the car shot forward to join the line of vehicles ready to be hoisted onto the boat.

'Hoy, you can't do that, you are not allowed.' The soldier rushed after her, his face as red as an overripe tomato.

'Too late, my man. I've just done it. There's a war on, don't you know? I'll be dining with the war generals next week and I'll mention your attitude to them if you don't keep out of my way.' Her Ladyship was hell-bent on moving towards the boat.

The soldier gave up and went away to bother somebody else. Catherine, Gelert and her gallant rescuer motored to the head of the queue of waiting vehicles and were soon ensconced safely on the decks of the boat.

'Call me Fiona. Lady Hemsworth is my title for the general public, but I'm Fiona to my friends and I feel that you and I are going to be friends. I like a girl who has pluck and refuses to be put off by rules and regulations. Who are you and where are you headed?'

'My name is Catherine Waterman – I have been training to become a VAD nurse in Somerset. But now I want to nurse at the Front.' Catherine did not want to reveal her true mission of finding Ben, in case Lady Hemsworth did not approve and Catherine was left stranded again.

'Good, we'll find you a place, maybe at my hospital. The important thing is that you are here to help. Keep close to me, my dear, some of these men are a bit rough and you are just a slip of a girl.'

Catherine recalled the friendliness of the soldiers on the train and also the fact that she was nearly six foot tall, but she did not want to annoy her benefactor so she meekly replied, 'I will, your lady… I mean Fiona. I'll take great care.'

Lady Hemsworth had a word with the captain or rather one of his minions, securing a cabin and ordering tea. Gelert stretched out on the floor at their feet and grunted softly in his sleep. Catherine welcomed the calm after all her perilous adventures and sipped delicate Assam tea flavoured with a slice of lemon. It was soothing to be away from the hordes of boisterous soldiers with all the chaos that attended an exit from the docks. *This is the life,* she thought, *this is the way moneyed gentry live; even in wartime, life is more comfortable for them.*

Her eyelids were drooping. She was almost drifting off to sleep whilst listening to a long monologue by Lady Hemsworth on the virtues of sphagnum moss as a dressing for wounds followed by a discourse on the benefits of beef tea for invalids. Fiona did not seem to need any kind of response and her voice had now assumed hypnotic tones. Then when her young companion was at her most vulnerable point, Fiona pounced, flipping Catherine out of her trance.

'Now, young lady, tell me the real reason why you are travelling to France all on your own. There are ways and means of getting oneself attached to a unit of nurses and sent over to France. You seem like an enterprising intelligent person and yet here you are travelling on your own. You must have a reason –

come on – let's have the truth and maybe I can help you achieve your mission.'

Catherine, now wide-awake, chose her words carefully. 'I am trying to follow my sweetheart – a soldier who serves with the Canadian troops. He is stationed at a place called Vimy Ridge. I fear he will die before I can tell him how much I love him.' She left out the suspicions about a baby, in case that was too much for Fiona to deal with. If she thought Catherine was with child, she might send her back on the next boat, saying wartime France was no place for a woman in an interesting condition. Fiona clearly had her own rules for life and Catherine was not sure what they were.

'Your soldier must be with Byng's lot then. We'll see what we can do to make your journey easier. I'm always fond of a love story and we must keep sight of the joyful part of this life in these difficult days.'

Catherine was taken aback; it all sounded so simple. After the despair and doubts of the morning, she felt her head was spinning again so she laid her head on the stiff linen pillow of the bunk and gave in to a deep dreamless sleep.

In the morning, travelling along the muddy roads, Fiona resumed the topic of the mission. 'My dear, I know a lot of the generals and I can give you letters to help you on your way. Where were you stationed in Somerset? I know the county well. I've relatives scattered in every nook and cranny'

'Kingcharlton, not far from Bristol and Bath. An old building is being transformed into a memorial hospital for soldiers to have rest and recuperation.

It's a very quiet little town.' Catherine wondered quite how powerful Fiona was. This new friendship looked promising.

'Isn't Kingcharlton where Major Bowmaker has a place – an old Somerset farmhouse? I know him. Don't tell me you have been working in the hospital he is building? If you are good enough for him, then you are good enough for me. I'll help you on your way, my dear.' Fiona looked very pleased to have found an acquaintance with connections to Catherine, someone who could confirm her *bona fides*.

They stopped to let Gelert stretch his long legs, have a sniff and make himself comfortable. Then it was back to the long, winding road. Catherine was relieved when the tall towers of the old chateau that Fiona had taken over came into view. Automobiles were not the most comfortable of rides on these ill-kept roads. Fiona's friends rushed out to greet them, mostly aristocratic ladies like her. They were smartly dressed and full of fun despite the grim conditions. There were other females present – young women who, like Catherine, had wanted to be part of the action in France and not stuck at home under the supervision of their mothers. Catherine was to learn that Fiona favoured a positive attitude as part of the healing process so each evening she and her friends would dress up in glamorous gowns for the last ward rounds of the night in order to raise the morale of the patients. She had some warning words for Catherine. 'You must brace yourself – you'll see some truly awful sights. Very often all you can do is bring them comfort in their last hours. Always appear positive and in charge of the situation.'

Catherine remained for a few days to help with the hospital chores whilst Fiona contacted her large group of friends to see if anyone could give Catherine a ride closer to her goal of reaching Vimy. Fiona was obviously a very powerful lady, as it did not take long to arrange Catherine's departure in search of Ben, with letters of introduction to help her all the way.

Chapter Twenty

Catherine surveyed the sorry remains of the chapel at Souchez – only one corner was left standing – a meeting of two ragged walls, giving the illusion of shelter. Dull thuds of bombs sounded in the distance. They never seemed to stop. The smell of cordite and mud filled the air.

Cold wintry winds blew across the battered land. Ben drew Catherine into the shelter of the wall, snuggling up to keep warm. She raised her face to his, gazing into his earnest dark eyes with their long black lashes. She stroked his weary face with tender fingertips. His lips brushed her cheek gently. Her lips were dry and cracked with the wind and cold – how would they feel to him? He kissed her softly then passionately. They could feel the heat rising in their bodies and longed for a place to make love. *This might be my last chance to show him how much I love him,* she thought. It really was much too cold for any lovemaking but the intensity of their passion for each other might keep them warm. Were they both thinking the same thing?

Leaning back on the wall, Catherine noticed carvings like ancient wall paintings on the limestone blocks. Ben explained that his companions were using their knives to leave a memory of themselves – eerily like an inscription on a gravestone – their name, their platoon, their country signified by a maple leaf. Catherine ran her fingers along the grooves tracing the letters. Her once-beautiful nails were ragged and grubby.

How poignant these crudely carved words were. Would the walls survive the war? Would anyone apart from the troops ever get to see the messages? Having experienced the battlefields and acres of mud, she thought that the walls would soon be bombed out of existence, taking the carvings with them, but she wanted to believe it would turn out differently. She had to stay positive.

'Shall we carve our names?' said Catherine. 'Write details of our lives, leave a statement of you and I as a couple and if nobody else knows of our love, at least it will be here – set in stone.' Catherine smiled, a weak little gesture of lost hope. She had the most awful feeling that they would never reach the stage of formally telling their parents of their love for one and other. As if on cue, she felt a butterfly flutter in her abdomen.

'Ben, the baby, I felt him move – the first quickening and it's here with you.'

'How do you know it's a boy?'

'I'm sure of it – a tall handsome boy like his father. Are you pleased about it or will we be a burden to you?'

'Not at all, Catherine, please don't say that. When all this fighting is over, I plan to return to Canada and find me some good farming land near Vancouver where the soil is so fertile that plentiful vegetables grow overnight – the fish just swim out of the deep ocean into our nets.' He took her hands in his and stared intently into her eyes as if to burn the words on her memory. 'You and I can make a proper homestead. I shall need a son to help me with the harvest. Not that I wouldn't welcome a daughter helping you bake the bread and tend the chickens.'

There was a time not so long ago, when Catherine would have torn a comment like this to shreds. Women have brains and should have the right to use them, she would have said, but this was not the time or the place. Besides she would be a frontier wife and have equal say in the running of a homestead.

They used Ben's penknife to carve their names, which must have blunted it forever. There was a debate as to whether to call Catherine by Ben's surname as Catherine Trueman, but once again Catherine experienced a feeling that made her shiver – like having a ghost walk over your grave – so they settled for Catherine Waterman.

'What's in a name?' said Ben. 'Our love will last forever. You're the only girl for me.' Catherine's response was to kiss him passionately on the lips.

Ben placed his hand on her tummy.

'You won't feel anything through all that thick serge,' Catherine laughed. 'It was only a tiny flutter deep inside.'

'So how can you be so sure,' asked Ben, 'surely you can't know yet.' He had grown up on a farm and knew the workings of such things.

'Women know these things; they are felt deep in their hearts.' Catherine smiled. She wanted to maintain an air of mystery for as long as she could. Ben patted her tummy.

'My son,' was all he said. 'At least if I die in this next push forward, I will leave a son to survive me.'

'Don't say that,' said Catherine, stroking his roughly shaven chin. *How did they do that,* she thought, *keep shaving whilst the world is blown apart around them?* She sought for the right words to comfort Ben. 'Don't think in that way: think instead of bouncing him on your knees when you come home on leave. Think of him growing up to play sports. If he is born in Cardiff, he could play rugby for Wales. Think of happy times, my dearest darling, or I shall surrender to tears. Let us not be sad.'

Ben hugged her tightly, a sense of urgency in his voice. 'But you must promise me you will tell him all about me, if I die in battle. Also, tell my mother and sisters about my baby son.'

Catherine tried to reassure him: 'Of course, my sweetheart, they shall know all about him.'

'You are going to Cardiff for the birth? Will your mother and father have you back?'

'They will, I am sure. They will be very cross, but they will support me. They may suggest adoption, but I will stay strong. I will keep your baby son safe for you until you return to claim us both.'

They fell silent at the thought of what was to come. Standing in the crepuscular glow of the evening, they watched flying bombs trace red and green arcs across the darkening sky.

Discretion had long passed. Other couples were making use of the night falling to say their fond farewells. They knew that their men would soon be entering the labyrinth of chalk-white tunnels, entrapped until the ends were blown away so that they could exit the tunnels and walk at a steady pace towards the guns of the enemy.

Ben had explained it all in hushed tones to Catherine when she had first arrived – the plans of Byng, their leader. The animation as Ben described the plan never ceased to entrance her. He had no wish to kill other men but he approved of the planning, the comradeship, the equal partnership of his troop. She wished that they could stay there for ever – that time would stand still for them. This would be their last meeting before the battle. They clung together gazing at the stars and praying for a miracle to bring them back together again.

Chapter Twenty-One
Easter Monday 9th April 1917

In the underground caverns beneath the fertile French soil, where not so long ago fat sheep and cattle had grazed peacefully, it was cold and dimly lit. Ben Trueman, tired of standing still for so long, shifted his rifle from side to side whilst wiggling his cold toes in stiff boots. It would never do to get cramp at a vital moment.

He tried to keep his mind on the battle plan, but it was almost impossible as Catherine's face kept appearing in his dreamlike state. The weird just-before-dawn atmosphere was not conducive to logical thinking. Instead, it produced unbidden images in his fevered brain. Visions of their awakening at the cottage – that special time together – ran through his head like the moving pictures in an electric theatre: the plans they had made; the feel of her body in his arms; the scent of her skin as he had gently unwrapped her; the ecstasy as he claimed her for his own.

The soldiers had been down below for some time, living in the hewed-out caverns. It wasn't too bad being in the subways, as they were called. They were pretty big, with food areas, bedding spots and latrines. The walls were covered in carvings like the ones at Souchez where he and Catherine had scratched their love messages on the limestone blocks. These were the work of men waiting underground for several days at a time, with a need to leave something behind in case they were blown to smithereens. Yielding to a primeval urge, they had identified themselves with name, rank, most with a maple leaf and some with a message for their relatives anxiously waiting back home. Ben knew that his friends were identifying themselves as Canadians, fighting together as a new country. His buddies had commented that although the flag they followed did not carry a maple leaf, the shiny new badges on their caps and epaulettes told the world of their pride to be bearing the silver insignia of their national tree. They were the men from the "Land of the Maple Leaf" – ready to charge and defend all that they held most dear. Ben had carved a message for his mother, father and sisters back home.

It gave him comfort to think of them observing this Easter weekend with simple rituals of food and church. When they were little, his sisters had made Easter bonnets, making him wear one for a joke. He pictured them as they looked when he left home, young ladies chattering and preening themselves in the mottled mirror over the fireplace in the log cabin. He visualised his mother preparing the Easter meal, then standing back to survey her table with chapped hands deep in her apron pocket, a smile on her work-worn face. Although the fare was humble and the china came from the penny market, all had to be done with due ceremony, ready for when his father came into the house, back from his fields and animals.

Would his mom have received the letter with the spray of red poppies and blue cornflowers pressed between thin sheets of paper? He had wanted her to imagine him walking in meadows full of wildflowers like the ones back home, not sinking in a field of churned-up mud.

His swirling thoughts again turned to Catherine. Would they ever meet again? Would he survive the ordeal he was about to undergo? It would be fine if all went the way Byng had said it would. He was a great man that Colonel Julian Byng, full of new ideas and battle strategies. When Ben had answered his country's call for more men to help the British troops in France, he had never envisaged that he would end up below the ground – deep in a tunnel with so many other men, waiting to march out into the dawn light to capture a hill where the Germans had been entrenched since the beginning of the war.

He had thought he would be issued with a rifle, told to clamber out of a trench when the whistle blew, then march forward in a line to be shot at like a row of fairground ducks. But Byng had other ideas about how to advance – he had said that they could capture the hill if they carried out his instructions correctly. He had made them practise, over and over again until they could carry out the manoeuvres in the dark. Each man had to be aware of the specific locations of the members of his unit at all times – he had to know what each man's tasks were and how to perform them himself if necessary. Byng had split the men into small units to make them into a tight-knit teams.

If the leader fell, one of them would take over and carry the team forward; and so it would go on till the last man standing. Now all the units were lined up in the twelve tunnels, each one a mile long, leading from the subways.

Ben felt stiff and chilled so he tensed all his muscles to send fresh blood racing round his body to warm himself. He shuffled around as much as he could in the tight space. Not long to wait for the signal now. The rumour was that it was snowing outside. Maybe this would make the German machine gunners less accurate with their aim. Ben hoped so.

White snow falling, white chalk tunnels under the ground, white cliffs of Dover. It was a strange world with caverns like cathedrals under the ground and soldiers, fighting in twisting tunnels like badgers and dogs, but with shovels and pickaxes

The instructions for the advance kept playing over and over in his head. Could he remember it all? His platoon was not going to fight underground but emerge into craters as the ends of their tunnels were blown out. They had entered this safe space far behind their own front lines to keep the operation secret so when they left the tunnels, they would be much further into *no-man's land* than the enemy could have anticipated. Also, another of Byng's brilliant ideas, there would be men to "mop up" – following the advancing troops at a distance. It was a common ploy of the defending enemy soldiers to hide in shallow holes, emerging to shoot the advancing men in the back. The "moppers up" would deal with snipers as they emerged, permitting their own troops to advance safely. Wave after wave of Canadian and English soldiers would move steadily forward to claim Vimy Ridge.

Ben looked at the men in his company leaning against the chalk white walls like him, and felt a sudden urge to confide in one of these comrades, to leave the news that he was likely to be a father, that whatever might happen to him on that day, he was leaving a footprint in the world, that he was starting a new generation who would benefit from this war to end all wars.

'Euan,' he whispered, 'Euan, if I don't make it today, tell my folks that I'm going to be a father. There's a nurse from Somerset carrying my child.'

Euan nodded, but whether he took it in properly or not was hard to tell. All the men were stony faced, adrenaline pumping – just holding themselves together.

Ben's thoughts returned to his sweetheart. Only by focussing on her could he stop himself from going mad.

*

The end of the tunnel exploded outwards, giving the soldiers access to the *no-man's land* between them and the enemy lines. They stumbled out over the debris of the explosion; their faces stung by the frozen air. The weather was foul as they emerged from the mouth of their tunnel. Sleety rain was falling, clogging up their eyelashes and reducing visibility. Ben blinked to clear his eyes and started up the hill as he had been instructed, blindly following orders.

Others were doing the same all around him. As they emerged from the security of the tunnel, they became fighting animals, moving steadily up the incline, expecting no resistance at all. Humanity was lost as a half-blind army marched on, intent on winning a victory. They had faith in their instructions from Byng. The days of continual shelling should have cleared the area of all the German soldiers so that as long as they could get to the top of the hill, the land would be theirs. They struggled on, steadily gaining ground. Ben followed his troop upwards – he was nearly there. He could see triumphant men at the summit when he felt a thump on his back. His knees buckled and he staggered helplessly. A German sniper had emerged from a foxhole and fired at him as he climbed. The "moppers up" had missed that one.

When Ben's knees could no longer hold him up, he crumpled to the ground. Unable to move, he listened to the roar of his comrades breaking through the German frontline, taking the hill. His frozen fingers scratched the ground as he tried to claw his way up again. The snowflakes began to cover his fallen body, like a snow-white linen eiderdown. Ben slipped in and out of consciousness. He dreamed of Catherine in the cottage in the Cotswolds, her face alight with happiness saying, "Yes" to his proposal. How pretty she had looked lying flushed and naked among the bedclothes.

He dreamed of their last encounter at Souchez. Through the mist, he saw her figure coming towards him with wide-open arms. "Stay here with me awhile. I will keep you warm. I will never leave you now." Above he heard shouts of victory from his comrades, then all conflict ceased, peace descended – the sound of battle faded away.

Later a hailstorm of bombs fell, and Ben's body was no more.

*

Back at base camp, Catherine was wondering how the battle was going. The baby gave an extra vigorous twirl inside her and she gasped – more news to tell Ben when he returned.

Reports were seeping in of a victory at Vimy Ridge but nobody seemed to know what had happened to Ben. Comrades had seen him in the advance but not afterwards. It was suspected that he must have fallen but there was no confirmation of this – no body to carry back and bury. The men suspected that one of the many enemy shells might have obliterated him, but they did not want to tell Catherine this. They preferred to leave it as a mystery – one that could not be solved satisfactorily for Catherine. It was then that she fainted.

From then on, nobody could persuade her that Ben was dead and gone.

'Show me his body,' she would say to those who tried in vain to calm her down. 'Show me his uniform and his dog tags. Then I will believe you.'

Eventually it was decided that she should be ordered home to her relatives who could give her the help she so badly needed. Friends of her family rallied round, and she was ferried across France and then the English Channel and finally to Cardiff to her mother and father.

Chapter Twenty-Two - 2017

Lizzy was sitting by the window watching the birds collecting twigs for their nests. Their busy actions seemed to be reproaching her for her lack of energy in following up the mystery of the metal tin. She could be sifting through the countless WW1 sites on the Internet, to find details of Canadian soldiers stationed in Britain or using the records of the Red Cross to identify the VAD nurse named Catherine. She might be able to discover what had happened to both of them. Maybe Catherine had crossed over to France to nurse closer to the battlefields? Had her soldier fought there? Had he survived? Were there relatives living now who would like to have the tin full of memories?

Two hours later, she had no more information than before. Lizzy was thinking how much she hated technology and how pleasant life was before some idiot invented them, when inspiration struck. If computers were not helping her, there was somebody who might be persuaded to reveal more of the mysterious story. She could pay a visit to the nursing home to see if Mavis Hollis was still holding court there. As a bonus, there was someone else who would enjoy a trip out. As she jangled her bunch of keys, Wellington pricked up his ears and plodded to the front door.

When they arrived at the nursing home, Mavis was not alone; there was a visitor at her side, a woman who looked like her twin – how odd that some families produced children that looked almost identical. Maybe it was the perms – they obviously visited the same hairdresser, abundant curls sprayed into immobility and their clothing – neat little jumpers in pastel colours. Shiny dainty shoes and beige tights, everything neat: ship-shape and Bristol fashion. Lips and nails painted in the same ruby tone enhanced the visual image of twins.

Lizzy envied their serenity. They made her feel as if she had been pulled through a hedge backwards. She raised a hand to her hair, trying to push her wind-swept locks into place. The two women wore a look of superiority as they ran their knowing eager eyes over her.

'Hello, Lizzy, are you looking for your mother? I think she's gone for a nap in her room. This is my sister, Irene, the baby of the family.'

'Hi Mavis, I'm not looking for Mum at the moment. Hello, Irene. Nice to meet you.' Lizzy smiled at the newcomer and tried to avoid shaking hands, as it was obvious that Irene shared the same fondness for heavily ringed fingers as her sister.

'No, I haven't come to visit Mum; it's you that I have come to see, Mavis. I was wondering if you had thought any more about that nurse, Catherine – the one I asked you about at the hospital – you know, the other day.'

Mavis stared blankly back at her as if she was about to deny any such conversation, when her sister spoke out.

'Mavis! Don't be so mean. Go on, tell her. Why shouldn't she know? Most of the village did at the time. What can it hurt? So many years have passed. Go on, tell her.'

Lizzy held her breath. Mavis looked unmovable. What would make her share this information? Suddenly an idea swooped into Lizzy's mind so simple it might work, people liked to share information. What could she barter with? It was obvious. Lizzy dived into her handbag and produced the tin nestling inside a freezer bag.

'This is why I am asking questions,' she said holding out the tin. 'I found this battered object outside the grounds of the workhouse or rather it found me. I am calling it a memory tin, because it contains photos and letters belonging to someone called Catherine and a soldier from the First World War but as most of the ink has faded there are only a few clues. Does this explain why I want to know? I came by the tin by accident.'

'That must be Catherine's tin; the one Nan found and lost again. Fancy that, after all these years,' Mavis and Irene stared in amazement as if Lizzy had produced a white rabbit out of a top hat.

Lizzy entertained the stunned sisters with the mysterious episode of the lorry at great length. This incredible tale produced many expressions of surprise and disbelief as Lizzy held out the contents for inspection. The two women didn't want to handle them, not even the *Vesta* matchbox shiny as a new pin thanks to Tom's ministrations. 'Full of germs they'll be after all those years under the floorboards,' the sisters explained.

'Go on, Mavis, tell her. You've got to explain now. If you don't, then I will.' Irene sounded quite indignant.

'No you don't, Irene. It's my place to tell, as I am the oldest. We only know what our Nan told our mum. To be honest we don't know whether she knew the whole story or that she remembered it quite right. She was only twelve that year and,' Mavis leaned in close to Lizzy and whispered though there was no one anywhere near them to hear, 'she couldn't read very well.'

Irene chipped in, anxious to make sure that the facts were accurate. 'Nan couldn't read at all, Mavis, to be truthful. She missed a lot of school looking after her brothers and sisters, and the teaching wasn't all that good in those days.'

'I know,' said Mavis, 'but it wasn't only our Nan what couldn't read. Different world then! They didn't bother much with children if they thought they would end up working on the land or going into service. But she had an excellent memory, never forgot a recipe or a person's name. 'Twas a sort of compensation for not being able to read, I suppose.'

Lizzy sat patiently, waiting for these two sisters to settle their differences and reveal to her what they knew. It surprised Lizzy how comforted she felt by their presence – their confidence in themselves and what they knew. They must not be rushed or they would take umbrage and nothing would be revealed, ever. It was amazing that they had contemplated revealing family secrets to her. Even now, Mavis looked a little unsure, but Irene seemed keen to talk – to let Lizzy in on their secret.

'This Catherine, why are you so interested in her? Somebody you don't know, from a hundred years ago.' Mavis gazed intently at Lizzy as if studying her face would produce clues to her sincerity.

'I know it must seem strange to you but it's a bit of history, isn't it – a connection to somebody who dropped a tin a long time ago.' Lizzy hesitated, seeking an explanation for her behaviour, which must seem very odd to the sisters. She continued: 'You see, I've been in the doldrums for some time. My husband died suddenly – a hit and run accident – walking home along that narrow country lane from the Ploughman's Inn one evening. This is the first time I have felt remotely interested in anything at all. That's all I can say really. You must think me mad – maybe I am.'

Both sisters leaned forward to pat Lizzy on the knee. They seemed shaken by the loss of Lizzy's husband. 'No, no, my dear, we don't think you're mad. It's just that ferreting about in the past sometimes produces unwelcome results but we both think you are genuine. We're just curious.'

Lizzy felt reassured by this statement. 'I was wondering if Catherine could be a distant relative. I've heard the name Waterman before. Been racking my brains to think what the connection was. There was a letter, you see, or so my mother said. A distant relative of my father wrote to my parents, something about an aunt nursing in this area in the First World War. My parents weren't interested, didn't follow it up. My mother mentioned it casually to me one day and then denied all knowledge of it later on. Obviously, it's too late to ask her about it now her memory is so patchy. My parents never spoke much about the family or relatives so I've no knowledge of my background like you do.'

The sight of the tin and its contents had clearly intrigued Mavis and Irene, and soon the information was tumbling out of their mouths in a rather muddled fashion. It would take some time for Lizzy to sort it all out. Now was the time to sit and listen – questions could come later. Mavis began the story, long-preserved by the family, with the air of an ancient tribal narrator in front of the whole community.

'The friendship began when our Nan, Daisy, met Catherine on a dark dismal night in September 1916. According to our mum, Nan said that Catherine was a lovely person, friendly and kind to her. Not stuck up at all, though her sister, Annie, was a bit hoity-toity, kept to her position always. Nan always hung about near Catherine, not too close but in the background. That's how she knew what happened. Nan would be that pleased to know that the tin has been found – she loved Miss Catherine. It went with her everywhere, buried deep in her pocket. She kept some special letters and photos of her and Ben when they first met and also a little silver thing that Ben had given her as a keepsake. Nan took a quick peep inside when it got left behind. It was meant to travel in Catherine's pocket but somehow it ended up under the bed. Nan found it when she went to strip the bed. But it was too late to return it to Catherine.' Mavis paused for breath.

'Our Nan had to hide it quickly, so she popped it in her bloomers before finding a little hidey-hole in a boot cupboard in the back kitchen. She thought nobody would notice it right back in the cupboard with all the boots in front to hide the hole. However, when she went back, hefty wood planks had been nailed across the opening. Nan didn't know that the rat-catcher man with his little terrier had been called in to sort out the rats' nest. All the rotten wood was pulled out and the dog sent in to finish off the offenders. In the following skirmish the tin must have fallen under the floorboards. Those little terriers have a terrible strength when they get their dander up even though they are not much bigger than a rat themselves.

'Did Catherine go to France then?' Lizzy felt secure enough to ask a question.

'Oh yes, she went, and she came back later after Ben had been listed as missing. She came back to retrieve that tin, but Nan was quarantined with scarlet-fever, so they weren't able to meet. She couldn't even let Catherine know that her tin was lost.' Mavis paused, looking at Lizzy to see how she was coping with all this information and then went on.

'When she couldn't see our Nan, Catherine went to find the Major, who told her that Ben had been killed on the first day of the battle at Vimy Ridge. Catherine wouldn't believe that he was dead. That news seemed to drive her to the edge of madness. She returned to France and was never seen again in Kingcharlton. Just to show you what a lovely lady she was, amid all her sorrow she thought of her friend, our Nan. Her last act before she left was to send boxes of goodies to Daisy's cottage – lovely fresh food and lots of clothes. It was like the Christmas they had never had before. The family shared their bounty with their friends. It would not have lasted long anyway as there were no fridges for folks like us in those days. Miss Catherine would not have thought of that, as she never dealt with food except at the dinner table. We never found out what happened to her after the war ended. We heard rumours of course but nothing definite.'

Lizzy's head was buzzing. She leant forward and screwed up her eyes in an effort to remember all these facts in case she never saw the sisters again.

Mavis continued. 'I suppose we should show you the tin we have. It's full of letters from Ben's mum. It's bigger than your tin – just the right size, kept the letters nice and neat. It's a cigarette tin, *Craven A* brand - they all smoked like chimneys in those days – helped them through the war. Oh dear, I'm losing track of what I want to tell you – letters, that was it, letters from Canada. They've got addresses and all, which might be helpful with your search. We could find the tin if you want; it's with a lot of other stuff in the attic. You might as well have it to see if you can solve the mystery of the baby.'

'What baby?' stammered Lizzy.

'Catherine's baby. Our Nan always maintained that she was in the family way when she left for France, but she never saw any baby. It was a mystery what happened to it. There were rumours that she gave it away.'

Lizzy hardly dared to breathe; this information sounded really promising. It fitted in with the little she already knew. She sat very still, looking interested but not too interested, not excited or anything but just absorbed.

'Ben, what about Ben, and what's Vimy Ridge?' Lizzy moved her chair a little closer so that she would not miss a single word.

'Ben's the soldier in those photos; he came from Canada to fight. She met him out at Charlton Farm, at the tea parties Major Bowmaker set up for soldiers on leave. All officers they were though, it was not for the likes of our family. Catherine was really taken with him. Vimy Ridge is the place where he got killed. They never found his body.'

Lizzy was feeling rather dazed by the flood of information and her confusion must have showed on her face for Mavis paused. 'The story is a lot to take in. I can see you look a bit befuddled. The fact that there are two tins in two different places makes it complicated. We've heard the tale so many times it all seems quite straightforward to us, but I can see you are getting confused. I'll see if I can make it a bit clearer – tell it a bit straighter.' Mavis took up the pace again.

'There was a *Craven A* cigarette tin, red and white it was with a black cat painted on the front, fifty ciggies in a tin. It held Ben's letters from his family. He gave it to Catherine to keep safe when he went away. Catherine left it with our Nan when she left to go to France. She kept the treasures closest to her heart in a small pastille tin that the cook had given her. It was just the right size to carry in her pocket.

She thought she had it with her when she took off to join Ben in France but it had fallen out in her rush to travel. Nan tried to save it but failed. Nan kept the big tin safe, she brought it home and hid it in the larder on the very top shelf out of sight. When they pulled down those Woodbine cottages, the family got a nice new council house – inside bathroom and all. Nan took care to take the tin with her – kept it with her all her life. They were important, you see, they were letters from Ben and his family.'

Mavis took a deep breath when she finished her tale and sat back to see the effect this information had on Lizzy.

Lizzy beamed at Mavis to disguise her belief that the sisters' story was not yet complete. Her suspicious mind was shouting at her - *there's more to come.* But so much had been revealed today that Lizzy was satisfied for the moment. She was surprised when Irene spoke out again.

'There was a man who came asking about Ben Trueman. He came from Canada. Do you remember, Mavis, he was asking about Ben's time in the village? But nobody told him anything, him being a foreigner. We know how to keep our secrets safe in Kingcharlton.'

The light was fading outside, and the tea trolley had long departed. One of the care workers put her head around the door and announced that the evening meal was being served in the dining room. Time for visitors to leave. Lizzy stood up.

'Would you like a lift anywhere, Irene? It's the least I can do after you two have been so helpful.'

‘Oh, that’s very kind of you, dear, but not needed. My hubby will be waiting outside for me. He always picks me up, just in case, you know. Such funny people about nowadays.’

*

Lizzy staggered out, reeling under this waterfall of information. ‘Wow, Wellington, what a result.’ she murmured as she bundled him into the car. ‘I can’t wait to tell Tom about this – another tin and a missing baby.’ She had not been expecting another tin. The *Craven A* cigarette box, that was a surprise, holding more information, maybe in better condition than the items in her little tin. Would the sisters keep their promise to search for the missing container? If so, how fast would that be?

Things could be moving on at last.

Chapter Twenty-Three - 1917

The household was caught up in a whirlwind of activity; all normal routines had been abandoned and Fred Waterman could find no area free from comings and goings, from the frantic commands issued by his wife, which were then rescinded, and fresh orders shrieked out. So, he did the only sensible thing in the circumstances; he took himself off to his office.

On his walk into the heart of the city of Cardiff, he pondered on the telegram that had thrown the whole family into this frantic activity: Catherine was on her way home and she was not well. He thought of the battlefields and the stories that he had heard in his club, tales of wrecked bodies and mutilated limbs whispered in hushed voices in quiet corners, away from the circle of armchairs where the men lubricated their stiff upper lips with cognac, to bluster of King and Country and moving the line forward.

His mind wove webs of possibilities: how would she be, this rebellious young woman, who had worn her youth so lightly when he last saw her, believing that nothing was impossible, that all would eventually be well. Had they shielded her too much as she was growing up, not thinking that she would choose to abandon the future they had planned for her as the wife and mother, comfortable in the home of a well-to-do young man of her own class? Should Fred have been firmer with her, forbidden her to train as a nurse? Should he have insisted that she stay at home with her mother and sisters to lead a quiet life?

What did "not well" mean? His train of thought entered a tunnel of darkness: he had heard talk of men who were driven mad by the pounding of the guns and the bloodshed, whose limbs shook uncontrollably and so much more too awful to contemplate. The armchair men at the club had branded these men cowards; but he could not bring himself to accept this point of view. He was not one hundred percent sure whether he would have been brave in such circumstances.

It was not like the battles in the Boer War where there was constant sunshine, and the British Force was indisputably superior. That had seemed to be a heroic struggle; the casualties had not been so horrendous. How many young men had taken the King's shilling believing that the present war would be the same? Reality dawned too late when they languished in trenches being forced to climb out at the shrill of an officer's whistle to become casualties, mown down in *no-man's-land*, by an *enfilade* of machine gun fire.

'Morning, sir.' Fred Waterman's dark musings were interrupted by the cheery greeting of the security guard standing at the door of his office. The old soldier standing stiffly to attention in his military-like green and gold livery did little to put Fred's mind at rest.

'Good morning, Mr Waterman. Mr Evans would like to see you as soon as possible.' The efficient young woman at the desk smiled and handed him a folder. All thoughts of home and Catherine's return must now be put to one side as he dealt with the day-to-day business of running an office.

Back at The Firs, Park Row, the level of activity had not diminished. The same thoughts that were troubling the head of the household were running through the heads of each and every one in the building, right down to the little maid who laid the fires each morning. They might be phrased in different terms and assessed from different angles, but there was no doubt that a common wave of tension was rippling through from cellar to attic as fresh linen was brought to Catherine's room and fitted with military precision onto the plump and comfortable mattress. Pillows were pummelled into shape and the bedspread shaken and flattened to lie smoothly without a wrinkle. Windows were flung wide open to air the room and all the furniture was polished so that it shone like myriad mirrors reflecting the faces of the workers.

Annie had been despatched to the shops to buy some fresh flowers. At last, everything was in place and there was nothing more to do but sit in the living room and wait. Even the servants in the basement kitchen breathed a sigh of relief as they gathered round the scrubbed wooden table to receive a cup of over-brewed tea from Cook.

It seemed like a lifetime before there came a clip clopping of hooves over the new-fangled tarmac of the road. A collective shiver ran through the building. This was a new experience, a woman coming home from the battlefield. There was nothing on the pages of the book of etiquette to advise on how to handle such a situation. Her mother shivered and remembered her fiery daughter: her rebellion against the lifestyle expected of a woman of her status. Would she still be so rebellious? She would have nursed unknown men in such intimate circumstances that were beyond belief to Florence Waterman. Her sewing circle was alive with tales of bold young women who were nursing and living unsuitable lives at the Front. All those years of careful chaperoning, and now this beloved daughter had spent months in the presence of unknown soldiers. Florence sighed as she rose to her feet at the shrill sound of the bell and the rough tones of the as-yet-untrained maid who opened the door. Bother the girl, she had still not mastered the phrases she should use or refined the harsh Irish brogue.

The door closed with a bang, and then there were sounds of coat and hat being discarded with questions asked in husky Irish tones. Would the girl never learn the correct procedure? Florence waited with trepidation for her first sight of her daughter.

The door of the drawing room opened, and Catherine entered. There was no question that she would make a scene or be rebellious. She looked exhausted and defeated, diminished somehow from the figure that had marched around the house lecturing her parents on the rights of women. Her face was altered in a strange undefined way. Florence suddenly experienced a premonition: she had known women whose faces had altered in such a way, women who were in an “interesting condition”. Oh no, not that. Were all those tales true?

‘Hello, Mother, how are you?’ Catherine’s tone did little to allay Florence’s fears. She did not seem to be happy to be home.

‘Dear Catherine, how wonderful to see you. You look simply exhausted, my dear. Was it a terrible journey? Come and sit by the fire.’

Florence found support in the simple manner of behaving as if this was a normal day, and Catherine was a guest calling in for afternoon tea. She rose and rang the bell. As an afterthought, she planted a light kiss on her daughter’s cheek. Catherine smelt of the outside, of smoke and cheap soap, her skin was rough and uncared for. Florence decided to keep up the pretence that this was an everyday occurrence and etiquette must be followed. She spoke to the waiting maid.

‘Nora! Ask Cook to send in a tray of tea, please, and ask her for some sandwiches and a selection of cakes.’

Nora was standing entranced by this visitor who had actually been to France and witnessed a battlefield. She knew that the whole kitchen would be waiting for a description of Catherine. She was trying her hardest to take in every last little detail; from the way she did her hair to the boots on her feet. Very shabby they were too, not at all like the usual footwear for the ladies of the household. Why, they were nearly as rough and ready as Nora’s own boots.

‘Get on with it, girl. Why are you still here? Off to the kitchen.’ Florence was becoming very agitated.

‘Yes, Mam, to be sure, Mam. Cook’s got some really nice scones. I’ll ask her to put some of them on the tray, shall I?’

‘Goodness, girl, will you never learn? It is Cook’s position to choose what goes on the tray. You have merely to convey my instructions to her. Off you go now.’

Mrs Waterman’s rattled nerves made an impact on the gaping girl and she rushed off to regale the kitchen with news of Miss Catherine and “goodness knows how the mistress seemed in such a state and no mistake – much worse than she usually was.”

‘Please don’t bother yourself over me, Mother. I have become accustomed to a much plainer way of life than this. We often went hungry over there. We just had the same rations as the men, the same living conditions.’

Florence blanched at the thought of her daughter experiencing the same living conditions as the men. This sounded much worse than she had been expecting. Thoughts of Catherine wafting through a ward with a lighted lamp faded away, to become replaced by something much worse. She wished Frederick were here to help her with this awkward conversation. Wasn’t that just like a man to rush off to the office when he was most needed? Unthinkable images were filling her head and nothing that Catherine had said or done so far had dispelled them.

‘How are you, my dear? We saw from your telegram that you had been unwell and that you had been sent home to recuperate.' Stick to the given story; that was the way forward for now. There was plenty of time to delve deeper into the nature of Catherine's illness.

'I suppose that is one way to put it, Mother, but the one thing my experiences over there have taught me is that it's better to speak plainly: to speak the truth. I am not unwell, though I am very tired. I am going to have a baby. They tell me that the father is dead. I don't believe them. They say he died a hero at the battle of Vimy Ridge, but there was no body. Not a trace! Not until they can give me some evidence will I believe he is dead. I have come home to give birth to the child. Then I am going to return to the battlefields to look for my hero and help those weary souls over there. I can do no less. Having seen what hell they are all going through, I could not possibly abandon them.'

It was unfortunate that Catherine chose to unburden herself just as Nora was bringing in the first instalment of the tea tray. She nearly dropped the loaded tray, as she told the enthralled kitchen afterwards, and the mistress's face – sure it was a sight to be seen.

Florence was speechless. The situation was totally beyond her control. She had expected that at a later stage, there might be some delicate questioning in a quiet secluded room. She had even hoped there might be a scene in which a newly bathed and pampered Catherine would burst into girlish giggles of amusement at her mother's fancies and declare herself untouched by a man's hand.

In no way had she anticipated this wild outburst; though it wasn't wild really, it was very calm and collected. That was what made it seem all the more terrifying, for Catherine seemed to be beyond being told how to behave. If her daughter had burst into tears and begged her mother to forgive her, asked her for advice and help, Florence would have felt some degree of hope of "managing the situation". They could have sent her away somewhere discreet to recuperate and then she could return to settle down to normal life. A baby could be adopted or farmed out. If the pregnancy was not far enough advanced there was even the possibility of hiring an expensive consultant to deal with the problem. But that would be impossible now it was out in the open.

Florence rose to her feet and holding firmly onto the back of the chair to steady her wobbling knees, she addressed a wide-eyed Nora still holding the tray.

'Put the tray on the table, Nora. Now, I want you to listen carefully to me. Are you listening?' Nora nodded. 'What you have heard was a very private conversation. Miss Catherine is not well and does not know what she is saying. You are not to repeat one word of what has just been said or I will send you straight back to Ireland with no references. Do you hear me, do you understand – not a single word?'

Florence did not believe for one moment that Nora would stay silent, but she did believe that Nora would convey to the kitchen how stern the mistress had been and the kitchen would understand. She knew she was a fair mistress, and she believed her staff to be loyal and she hoped that they would keep the secret within the household. She would have to send Catherine away of course and then anything that might slip out could be dismissed as mere servant gossip. How she wished Frederick would return so she could share her burden with him.

*

Catherine rose from her comfy seat in the drawing room, her weary limbs shrieking in protest at having to move again. How soft the carpet felt through the thin soles of her battered boots. As she walked, she glanced behind her, imagining that she saw footprints – that her boots had carried mud from the battlefields into this tranquil room. That was not possible, of course, for she had travelled many miles since that first footstep on English soil. Maybe it was guilt at disturbing them all in such a belligerent way, that played these tricks on her mind.

The stairs were endless, wide steps cushioned with brightly patterned carpet. She stumbled and caught a toe on a brass stair rod. The leather, worn paper-thin by continual use, offered no protection; she almost cried out with pain, she who had endured so much with no complaints. She fought to stay calm until the bedroom was reached. Many times, she had imagined that room when lying on a canvas camp bed, longing for sleep to come; the clean sheets, soft blankets and thick curtains to shut out the world outside, to keep at bay the visions of blazing lights, red, yellow and green, the shrieking of the horses, the cries of men in no-man's land, the muted moans of her patients in the dimly lit tent.

Clinging to the solid balustrade, she was grateful for the reassuring shape of familiar wood beneath her fingers. The curves she had traced as a child brought back memories of peace, security and laughter. She and her sisters would poke their rag dolls through the elaborate carved banisters, allowing them to fall to the multicolour tiles below as the maid was passing, to see if they could make her jump. How long ago that all seemed. Just a few more steps and Catherine would be safe. Then she could let go.

The room was as she had left it, freshly cleaned and sweet smelling. Her nightdress case, embroidered with bunches of roses, lay plump on the eiderdown and she knew that if she opened it, there would be a freshly laundered garment inside. What would her mother say if she knew that Catherine had often spent days and nights in the same unwashed uniform? How could she explain how her life had been in Flanders?

There were no words in her mother's vocabulary to describe the battlefront or the devastation across the land; the ruined villages and broken trees, the deep sucking mud which pulled men and horses down, the yellow gas that rolled towards the trenches causing them to choke and lose their sight. Catherine saw again the lines of men who had endured a gas attack holding the shoulder of the man in front as they moved like a human caterpillar, blindly following the leader. She shut out such thoughts as she slumped in her easy chair and looked around, catching sight of herself in the triple mirrors of the dressing table. Could that gaunt face with bird's nest hair belong to her? Three images from different angles stared back at her and all told the same story.

Ghosts of her former self filled the mirror. There she stood her new nurse's uniform, all spic and span, waiting for patients who needed her help, then her first grownup ball, her newly put-up hair, decked with multi-coloured silk flowers, her pearly-white shoulders modestly protruding from ruffles of rose-coloured silk, her face, flushed with excitement. Now that face stared back at her, wan with travelling and devoid of all hope. Catherine thought of the shocked faces in the drawing room below. How could she have spoken to her mother in that horrid manner? She had intended to approach the subject of the pregnancy in a calm manner, to seek her mother's help gently. But fear and exhaustion had driven her to blurt the truth out in such a way. Fear that she would have to fight the whole family to bring this about had made her aggressive. She hated the person war had made of her.

She wanted to keep the baby; it was all she had left of Ben. There was no way she could give this baby away to an anonymous family. But then there was no way that she could tend the child herself. She must get back to the Front, to help those damaged men who lay in pain waiting for the most basic of medical care. How could she neglect them now that she knew how terrible it was? How could it all be resolved? She had envisaged her mother taking care of the infant until the war was over when she could come home, but now she realised that this fantasy was just the result of lack of sleep combined with the feverish planning of her overwrought mind. It had all seemed to be so straightforward whilst she was "over there".

Then she thought of her older sister, Beatrice, who had been married for several years with no sign of a baby. Maybe they could care for the child, pretend it was their own to avoid any scandal. That was if the infant survived, it had not had the best start to life. Had the tiny creature been injured in some way through being carried in its mother's womb as she tended the wounded soldiers, then crossed the miles of battered land and choppy sea to come home to Cardiff. Her body was aching from top to toe.

She began the laborious process of unwrapping the layers designed to conceal her swelling shape. Clothes fell to the floor around her feet. Stepping out of them in her underwear such as it was, she took the pristine nightdress from its case, pulling it over her head to form a tent under which she could modestly remove the rest of her garments. In her haste, she had not undone the tiny buttons at the neck. The flimsy muslin ballooned around her head, making a fragrant tent, smelling of lavender mingled with soapsuds. Sunlight filtered through the delicate material, enclosing her in a childlike world of blissful ignorance. No harm could reach her in this scented cocoon. She sank to her knees, lingered in this halfway house, being neither here nor there, till a knock on the door shattered her peace.

'It's just me, miss.' Nora's cheerful tones boomed through the door. 'The mistress thought you might like some more tea. I've got a tray here. Will I bring it in?'

Catherine hastily pulled down her nightdress. Reality returned with a thump. 'No thanks, Nora. Please take the tray back to the kitchen. I just want to bathe and sleep. Also, find my mother and tell her that I will be down later, when I am clean and rested.'

'Right you are, miss.' Nora's boots clumped away along the landing. How could they clump on carpet? But that was Nora. The world seemed not so hideous when girls like Nora existed to clump about in a cheerful manner.

Catherine lay on the bed and closed her eyes. She could hear a birdsong outside, it was all so normal, or what had once been normal to her. Her nerves were jumping like galvanised frogs. The quiet house seemed unsettling after all the noise of the battlefields, the boredom of trench-life and having to stay alert day after day.

She should be able to relax now. It had taken all the energy she possessed to get herself home. *I should not have been so rude to Mother,* Catherine thought. *I behaved badly. It must have given her such a shock to see me in such a state. It's not her fault that my life has gone awry.* Catherine opened her eyes and started at the ceiling – she could not sleep.

I've got to stay strong for the baby. I must put aside all my ghastly memories and behave in a civilised way. They are only trying to be kind to me; it's not their fault that they haven't the faintest concept of what life is really like out there. I must let them help in any way they can and accept it gratefully.

It was all becoming hazy; the room was drifting and swirling around her. The battlefields had receded for the moment though no doubt they would come back as nightmares.

Chapter Twenty-Four - 2017

Lizzy was tempted to throttle Peter before they reached Dover. She had studied the glossy brochure from cover to cover and decided that a tour of the battlefields and cemeteries would be a logical next step in pursuit of the truth. They might be able to question the "experienced guides" about the best way to uncover the history of the wartime couple. All the arrangements for travel seemed well organised, a luxury coach with all comforts and plenty of stops to stretch their legs. But she had not realised how much Peter liked to talk. He had an impressive file of notes and had planned each day meticulously. Gone was Lizzy's plan to wander around quietly and soak up the atmosphere. It seemed that he had planned a list of activities for every day and was intent on explaining them all to her.

Finally the sight of the ferryboat blocked out the words buzzing in her ear. This was the real thing at last. The coaches rolled into the gaping mouth of the ferry where all was activity with busy workers shouting orders as they packed vehicles tightly onto the garage deck. When the coach staff gave instructions about leaving the coach Lizzy was disappointed, wanting to stay where she was, to curl up in her seat and sleep. She wouldn't go hungry – her backpack was full of snacks. But staying on the coach was not allowed so she stumbled down the steps behind Peter.

The impact of the foetid air combined with the noise was almost unbearable after the peace and warmth of the coach. Lizzy was already regretting that she had allowed herself to be lulled into a state of relaxation by the rolling wheels on smooth tarmac. It would have been better to stay awake and alert. Rousing her flagging body was such a shock to the system.

The noisy central dining room with long queues for hot food looked horrendous. Lizzy found a little cafe selling sandwiches and coffee. *I'll buy myself a sandwich and a coffee. It smells good – I hope it tastes as good. There must be a corner where I can hide myself away and watch the waves roll by.* Lizzy found a spare bench and tucked herself in, away from the swirling crowds. The coffee was surprisingly good, really hot and full of flavour. She chomped her crayfish and organic rocket sandwich and began to feel better. She had no idea where Peter was, probably eating in the great hall. They had become separated between the car deck and restaurant deck when great crowds of hungry travellers ascending the staircases swamped them. But yet another surprise awaited her later when they returned to their coach. Just like the appearance of the tin, something or rather somebody was going to jolt her out of her hermit-like existence once more.

'Hello there, folks. Let me introduce myself.' At the front of the coach, holding a microphone and looking very self-assured stood a tall fit-looking figure wearing dark glasses, mirrored like an aviator. *When did he join the coach?* Lizzy thought. He must have joined them on the quay side when they returned to the coach. He looked like a would-be lady-killer, an amateur *Don Juan*, as he took off his glasses and surveyed his coachload of potential victims. And then replaced them with a flourish as if to maintain an air of mystery.

'Hi there. Call me Jonny. I am your military expert and guide for the week. Here to make sure you don't get lost, to give you some background to the places you will be visiting. Ask me any questions you like.'

Lizzy took an instant dislike to him. The horrors of the ferry had made her irritable and he looked arrogant, very self-satisfied and overly confident. Lizzy's weary heart sank lower. What with Peter sitting at her side with his plans and the guide talking non-stop, she felt surrounded by dominant men. This stranger in their midst strutted up and down the aisle with attitude, constantly tweaking the collar of his navy-blue fleece. In a theatrical gesture he whipped off his stylish sunglasses now and again to reveal startling blue eyes that looked as if they could search out any weakness or inner secrets. He surveyed his captive audience.

'Tell me about yourselves. What do you expect to achieve from this trip? Does anyone have a personal mission to find a relative's grave? Is there anybody wanting to visit a particular battlefield where their loved ones had fought?' His strident voice rang out with authority.

A woman somewhere in front of Lizzy seized the opportunity of a spot in the limelight. Her harsh voice rang out as she insisted on telling multiple stories of her grandfather's wartime experience. Lizzy shrank down in her seat zoning herself out of the situation. She did not want him to question her and Peter; she did not want to speak to Jonny or discuss her mission. Surely the fact that she was travelling with Peter Catchpole would put him off. If not, he must be as thick-skinned as a Jaffa orange. She took a chance and peered out carefully to see if he was getting close to them. He was a handsome man. His hair was sculpted in waves framing a lean face, with high defining cheekbones. Was he wearing moisturiser? His voice when he stopped shouting was melodious, husky, well spoken. He had the appearance of a man who made a living by making well-off women happy. Maybe this was a side-line of his, seducing single females whilst guiding people round the battlefields. Lizzy closed her eyes once more, pretending to be asleep as he neared their seats.

However, Peter proved to be the deterrent she had been praying for. As soon as the guide stood over them oozing charm Peter seized his moment of glory by reeling off facts, figures and questions he would like answered. Mr "Call-Me-Jonny" realising that he was losing control of the situation quickly sidled off with the excuse that he must check their next comfort stop. *We will not be receiving much personal attention from him this week,* Lizzy thought as she opened her eyes for a second to catch sight of his scornful profile.

The roads were very clear and well-maintained, the traffic minimal, the driving so smooth that Lizzy actually dropped into a light sleep, only disturbed when the coach slowed down and stopped outside a hotel. Stiff limbs were unfolded, bits and bobs gathered up, overhead bags retrieved carefully, as a slow stumbling crocodile made its way out of the coach. Extremely weary, Lizzy was managing well until a random walking stick fell in front of her at the top of the steep metal steps. Falling helplessly, without any means of stopping herself, all was lost until two strong arms grabbed her in a vice-like grip.

Thank heavens for that, it could have been broken limbs and a ruined trip. Glancing up about to heap praise and thanks on her rescuer, she froze, caught in the glittering gaze of the man she had decided she hated. She drowned in the bluest eyes ever, she swam in their depth and her heart fluttered, swooped and righted itself. For a time all action around them halted. They were caught up in an amazing moment – two people in a bubble. He seemed reluctant to let her go. Then someone behind coughed and the loud lady with the loud voice started making comments on thoughtless people. Lizzy looked away, annoyed at herself for reacting like this.

'Are you alright? Would you like some help with your luggage? Shall I get you a brandy? You look very pale.' The tone of his voice had changed to helpful and alluring.

Her whole body was shaking at the thought of how the fall might have ended. Alarmed at her body's response – like a lovesick teenager with a crush – she wanted to find a quiet place to recover all on her own. 'No, no, I'm okay. Just a bit shaken. Peter will help me with my luggage. I need a strong cup of tea and lie down for a bit. Thank you.'

The whole incident was confusing with such mixed emotions that she had to get away without any conversation. Forgetting her manners, she hobbled off after Peter in search of their suitcases. It was only later that she thought this must have seemed rude. But her tired mind had flashed up a vivid picture of the hypnotising gaze of a wolf and a sacrificial lamb. All she wanted was to escape. This was not meant to happen. Romance and heartbreak were not on the agenda. Losing Gerry was so painful; she wanted no attachment to another man. No one was wheedling his way into her heart again, especially not this one who looked like heartbreak material if she was not mistaken. But how could she fight her feelings if they betrayed her so suddenly, snapping into disoriented teenager mode? The seeds of attraction buried deep inside her, moving from long dormant stage to starting to come alive in that one instance. She must quickly bury them again.

*

At the reception desk, Jonny was watching his party book into their rooms and considering his options for the trip. Usually, at this stage he was weighing up all the women in his charge, working out if any of them were available. Luring spare women into his bed was easy, too easy sometimes because what he really liked was the hunt and a bit of a challenge. His talents enabled him to get his own way surprisingly often;

handsome, charming, witty with a good line in empathetic flattery guaranteed to appeal to lonely or bored women. A touch of kindness, a good line or two and they were like putty in his hands. As he explained to his friends, there were so many bored women out there. All they really wanted was attention, easy to give whilst he was away from home on the prowl.

His mind flicked back to Miss Prim and Proper. He thought he knew the type well but there she was following her quirky companion around; what was that relationship about? She was not bad looking, abundant red curls with a few streaks of silver, lovely eyes, rather frumpily dressed: sturdy walking boots, practical walking clothes, no spirit, no sparkle. Her life must be pretty dull. Briefly, he imagined her in an outfit of his choosing; a slinky black dress, with a couple of glasses of red wine inside her.

She didn't seem very excited about the trip. Was it a pilgrimage to find a relative's grave or research for a book? That made people serious sometimes. There was always a budding author on board, hoping to catch the moment, as they were in the centenary years. There had been no request to find a special grave. It was intriguing; he loved any mysterious encounter. This lady was not a great conversationalist; look at the way she was not interested in his first overtures - maybe not worth bothering with. She seemed like hard work.

But wait, what about the connection when their eyes met as she nearly fell into his arms? She felt good, a whiff of exotic perfume, and the sensation of lovely skin and generous curves beneath all those bulky clothes. It was a fleeting glimpse of the pearl in the oyster. Helping her off the coach was automatic – mustn't let anyone fall, bad for the company – could be injuries leading to compensation. But he had been trapped for a moment in the gaze of her eyes: a tantalising shade of green. He was reminded of a painting seen when he had been an art student: a mermaid combing her long red hair sitting on a pebbled beach with her scaly tail wrapped round her and a pearly necklace adorning her white neck. Miss Prim had that otherworldly look. Here was an extremely passionate woman if he was any judge and he thought he was by now. She was keeping her passion well hidden – why would that be? That had been a revealing moment when the curtain was drawn back. He would have dismissed her as an option altogether if it had not been for that electrifying experience of eye contact.

Intrigued at the challenge in spite of himself, Jonny resolved to speak to her later in the evening when all the guests usually gathered together in the bar for a drink and a chat. Perhaps he could get her away from the protective custody of her companion. Jonny was sure his charm would work its magic if unleashed on this unsuspecting female. But he was out of luck that evening for Lizzy, who had endured quite enough of bothersome guides and Peter talking non-stop all day, opted for a soothing shower and an early night.

*

Lizzy stood at the gates of the first cemetery, stunned by the rows and rows of white headstones stretching ahead in symmetrical order. She had not expected this place to be so tranquil – such a peaceful experience. Birds were singing in the trees; the sky overhead was the azure blue of a summer's day with white fluffy clouds floating along.

What a contrast to the graveyards back at home, often neglected, overgrown and gothic in appearance with tilted gravestones covered in lichen standing gloomily within broken walls. Gigantic yew trees laden with red berries like Christmas lights lined the paths where only black crows walked.

Her expectations had been hazy, but the reality of it was overwhelming. People were walking on neatly mowed grass. Where should she start? Peter had rushed off to find the book holding the names of all the soldiers buried within these walls. Apparently, each cemetery had such a book to enable visitors to find lost relatives. His interest in the cemetery was facts and figures. She was interested in the human stories behind these white stones. Still, it would give her the chance to walk leisurely around and stop to stare if she wanted to. Jonny the guide had been hijacked by the woman with the ugly voice who insisted that he accompany her and find a particular grave belonging to a relative. Lizzy supposed that he had to spend some time doing the work he was paid for. It left her in peace.

She paused at the gravestone of a soldier killed at the tender age of nineteen. The stone was pristine, stark white, with every word as clear as when it was carved. The words were heart-breaking. Did this young lad still receive relatives bringing flowers or was he lying here forgotten by those at home? There were shrubs planted in a narrow band of soil at the foot of the stones, with small rose bushes she recognised from home. The War Graves Commission had done a wonderful job in laying the soldiers to rest with the honour they deserved.

In her solitary state far from the other people on the trip, she felt at peace with the world. Absorbing the sights and sounds of this memorial ground, where soldiers lay sleeping peacefully after the chaos of the battle, her own petty troubles melted away. She stopped once more. A particular gravestone had caught her attention – no details apart from the words "Known unto God". Tears were rolling down her face. This was unbearably sad, this man with no name. And he was not the only one, when she looked there were so many unknown soldiers all around him. She was hunting for a tissue in her pocket when Peter bounded up, full of information.

'What's the matter, Lizzy? What's upset you?'

Lizzy was still speechless, wiping the tears away with her hands. To her surprise, Peter produced a snowy-white handkerchief from his breast pocket. With a flourish worthy of Sir Walter Raleigh, he handed it to Lizzy. 'Mother said, "Never go out without a clean handkerchief in case of emergencies" and I guess this could be called an emergency.'

'Thank you,' Lizzy gulped, burying her face in the soft linen. 'Thank you very much, this is just what I needed.'

Peter's face assumed a self-satisfied grin, which almost wiped out the generosity of his gift. 'What's upset you then?'

'The sight of all these graves with this inscription.' Lizzy pointed to the words that had reduced her to tears. 'So very pitiful to be unknown, and so sad for the parents at home not having a place to grieve or to pay their respects.'

Peter replied as if he was reading out from a book.

'Rudyard Kipling chose those words for the stones of unknown bodies. He helped the War Graves Commission. Don't worry. Everyone has a memorial somewhere. This soldier will have his name on one of the lists carved into the big memorials, like Menin Gate or Vimy Ridge for the Canadians. Some of the soldiers have their names in two places if the authorities make an identification of a body after the name has been carved on a huge memorial stone.'

Once again, Peter seemed to miss the emotional side of life. He was marvellous at organisation and practicalities, but his feelings were blunted somehow. His handkerchief was just what was needed, soft and clean, smelling of soap. Lizzy buried her face in it and then clenched it in her hand like a child's comforter. Her tears had been shed not just for the soldiers but also for the loss of Gerry and the miserable period since his death. It was as if a great mass of sorrow had been trapped inside her, unable to escape. She had been holding it back, not wanting to distress her children with her grief. Now it could no longer be contained, flooding out of her like a torrent from a broken water pipe.

Lizzy was thankful for Peter's presence when the deluge came, because she realised that his lack of emotion stopped her from feeling guilty about being so emotional. He neither condemned her nor suffocated her with help. He just accepted her as she was and dealt with it. That said, he was still irritating in some ways. He never stopped talking. It was like the contents of an encyclopaedia being poured into her ears all day long. It tainted her way of thinking; it spoiled her pleasure in the unravelling of the tale of Catherine and Ben. She was not interested in the facts and figures of each battle. She wanted to weave her own imaginary story around this mystery couple.

Chapter Twenty-Five - 1917

A wild wind set all the trees aflutter as Catherine and Nora travelled across the Clifton Downs watching the undulating back of a high-spirited dapple-grey mare. Catherine had hoped that her brother-in-law Arthur Mortlake would send his gleaming motor to transport them as she hoped for a comfortable ride. How silly was that. He was using it for business purposes no doubt. Good, maybe she would have her sister Beatrice to herself if Arthur was away from home. Large heaps of fallen leaves decorated the grassy areas causing Catherine to shiver at the thought of the colder weather when her baby would be born. She drew the collar of her voluminous concealing cape tight against her throat and told Nora to pull her head in from the window. She emphasised that their arrival at Hilltop House was supposed to be discreet. It was time for a little chat with Nora.

'I'm relying on you, Nora. You are my only friend in this household. You must not gossip to everyone you meet. You can be friendly without giving my secret away. Promise me now before we arrive. We are supposed to be coming for a little holiday and nothing else. Promise me now.'

'To be sure, Miss Catherine, I will say nothing, not a word about the baby will leave my lips, cross my heart and hope to die.'

Catherine suppressed a sigh, thankful that the clattering hooves would muffle their conversation from the driver and footman up front.

'Good girl. Remember – that's the last time you will mention the word *baby*. Now tidy your hair before we arrive, the wind has blown it into a veritable haystack. This is a very formal household we are entering, much like my parents' home in Cardiff. You will have to be on your best behaviour.'

Nora's face assumed its habitual grin, showing the gap in her two front teeth. 'To be sure, miss. You can trust me.'

All conversation was put aside as the horse put on a spurt at the scent of home and a warm bowl of mash. The animal's flanks were quivering with energy and Catherine feared it might bolt at any minute, scattering passengers and luggage all over the sprawling Downs. Nora bounced about from one side of the carriage to another, she was squealing with delight one moment and then cowering in the corner the next, hands firmly placed over her eyes. The train journey from Cardiff General to Bristol Temple Meads had amused her, picking out sheep and cows in the fields. However, the long dark tunnel under the murky waters of the Bristol Channel found her hiding under the travelling blanket with cries of: 'Will we be out soon, miss? Are we really under the water, miss? How do they keep it all out if it's over the top of us? Suppose there was a leak, like it started dripping and filled the carriage right up.'

A minute later, she was aghast at the sight of the Clifton Suspension Bridge and immediately stuck her head out through the window again so that wild chestnut curls were blowing freely in the stiff breeze, all promises to behave immediately forgotten. 'Will you look at that, miss. How does it stay up there, not blow away in the wind or drop down out of the sky? Just look, Miss Catherine. I should be afeared to walk across it.'

The Suspension Bridge with its outspread arms appeared to hover like a seagull over the dark brown waters below, where miniature ships laden with goods sailed towards the docks. It was a slow and winding journey up the river to unload on the bustling quays where crowds of men patiently queued for the privilege of being selected for a day's work. The bridge was a famous landmark, a marvel of Isambard Kingdom Brunel's vivid imaginative powers – suspended as it was between pillars on either side, appearing to hang like a baby's cradle from those seemingly flimsy supports.

Catherine hauled Nora back in, thinking that this one would never make a lady's companion – her lust for life was too great to be stifled. 'I'll explain later. We might take a little walk that way and even venture across to the other side, to Leigh Woods and the countryside beyond.'

Sometimes Nora's incessant prattle made Catherine's head ache but she was glad of the distraction from her thoughts of Ben and their last meeting. The smell of him haunted her, the touch of his unshaven cheek against hers, the warmth of his embrace when nothing else of the outside world intruded. Her mother's decision to send Nora along as her maid was a sensible one, Catherine realised. Nora's excessive sociability and relish for gossip would mean that the news that Catherine was pregnant would be spread throughout Cardiff as fast as the butcher's cart could travel. And then there were her relatives working in the city in various households; an aunt cooked for a family not far from the Waterman household. No, it would be safer to send her to Bristol with Catherine where nobody knew them. Beatrice and Arthur would know what to do, how to contain the secret.

Catherine's thoughts turned inward again to her private world, living that last meeting over and over again. Nora's prattle did not interrupt Catherine as she could let it buzz around her whilst she dreamed of Ben. All too soon the groom hauled on the reins to bring the horse to a halt. Clouds of steam were rising from its damp flanks, mingling with the autumnal mist of the morning. The baby stirred, awoken by the sudden stop, kicking small limbs like fluttering wings deep inside her. He or she was all Catherine had left of Ben now and nobody was going to take this precious child away from her without a struggle. Try as she could though, she could not yet visualise herself as a mother with a baby in her arms. Perhaps all that would come later.

Her head was in the most enormous muddle; she was unable to think clearly. All the noise, clatter and destruction of the battlefields lingered in her dreams. The confidence that she would always make the right decision had deserted her completely. Leaving Cardiff had seemed to be a sensible solution for avoiding her mother's overwhelming solicitude and her father's troubled face whenever he entered the room, but Catherine wondered if Bristol would be any better. She thought of herself as a little coracle pushed hither and thither by other people's plans. Her emotions were mixed on leaving Cardiff and the security of her home to stay with Beatrice and Arthur for as long as necessary. The formality of the household and long walks on the Downs might give her time to think, time to work out what was best for the baby and also help her to soothe her aching heart.

Catherine gazed at the elegant Georgian house, gleaming white in the autumnal sunlight. She could see the large front door held open by the maid, and a manservant waiting for them to enter before carrying their luggage through to the kitchen area and up the narrow winding backstairs. A moment of panic had Catherine wanting to tell the driver to turn the carriage around and take her back to the station. For a moment, she imagined herself returning to the battlefields with the baby in a bundle under her arm or in a small cart such as the refugees used to ferry their infants away from the carnage. Somewhere out there, Ben still lingered – she was sure of that. The madness passed. Like the well-bred young lady she was meant to be, she gathered her skirt, holding it high above her gleaming black button boots as she gingerly negotiated the wobbly carriage steps with the help of the groom. Smoothing down her skirt, she marched up the path and over the patterned tiles of the lobby into a hallway smelling of beeswax and lavender.

What sort of reception will we have? Lizzy wondered, as she allowed the maid to remove her concealing cape. She had always been a little afraid of her sister's husband, so stern and self-righteous, but Catherine's time on the battlefields and in the nursing stations in Flanders had robbed her of all civilian fears. Arthur's sermonising would pass right over her head just like much of Nora's chatter. Beatrice, her sister, was a different matter – gentle and kind, who seemed to have the knack of twisting Arthur around to her way of thinking with just a little shrug of her dainty shoulders and the merest hint of a tear. It was she who had suggested the plan of Catherine coming for a visit to her older sister. It would be more difficult to face her questions. This seemingly gentle creature had a spine of steel and the stubbornness of a mule.

They might both be waiting for her in the drawing room to receive her properly. Arthur had his position to maintain. He was a stickler for etiquette who wanted not a hint of scandal. Catherine would not have dealt with her pregnancy in this way, but the family had decided, and she was tired of arguing, worn out with grief. She would go along with their plans for now. She checked Nora's appearance and straightened a few items that were straggling. Catherine produced a tiny pocket-handkerchief and tried in vain to dislodge smoke smudges from Nora's cheek. She wanted her dear little companion to be accepted into this unfamiliar household.

'Off you go to the kitchen with the other servants. I expect they will show you what the daily routine is and find you some refreshments.' She smiled at the other maid to ensure her request for food and help for Nora was dealt with properly.

'Remember what I said now.' A stern look and a finger drawn across her lips made Nora's face look serious for a moment or two. 'Best foot forward, Nora.'

Catherine took a deep breath, straightened her back and entered the drawing room, prepared to do battle. As she had hoped, Arthur was not there, only her dear sister who rose to meet her and flung her arms around her in a rose-scented hug.

Her sister's warm embrace disarmed Catherine and she melted into her arms with tears in her eyes. 'Oh Beatrice,' was all she could say.

*

Ben's son came bawling into the early morning light, impatient to be getting on with his life. Along with his powerful vocal chords, he possessed masses of dark brown hair and a bold face, angry at his confinement. His chubby arms and legs waved energetically in the air before the midwife wrapped him in a clean white towel. Anxious to be free of his exhausted mother, he looked healthy with a good pink colour, despite the long painful labour.

Born within sight of the Suspension Bridge to the tune of the gulls screaming overhead, he would be a true Bristolian, so playing rugby for Wales would be out of the question. Sounds of boat whistles and hooting horns echoed from the deep river gorge below as if to welcome the baby boy. Arthur had insisted that she move into a small nursing home for the delivery. It was too much to expect all that upheaval in his house. The neighbours would be wondering why the doctor was calling in his carriage.

Catherine was quite happy with that arrangement. She had grown tired of Arthur's disapproving looks. Now she was on her own she could devote all her time to working out what had happened to Ben. He must be somewhere. Bodies didn't just disappear without a trace, did they? The officers must be wrong. He was still alive, and she was going to find him.

Familiar sounds drifted up from the streets below. Life in the city was carrying on as usual: shopkeepers' carts clattered over the cobbles delivering all the necessities of life, whilst in the breakfast rooms of the tree-lined squares, businessmen crunched toast and marmalade, supped from plates of kedgeree or lamb chops, then wiped their chins with pristine napkins. Newspapers were unfolded and perused. Cooks, red-faced and flustered, were sipping their first brew of the day. Tea trays were being delivered to recumbent ladies who peered anxiously in their mirrors to see if hours of sleep had worked wonders on their complexions. Butchers' boys were whistling as they pedalled their bikes, their wicker baskets full of meat for the occupants of grand houses on the Downs. Milkmen were busy on their rounds, filling the jugs of kitchen maids and indulging in a little saucy backchat. The world was in the process of waking up to the usual routine of the day. This was the first day of baby Waterman's life, normal, vibrant and full of promise. The son of Catherine Waterman and Ben Trueman had entered the world on the 9th October 1917.

*

'What shall you call him?' asked Nora.

'Huw,' Catherine replied. 'That was Ben's second name. It's Welsh.'

'To be sure that's a beautiful name for a beautiful boy,' Nora whispered, stroking his face with wonder. 'His father will be proud of him. Can I hold him?'

'You will have to wait a while, Nora,' said Catherine, 'he needs to rest. You will have plenty of opportunity to hold him later, for you will be his nursemaid.'

Nora's round face beamed with pleasure. 'That'll be something to tell Mammy back at home – me a nursemaid. Will I be in charge of bathing him then?'

'You will, but not right away, he's only just arrived and he's very fragile. He needs gentle handling; he's not a baby lamb like the ones back home on the farm, which need to be shaken to take a first gasp of air. Let him sleep now. Off you go.'

Once Nora had left taking her exuberant love of life with her, bustling out of the door like a small tornado, Catherine lay back on her pillows and gazed at her son. She was glad that she had Nora to help; she would lean on the young girl's naïve confidence to deal with the difficult times ahead. Nora's unswerving devotion and solid belief that all would be well was what Catherine needed at the moment to cope with her family's disapproval and the uncertainty about Ben.

'Where are you, Ben? Your little boy needs you and so do I. You can't be dead. Please, please, don't be dead.' The words were muttered softly with an air of desperation.

Somewhere in Catherine's brain a tiny seed of accepting the truth was growing. Her intelligent mind was slowly processing all the information she had been given and it was moving to an undeniable conclusion. But for the moment she had managed to ignore it and believe that Ben was still out there somewhere. If she accepted what everyone had told her, it would feel like the end of all hope.

Catherine gazed at the tiny shape in the cot. She had expected to be captivated by him from the moment he was born. But she felt nothing, no matter how hard she tried. She was exhausted, sore and sleepy. Sleep descended as a merciful blessing. Mother and son snored in harmony.

*

Catherine was allowed back to Arthur and Beatrice's home after a few days as she and the baby had no problems. Catherine was feeding Huw herself in her role of a modern mother. She found the process somewhat painful, but Huw seemed to be thriving. She had not realised that the constant attention a baby needed would be so time-consuming though. Frustration and boredom descended at having to stay at home all day to feed her son. Catherine was restless, her mind buzzing with what had happened to Ben; she was wondering who could give her the correct information.

It pained her to admit it, but perhaps her mother had been right about placing Huw with a wet nurse for a few months. However, Catherine was determined to feed the baby herself. On one hand, it was an act of rebellion against her mother and on the other she was of the opinion that a poor fatherless child needed at least one attentive parent. Arthur Mortlake's house was a strict one and she was often expected to stay in her own room or the nursery. Once the child had been safely delivered and looked likely to survive it was decided that Catherine would not return to Cardiff but would stay in the house on the Downs. Quite who took this decision, nobody could remember. It seemed that Arthur had taken it upon himself to arrange matters. He thought that his wife Beatrice was benefitting from the company of her sister and was enjoying her new position as an aunt.

If Fred and Florence were surprised that Arthur would put himself out with this offer, they did not argue the point. In truth, they were grateful to be relieved of the burden. Catherine's thoughts on her situation were brought back to the present as Huw pulled away from her breast, came up for air and squealed like a little piglet, waving his arms in the air. He was a dear little fellow, but no matter how hard Catherine tried to concentrate on him alone, to be a good mother, her thoughts returned to Ben and her original plan to return to his side in France. Milk dripped down her front and she wept for her lover.

Chapter Twenty-Six - 2017

Lizzy gazed on the motionless body of her mother with bewilderment. Was this all it was? No struggle, no strung-out pain relief; just the breathing slowly stopping and then coming to a halt. Her chest rose and fell no more but stayed as a plateau. It seemed like an anti-climax to the days during the last couple of weeks when her mother had become increasingly demanding and vitriolic as if she knew she was fighting her last battle.

She wouldn't eat and she wouldn't drink, and she kept throwing the bedclothes off. Now, there was this quietness, this nothingness, and this lack of a person who had been her mother.

'Why don't you go and sit in the rest room whilst we tidy your mother up, make her look presentable.'

Lizzy knew what the nurses meant; there were things that they had to do that she did not want to think about or see, so she allowed herself to be led along the corridor to a quiet room where presumably they parked relatives in a similar situation to her, away from the rest of the inhabitants of the nursing home. They brought her weak tea and digestives. Ever afterwards the combination of those two would always make her think of death.

Outside the window was a garden where the trees were swaying gently in the breeze and birds were pecking the lawns. Everything was the same and yet everything was different. She had not known how she would feel when her mother died, and she was no wiser at that moment.

Now she would never be able to ask her mother about the past. That link with the former generations was broken forever and she would have to rely on the sisters for more information. How she wished she had listened more carefully, shown more interest in the long-winded tales of her once garrulous mother.

Now there would be the funeral to arrange, the guests to be invited, their names sought in the battered address book her mother had once filled with friends. Very few had visited in the nursing home, finding conversation impossible.

It was going to be a busy day with forms to be filled. But for now, she would take advantage of the quiet room, where she could gaze out at the sunlight and think of nothing. She did not know what she felt, only a terrible anxiety about something unknown.

She wanted no words of comfort, no sympathy. The speeches meant nothing. Her mind was numb, and she would have to wait until it was working again before she could speak to anybody.

Chapter Twenty-Seven - 1917

'Where are you going, Catherine? Surely you should not be venturing far in your state of mind?' Beatrice's face was a criss-cross of worry lines both for her impetuous sister and her baby nephew.

'I feel fine, Beatrice, the baby is fine! It is imperative that I find out whether Ben is alive or dead. As I am not his wife or a relative, no authorities will tell me anything. The only way to gather any information is to travel over to Kingcharlton to see Daisy and ask the Major if he or Charley have any news of Ben.'

Catherine did not want to explain to her sister that she needed news of her memory tin and the whereabouts of the *Craven A* tin. Where on earth was her tiny pastille tin? Waves of panic assailed her when she thought of the missing object. She must find Daisy and ask her if she knew where it was. It contained the only photos of Ben she possessed, though Charley might have some left in his photography room.

'Now that my baby has been delivered and safely hidden away here, there will be no scandal from what people see or deduce. They will think I have been in France all this time and have just returned.'

Catherine finished buttoning her coat and adjusted her hat to a more suitable angle, securing it firmly with a vicious jab of a hatpin.

'You don't mind looking after Huw? You are so good with him; you manage him so much better than me. And you have Nora as a nursemaid, and she dotes on him.'

Beatrice kept quiet for the moment. She was not confident that nobody but family knew about baby Huw. Nora knew the truth of the matter and Nora had connections in Cardiff as well as Bristol. Her large extended family seemed to have members all over the country. Maids always knew what was going on even if they pretended they didn't. They had days off, put on their best clothes and treated themselves to pots of tea and slices of cake in flowery teashops. If they had followers, they might have a stroll in the park to listen to the band and buy ice creams from the *hokey-pokey* Italian, who pushed along an ice-cream trolley. They chatted with the delivery boys who came to the back door. Any news passed from household to household all around the town.

What secrets did they share? They must talk about something – gossiping – spreading the whole wealth of knowledge seething below the placid surface of daily life. Surely some of the maids in Kingcharlton suspected something, if not all of them? What about that girl called Daisy, that Catherine was always talking about? The memorial hospital and the wounded patients must have caused quite a stir in the town and Catherine had been at the very centre of it all. They must have been gossiping about her.

Beatrice dropped a stitch. She was knitting a complicated matinee jacket for Huw whilst talking to Catherine and she suddenly noticed her error. Knitting was usually a soothing occupation but the worries twitching in her mind were causing her to be distracted. Concentrating on picking up the wandering stitch with a crochet hook, she checked her rows were in order and returned to the perplexing problem of Catherine and her erratic behaviour. Why would any mother with a darling little boy behave like this? If Huw were Beatrice's baby, he would not wish for anything. Why couldn't she have a baby to cherish?

There was no solution at the moment. Words had no effect on her sister. Catherine had always seemed rather unstable, dashing here and there with inappropriate plans. Now she seemed distraught with grief; the pleasure that must surely come with motherhood had not calmed her down at all. Until she settled down there was no way that Beatrice could alter her way of thinking. At the front door, she made one last attempt to persuade Catherine to act in a sensible manner.

'Try to be careful, Catherine. You are only going to hurt yourself with all this rushing about. You ought to be staying at home peacefully, allowing your body to recover and not going about in society where gossip will begin.' Her words were wasted as soon as they left her lips. Catherine swept out of the door and banged it closed behind her.

The Downs were covered with fallen leaves; they rustled under Catherine's boots as she walked to the bus stop to catch the omnibus to Temple Meads station. Walking calmed her spirits – she found the exercise invigorating. Her mantra as she walked was – 'I must find Daisy – I must find my tins – I must find news of Ben. Somebody will know something. It's that sort of place.'

The familiar sight of the impressive station frontage produced an enormous surge of hope. Daisy would surely have that tin Cook had given her so long ago. She could once more carry it in her pocket and feel its comforting shape as she moved about her daily tasks. She wondered about Daisy and her fortunes since she had been away in France. Had she grown plumper with some good food inside her? Would she be pleased to see her friend?

Standing under the station clock on the platform with a chill wind whistling through, her mood altered as she remembered her first sight of Ben in the glow of a lighted match. The memory of his handsome smiling face almost overwhelmed her, so she sought out the ladies waiting room to compose herself, dry her eyes and prepare for the battle ahead.

*

The train journey to Kingcharlton was not long. Catherine barely had time to find a seat and establish herself before the train rattled to a halt and she was getting off. Trembling with excitement, she strode through the village and started up the hill to the memorial hospital where she expected to find both Matron and Daisy.

Nothing had changed here. It was as if she had never been away, never travelled to France to see the battles raging, never carried a baby within her, never undergone the travails of giving birth or nursed a baby at her breast. All the ups and downs of her life: the merry-go-round of emotions that swirled inside her meant nothing to this tranquil place.

At the top of the hill, the workhouse was still brooding over the valley, but workmen had now separated it from the new memorial hospital with a waist-high wall, finished off with an ornamental arrangement of stone, known locally as "cock and hen". Her visit did not start well. The relief at having arrived at her destination safely was destroyed immediately when she sought out Matron.

'Daisy's not here today or for the next few weeks. She's confined to her cottage. Her family have been struck down with scarlet fever. Come in and I will explain.' Matron smiled as she ushered her guest into her private room.

Catherine stood as still as a statue – one very distressing thought filling her mind. Daisy, the one person who might know the whereabouts of her precious tin, was out of reach. All through her pregnancy and labour, Catherine had been comforted by the belief that Daisy would have found it and hidden it somewhere for her. Tears started to trickle down her stricken face. Beatrice had been wise in her words. Catherine should have stayed in Bristol. All she had been through, combined with the heightened emotions of childbirth, was driving her into hysteria.

*

Matron studied her with a practised eye and drew her own conclusions. There were women who showed no outward signs of pregnancy and childbirth apart from a swelling belly but there were other women whose pregnancy showed throughout their bodies, especially in their faces. Catherine seemed to be one of the latter; her present mood and actions confirmed Matron's suspicions. Even though she had delivered the baby, the tell-tale signs had lingered on.

Ushered into the cosy room where the fire crackled and the kettle sat on the hearth, Catherine muttered, 'Back to the beginning like "Alice in Wonderland".'

I must get her to calm down, Matron thought. *She needs to rest – be helped through this obsession to see Daisy. A nice cup of tea might help with plenty of sugar.*

'Sit down and we will have tea and toast. Have you eaten this morning? You look famished.' The pale face of Catherine and her shaking body alarmed Matron who was clutching a bottle of *sal volatile*, just in case. 'Daisy is back at home with her mother, my dear, helping with the little ones who have scarlet fever. They are in quarantine and you would not want to take that kind of infection back home with you and spread it to others more vulnerable than you.'

*

Catherine was at a loss; nobody knew about the tins except Daisy and she was now out of reach. Maybe Catherine would have to leave her small tin to fate and hope it turned up in a place where somebody might recognise her initials and the photos. The larger tin would still be safe with Daisy.

When Catherine raised her wan face to Matron's concerned eyes, something clicked into place and she realised that Matron had guessed about the baby. Beatrice was right. The birth of baby Huw was no secret in Kingcharlton although the inhabitants were not acknowledging it openly. Did they now view her as a scarlet woman? Had she lost her good name?

Matron spoke again. 'You could go down to the cottage and stand outside and shout out what you want to know but you couldn't have an intimate conversation. That area is so crowded with people that soon the entire village would know about your business. Nobody in that cottage can read or write properly, so it wouldn't be any use to have a written note delivered to Daisy. Would you like to write her a note and leave it with me for when she is out of quarantine? I could read it to her, if you like. The doctors are trying to keep control of the infection, it can spread so fast through a community as close as ours.'

She stopped to wait for Catherine's response and as there was none, she continued. 'Have you considered asking Major Bowmaker for news of Ben? His son is at home I believe – he might know what the situation is.'

'That's a very good idea. I'll go right now.' Catherine looked brighter and made to stand up and leave.

'I might be able to save you a journey. I think he will be visiting today to see that all is well with the patients at the hospital. You just sit still for a while then you will be in a fit state to question him as much as you like.' Matron put some bread on the toasting fork as if in an effort to distract Catherine from rushing off.

Having a plan set before her and feeling very dizzy, Catherine relaxed a little, sitting down as she was told, closing her eyes and listening to the gentle chitchat of Matron; she focussed on how she would talk to the Major. The tin situation could be resolved later – one step at a time. She must make the most of this present opportunity. To speak to someone who had military experience might put her mind at rest. He would know how to proceed.

It was bad news: the worst news in the world. Major Bowmaker was very kind, taking her hand in his big paw.

'Why my dear, poor Ben was killed at Vimy Ridge just as the victory was theirs. Charley knows a splendid chap who saw him drop. He checked for a pulse as he passed but there was none. You can trust the word of this man. But it could not be verified for some time because the fighting was so fierce.

'Unfortunately a misplaced shell landed close by. That was why there was no body to be buried. We would have written to let you know but you seemed to have disappeared. Nobody would tell us where you were. So sorry, my dear. You two made such a splendid patriotic couple.'

It was because of the baby that nobody would tell them where I was, Catherine thought, *they all wanted to protect me. What a mix-up. I'm going back to France right away, there is nothing to keep me here. He's not dead. They're lying. I will find where Ben is and take care of him.*

It seemed she had forgotten about poor little Huw lying in his crib. Stunned by the news, Catherine stumbled away from Major Bowmaker, Matron and the hospital to seek some peace on her own. Her steps took her to the top of the hill near Daisy's cottage where there was a bench by the blacksmith where farmers waited whilst their horses were shod. A small memorial fountain in honour of Queen Victoria stood close by with a copper cup attached for weary travellers along the Bath Road. Catherine took a cupful of water and then sank gratefully onto the bench to consider how to soothe her aching heart.

Nothing unusual happened in Kingcharlton without the news being spread over most of the village like a flooding tide. Once Catherine had been spotted, news was passing from door to door. Daisy in her cottage had already been informed that Catherine was in the village and longed desperately to see her once more. Daisy wanted to tell her about the tin – how it had disappeared when the rat-catcher man called. The fact that Catherine might be worried about her tin was always on Daisy's mind.

But she did not know that Catherine was resting on the stone slab by the blacksmith's forge, where the fire burned bright and the sparks flew high and wide, looking down on the crowded cottages below. The news did not reach her until it was too late to run up, stand at a distance and shout out the information. Therefore the whereabouts of the small tin could not be passed on and Catherine was none the wiser.

*

Catherine accepted that what Matron had said was true; she could not endanger her health and that of her new-born son by venturing into the very middle of that infected area. But she must find a way to help Daisy, her faithful friend and keeper of the tins. How could she ease the ordeal of being crammed in the tiny cottage with her extensive family?

The answer to Catherine's problem came to her as she watched the blacksmith making horseshoes. Holding a strip of iron with gigantic grimy tongs in one hand, he plunged the metal into the red-hot coals, drew the glowing iron out and beat it into shape. This action was repeated until the man was satisfied with his handiwork. Watching the steady rhythm of such familiar tasks in the countryside calmed her fevered brain. What would help a cottage full of invalids? Good nutrition; and so Catherine's thoughts turned to food. When she and her sisters were ill, they had been fed special invalid diets of chicken soup, beef tea and soft white rolls. While she could not hope to obtain all of these items, Catherine could provide some and so she set off for the High Street with purpose. Lists of nourishing foods danced in front of her eyes.

Chapter Twenty-Eight - 2017

Grey clouds floated across the sky bringing a threat of rain, not at all like the pleasant autumn weather of the last few days. No exciting events were listed on the calendar so it occurred to Lizzy that this dull day would be the perfect time to catch up on the housework. She had let her chores pile up whilst she was pursuing the mystery of the wartime romance. If she could find something entertaining to listen to on the radio, she could persuade herself that housework was fun.

Lizzy was hunting for dusters in the cupboard under the sink when the phone rang. Where on earth was it? She raced around the house following the strident ring tones. The chirrups were getting louder as she approached her knitting basket and delved in to pull out the noisy mobile. Just in time – a few more seconds and the call would have ended.

'Who's that? Irene? Irene Hollis? Oh, I remember – we met at the nursing home, you're Mavis's sister. How can I help you? What? You think you can help me? You want me to come round? Right now? Hang on a moment, whilst I find paper and a pen...Right here we are.'

Lizzy stared at the notepad in her hand. Apparently Irene did not live far away. How odd that they had lived their lives so close by, probably passing each other many times over the years and now their lives seemed to be intertwined. She must go and make herself presentable. These were the kind of women who expected one to look tidy, the sort of women who were so organised that they had routines; they would not give houseroom to dust mountains. What if they expected to be asked back for a cup of coffee? She would have to hire in a team of cleaners. What was this all about? Irene had sounded so mysterious, "something that might interest her". What could that possibly be?

She remembered the feeling of hidden secrets – of half-revelations and more to come if she did not upset them. They had mentioned a tin containing letters from Canada, which would be helpful for tracing Ben's relatives and they had promised to give it to her.

Irene opened the door of the neat little house to release the mingled aromas of lavender polish, honeysuckle air freshener and home baking. After Lizzy had removed her outdoor shoes, revealing the hole in her sock that she had meant to darn, she was ushered into the front room where dainty china figurines sat on pristine crocheted mats, and a miniature table stood by every armchair with a coaster awaiting a hot drink.

Lizzy wove her way across the room, praying that she would not stumble and knock something precious over. Mavis was already seated on a pale pink velour sofa, adorned with so many fluffy cushions that she had to perch on the edge upright. Or maybe that was her corset because it looked as if her neat figure was being held in place very firmly.

She looked exactly as she had the day Lizzy had met her – not a hair out of place, her fingers covered in rings. It must take quite a while to put those rings on in the morning: Mavis and Irene would not be leaping out of bed to pull on any old outfit and race out the door without their makeup and hair neat and tidy. Lizzy would have bet her last five pounds that both these women had a line of washing out before they went to fetch their morning shopping and that would all be before ten o'clock.

She admired this level of organisation – why could she not be more like this? No matter how hard she tried, a room always looked worse after any effort at cleaning. This room she was scrutinising was so pleasant to sit in. One did not have to move anything to sit down, there were no old newspapers or piles of books to be read, filling up every bit of the coffee table. But what did they do all day? Where was the evidence of their hobbies? Or maybe they put them tidily away in cupboards. Before Lizzy's mother went into the nursing home, she had been constantly chiding her daughter for her untidiness – had told her that there was no need to have all her hobbies spread out all around her. She could just choose one and keep the rest neatly put away, but Lizzy could never decide which one and preferred to have all her favourite items out on the sofa beside her.

'Thank you for the invite. It's lovely to see you again.' Lizzy had reached the comparative safety of an armchair by the window and had eased herself into it without mishap.

'We have some more information for you, but in good time, my dear. Best get comfortable first. What would you like to drink? Nice cup of tea do you? I have got some coffee somewhere, if you must, Mavis and I don't drink much coffee.'

Lizzy was finding it difficult to restrain herself whilst all the niceties were completed. She had rushed out of the house on the promise of some exciting news and now it seemed that it would be preceded by a tea ceremony as equally elaborate and prolonged as any Japanese tea party. But, as she remembered from their first meeting, these two sisters would not be rushed. They moved at their own pace and there was no point in becoming annoyed or trying to hurry them up. Lizzy decided to allow herself to sink into her comfortable armchair and enjoy the journey wherever they were going. It was certainly a welcome alternative to housework.

A hefty tray appeared in the arms of Irene whose grin followed it like Alice's Cheshire cat. There were bone china cups and tiny teaspoons, sugar lumps with tongs, floury scones on paper doilies with little dishes of jam and cream. Despite her impatience Lizzy dutifully accepted a plate emblazoned with pink roses and a napkin wreathed with honeysuckle strands, a tiny knife, a cake fork and one of the scones.

She felt very hot; the difficulty of manipulating all this china and cutlery was totally unnerving her and there was a scone to manage as well. She managed to eat something and drink a cup of tea with no mishaps but with no pleasure either. She politely refused another helping, at the same time complimenting the sisters on their cooking and presentation. Only then was she allowed to place her plate back on the tray and assume an interested expression ready to receive whatever it was they wanted to impart. She was lucky that they decided to leave the washing up till later. They cleared the table and sat down facing her, smiling that broad grin they seemed to wear permanently.

She wondered if there was actually nothing of note to impart – no tin found; that this was just a ruse to invite her to their home. Maybe they led very dull lives. She resigned herself to not learning anything new.

'Shall I start then, Mavis,' said Irene, 'or do you think you ought to do the honours? You are the oldest, after all.'

'Thank you, Irene. I shall indeed.' Mavis took a deep breath, looking suddenly serious.

'You have to understand, Lizzy, that when we met you at the nursing home, we didn't know you properly, not like we do now,' Mavis explained.

Lizzy nodded: she knew what they meant. They had to find out if she was genuine before they could reveal all of their secrets.

'We liked you of course, otherwise we wouldn't have said anything at all,' Mavis continued twisting her hands in her lap. 'We only told you what most people living in the village then, could have told you, or at any rate anyone at the workhouse and hospital.' She hesitated, looking rather nervous.

'But there was something that nobody but our Nan knew, a very big secret that she made our mother swear never to tell anyone. Of course, Mum told us, we didn't count, we were family and knew how to keep these secrets deep in our hearts. Then there was your mother – we didn't want to upset her, but now that she has passed on, what we have to say will not hurt her. We did not know whether she knew all the facts and peoples' attitudes were different back then.'

Lizzy was on the edge of her seat. What did any of this mean to her mother? 'What do you mean?'

'Mavis suspected she knew you as soon as you entered the room that first time.' Irene could not help getting an odd word in.

Lizzy was feeling lightheaded; there was a whistling in her ears and a sense of wobbling on top of a high cliff from which she might fall.

'What do you mean she recognised me? Are you going to tell me that I am related to you? Is that the secret you have been keeping?'

'Why no, course not, silly,' Mavis said, 'you don't even look like us. No, you look just like her, just like the photo that we have in our keeping. It's all here in this *Craven A* cigarette tin we are going to give you.' She patted a small package on her lap.

Lizzy smiled. They had found it after all.

'The tiny photo in your pastille tin looks nothing like Catherine really. This other photo in our tin is a much truer likeness.' Clearly Mavis was the type of woman to emphasise her superiority even in the case of battered old photos.

Seeing how mystified Lizzy looked, Mavis added, 'You are the spitting image of Catherine Waterman. You look so like your grandmother; you could be twins.'

Chapter Twenty-Nine - 1917

Despite the nostalgic name, Woodbine Cottages was merely a cluster of ill-constructed buildings in narrow rows, crammed together with no privacy, covering a damp rat-infested plot of land. The slope from the blacksmith's forge to the shallows at the bottom was so steep that the cottages seemed to be on the point of sliding down to pile up in the river.

It was not a normal day – such a thing had never been seen in Woodbine Cottages before. Small children, pushed outside to play by their mothers, whooped with excitement as a delivery boy on a bicycle negotiated the steep descent and narrow paths to stop outside number six. They ran behind, alongside, in front of the rider, nearly knocking the bike over with their enthusiasm. It did not matter how much he shouted at them to "mind the bike" and "get out of the way you numbskulls". At the sound of shouting, heads were thrust out of the doorways and a crowd gathered, eager to know what was happening. The delivery boy hastily knocked on the door of Daisy's cottage, heaved a huge cardboard box from the wicker basket attached to the front of his bike and made off speedily as the door opened a crack, shouting out, 'It's from Miss Catherine Waterman!'

There had been quite a tussle with the manager of Chappells Emporium to get her gift delivered. Catherine had stood her ground and offered an extra delivery fee and here was the box standing on the step. It was so large it covered the whole step and took most of the little ones to pull it inside. They all stood back whilst Daisy opened the flaps of the box. There was a letter at the top and they waited whilst she slit open the envelope in case it was all a mistake, and the box would have to go back. Although there had not been much time for writing lessons with Miss Catherine, let alone reading lessons, she had learnt to distinguish her own name and that of Miss Catherine, and interpret the kisses underneath. Such a pity she had not been able to meet up with her, but it would have been too dangerous. Unfortunately, Daisy could not read the question enquiring about the small tin and so the note was placed inside the *Craven A* tin of letters perched on the only shelf in the house.

The children meanwhile were exploring the contents of the box, full of good staple items such as any decent cook would keep in her larder: packets of tea, bags of flour, cans of peas and fruit, a pat of butter carefully wrapped in greaseproof paper, two loaves of bread, several jars of jam from different fruits, a tin of treacle and one of golden syrup, cheese and bacon, sliced by the grocer on his dangerous-looking machine, a huge box of biscuits, tins of corned beef and ham, a bag of sugar, and oranges, apples and pears from the greengrocer next door.

Catherine had not realised that there was no cool larder with marble shelves to keep the food for a long time because she was thinking of her mother's cook and her well-stocked larder. That didn't matter at all, for the family was so hungry and starved of delicious food that they managed to consume all the perishable stuff in a couple of days. What was likely to go off they shared with their friends in a makeshift feast. It went into the communal memory, when Woodbine dwellers and their descendants would say: 'Do you remember the day the hamper came down the hill? What a day that was. All sent by that young nurse at the hospital, that Miss Catherine, her that had the baby with the Canadian soldier. Bless her.'

Whilst the children were shrieking with excitement over the box, Catherine was steeling herself to enter the butcher's shop with rows of dead rabbits hanging from hooks outside. Was that blood on the pavement dripping from their little noses?

She shuddered as she stepped inside where the smell of dead animals hit her nostrils. She had never been anywhere near such a shop before. A pig's head sat in the middle of the window surrounded by various bits of animals. Catherine had become a vegetarian after listening to one of the afternoon talks given by an offshoot branch of the suffragettes. All sorts of movements were starting up and Catherine had attended every meeting she could find.

She drove the cook in their household demented by lecturing her on the merits of vegetarianism whilst the poor woman was faced with cooking large joints of meat for the rest of the family. Catherine was not really sure that she liked vegetables very much but once she had chosen a path, she showed great fortitude in following it. She did occasionally share a tasty morsel of lamb pinched from the table when no one was looking but at least she was trying to do the right thing.

The smell of the raw meat and the curious sensation of treading on sawdust were almost too much for Catherine and she began to feel dizzy, but she practised deep breathing and mindfulness as Dr Morgan had prescribed.

'Have you any cooked chicken?' she demanded of the ruddy-cheeked man behind the counter, wearing a striped blue and white apron, and a straw boater on his head.

'No, miss, all my meat is raw. You takes it home and you gets your cook to cook it for you,' replied the butcher confused by this odd question, never asked before in the whole of his butchering lifetime.

'Have you a wife?' Catherine enquired. The butcher wondered if this was to be followed by a proposal of marriage. He was used to imperious ladies but not one who seemed slightly mad. Yet she looked as if she had money, and in that case the customer was always right. *Keep the lady happy,* he thought.

'Why, yes, madam, I do, and a very good wife she is too. Looks after me a treat, she do,' lest there might be any misunderstanding as to his marital status.

'If I paid for it, would she cook me that chicken?' Catherine pointed a steady finger at the largest chicken she could see. 'Then could your boy deliver it to a cottage for me? The people are sick, they need some nourishment. I believe chicken is very good for invalids.'

*

The butcher, a good-natured solid man with very little imagination, was stunned at this request. He stood with his head on one side and considered the pros and cons of this transaction. Would he get into trouble with the law or the guilds that ruled what shopkeepers could undertake in their business? Would he now be pestered with requests for cooked meat? He took off his straw boater and rubbed his forehead.

Most of all, he was worried about whether Maggie would want to cook chicken for other people. He never knew which way the wind was blowing with her. She had moods from time to time. Fortunately, she was out at the back working on some bills for him. He was not good at paperwork, but she was quite at home with a pencil and paper, totting up figures.

'Maggie!' he bellowed, 'could you come out here and help me with a customer? She wants to ask you something.' Leave the two of them to it, he thought, keep out of any arguments that way.

Catherine repeated her request to the sturdy young woman who had appeared in the doorway with rolled up sleeves and a pinny over her plain serge dress.

*

Maggie was not the least bit disconcerted by the request. As she told her mother in the evening:

'The world is full of odd people. Not all folk do things the same way. It made sense, sort of, what she was saying, because how would you manage if you had no oven and you wanted to cook a chicken? I know the baker lets people cook meat in his bread oven when he has finished baking for the day when there is all that good cooking heat going to waste. But she probably doesn't know about the baker, being as she is a stranger and he's a bad-tempered man. So, I says to her, "Yes madam, I could do that for you" and we made a price between us. And she gives me the address – uses my pencil and my paper to write it down. Lovely handwriting she had – copperplate I think they call it. Only it was so twirly I couldn't quite make it out, so I asks her to put it in big bold letters so as I could read it.'

Her mother stared at Maggie in amazement at such goings-on in the town.

'"Oh, you mean capitals," she says, "like this" and she puts it all in big bold letters and I can read it easy as you like. Very obliging she was, though a bit pale looking. "That's fine, miss," I say. "I'll take it out the window now and it will be cooked later on when I finish my book-work, and then delivered to that house. They will have a shock and no mistake. They don't get meat to eat often there." She smiles at me and opens her little velvet bag and pays me the money there and then on the nail. "That's the sort of customer we want," I says to Noah, "those what pay up straight away and buy more than two sausages and a pound of tripe."'

Her mother nodded her head in agreement. Her daughter Maggie had a good head on her.

*

Catherine stood outside the butcher's shop, considering her next move, staring at the rabbit corpses. Would the smell cling to her? She feared it might. Pulling open the strings of her Dorothy bag, she searched for the tiny phial of her favourite perfume, lily-of-the-valley. Sprinkling a few drops on her gloves and her throat reassured her that she had eradicated the smell of dead animals.

She continued along the High Street, where she was pleased to see a number of useful shops. She pushed open the door to a draper's shop, greeted by a bell and a pleasing aroma of lavender and bleached cotton. Bales of cloth of all colours and designs were stacked on shelves behind the assistant at the large wooden counter. These seemed to cater for every form of life and occupation in Kingcharlton, from babies to school children, from ladies of the house to maids' outfits, from working clothes to fancy dresses. Catherine supposed they would all have to make their own clothing or employ a dressmaker, as there were no big clothes shops like Howells in Cardiff.

'Do you keep underwear for children and ladies?'

'No fancy stuff, madam, but plain cotton items, very serviceable and long lasting.'

'Show me some, please, a selection of sizes.'

Catherine did not remember how many sisters Daisy had or their ages though Daisy must have told her. There were no brothers to be catered for as they were away in France. She picked out a suitable selection and added some items for Daisy's mother. She arranged for them to be delivered. The errand boys of Kingcharlton were working hard. Next was the cordwainer's shop with boots of all sizes in his shop window. In this small village, the cordwainer also acted as cobbler, mending shoes as well as making them. Several pairs of well-patched, well-worn boots were waiting on his counter to be collected by their owners. Once again, Catherine purchased a selection with the assurance of Mr Jenkins the owner that they could be exchanged for correct sizes if necessary.

Now her energy was flagging, and her purse was empty, and her thoughts were creeping back to her precious tin, and Ben buried somewhere in a foreign land. The process of shopping had distracted her for a short time, but now she was sinking back into despair. A sudden frenzy of emotions and restlessness assailed her, and she spoke aloud as she hurried along.

'I must go to France. I can't stay here any longer searching for my lost tin and seeking to retrieve the one I left with Daisy. What good would a lot of letters and photos be to me anyway? Major Bowmaker could be mistaken. I must go to France and find the truth.'

She had wanted to stay in Kingcharlton to see from the distance, how her gifts were received but a mad mood took her so that she rushed to the station instead and jumped on the first train back to Bristol. She would return to see Beatrice and beg her to look after tiny Huw whilst she searched for Ben.

*

Back at the cottage, unaware of the chicken and other items that would soon be arriving, the children had finished unpacking the contents of the box, and had laid everything out on the table, enjoying the feast their eyes and their imaginations were having in anticipation of the meals their tummies would enjoy later. There was a multitude of brightly patterned boxes and tins. It was a dazzling display like a grocer's window. And last of all – right at the bottom of the box – there had been bars of chocolate and all sorts of little treats for the children.

Daisy's mother was quite overcome and sat with her hands in her lap watching the children and hardly believing what she was seeing in front of her. And so the sainthood of Catherine was ratified at number six Woodbine Cottages and the cigarette-tin, full of letters from Canada, was deemed a precious item to be looked after carefully and passed down through the generations until such time as it might be claimed. It survived another war with bombing and privations. But the Hollis family guarded the tin and its secret until one hundred years later when a stranger came calling, asking about Miss Catherine.

Chapter Thirty

Meanwhile in Clifton at the residence of Arthur and Beatrice Mortlake, there were serious matters to be considered.

'Where's your sister gone, Beatrice?'

Arthur Mortlake looked sternly at his wife, who was holding the gurgling baby in her arms, cooing and clucking with a contented smile.

'Should you be playing with the baby in the drawing room, with all the servants around. There's a temporary nursery upstairs until Catherine returns to her parents. I thought she would only be here for a short time – then return to her house in Cardiff, posing as a war widow. It's turned the whole household upside down.'

Beatrice winced at the phrase "temporary nursery". She so longed for children of her own to fill a permanent nursery, but nothing seemed to be happening. Secretly she was enjoying the fact that the baby seemed more attached to her than to her absent sister. It was a struggle to stop herself from pretending that Huw was her baby, lest she gave her feelings away to Arthur who was very sensitive about the lack of fatherhood so far.

'The baby's name is Huw, Arthur, and all the servants are on their afternoon off, so nobody is about to take any notice.'

'Stop trying to distract me, Beatrice. Tell me where your sister is today. Has she gone to register the child properly and is she really going to call the baby Huw? What sort of a name is that, surely it should be Hubert?'

'It's the Welsh spelling of Hubert. And it's the father's second name. His family emigrated from Wales to Vancouver before the turn of the century.'

'Lot of nonsense, and you still haven't told me where she is and why she is leaving you to perform her duties as a mother yet again.'

Beatrice sighed wistfully and cuddled little Huw more closely to her ample bosom of pink velour, which he seemed to enjoy.

'She rushed out earlier, planning to catch a train to Kingcharlton. Ben's whereabouts are still playing on her mind and she seems to think that village gossip might provide an answer. A notion still lingers in her distress that he is lying injured somewhere in a foreign hospital with a loss of memory. She wants to see Daisy – the little maid who took such a liking to her.'

Beatrice took a deep breath, ready to defend herself.

'I can't persuade her to settle down, Arthur, no matter how often you tell me to speak to her.' Beatrice was extremely agitated, and the words tumbled from her mouth in a muddle. Fearing that she might alarm the baby, she lowered her voice to a loud whisper.

'What would a country maid know about casualties? They are so cut off in Kingcharlton, it's a wonder that they know anything about the outside world.' Arthur was scathing in the extreme, irritated by his sister-in-law's ridiculous behaviour. As nobody knew about Catherine's tin, her behaviour seemed totally unreasonable.

'Servants always know what is going on, whether they turn a blind eye or not, and they pass it on to other servants in other households. News spreads like wildfire.' Beatrice rocked the baby who was becoming fretful. Soon his eyes closed, dainty eyelashes resting on rosy cheeks and all was peaceful once more.

'You're mistaken about their lack of knowledge of the war; many maids have brothers on various front lines – some very young, lying about their age. As long as they look sturdy, they let them sign up, especially after the heavy losses of the Somme.' Despite her indignation, Beatrice was still whispering so as to not disturb the sleeping infant.

At the back of the house, there was an enormous bang, as a door was slammed shut.

'Beatrice, Beatrice, where are you?' The sound of boots clattered in the hall and Catherine rushed into the room, pulling off her outdoor coat and hat as she came. She was evidently in a great state of distress, her face white with shock, her body trembling from head to toe. She was in such a hurry that she could not even wait for the maid to open the front door. Beatrice shivered at her sister's dishevelled appearance. Catherine's croaking voice shrieked out and woke the baby up.

‘Major Bowmaker says Ben’s dead. He said they were searching for me to let me know. My mind is in a whirl – one minute I believed what he said. The next moment I was wondering if he was misinformed. I can’t rest, I can’t sleep I can’t sit still until I have some proof. Whatever shall I do?’ She collapsed on the settee, her head in her hands without taking any notice of the baby.

‘You could look after your infant for a while,’ muttered Arthur.

Beatrice frowned at him and signalled him to leave the room to let her deal with Catherine. ‘Bring her a glass of brandy, Arthur, that will revive her.’

‘What good is brandy to me? I have lost the man I love and the father of my child. I must go to France, back to Vimy Ridge, and see where he is buried.’ Catherine hurtled out of the room and thundered up the stairs.

Arthur continued grumbling. ‘It’s a good job most of the servants are out of the house at the moment with this nonsense upsetting the peace. Our respectability will be damaged irreparably. We won’t be able to hire a decent cook.’

Arthur followed her out into the hall in time to see his sister-in-law raising clouds of dust on the stairs from her thumping heels. He closed the door firmly and stood in front of the marble fireplace with his thumbs in his waistcoat pockets. As if to confirm his position as master of the household, he studied a magnificent golden pocket watch hanging across his waistcoat and informed Beatrice of the time although she could see it clearly on the grandfather clock in the corner.

‘This is the final straw. I have reached a decision. We are going to move away from Bristol and take the infant with us. I have been offered a position in the north, managing a munitions factory with an excellent salary. And we’d better speak to the maids about the dust on that stair carpet. It’s not good enough.’

‘But what will Catherine say?’ Beatrice’s face was a picture of astonishment as she took in her husband’s words.

‘She can’t object. She spends no time with the baby at all. It’s a disgrace. I have waited long enough. That baby should have been registered by now. If she does not come down now to register him and promise she will return to Cardiff, I will take the child under my own wing and register him as our own.’

‘Can you do that, Arthur? Won’t the registrar know it’s not our baby?’

More thumping on the stairs and the front door banged again. Arthur peered through the net curtains. He turned to Beatrice and smiled.

‘She won’t be here to say anything. Her son is the last thing on her mind. She is dressed in her nurse’s uniform and is carrying a carpetbag. I think she means it when she says she is going to France. As to the matter of registration, I know a man at my club who could make it happen. He owes me a favour or two. It could be sorted out tomorrow, if you agree.

Arthur smiled and patted his wife’s shoulders. She was the one weak spot in his solid armour. But he took care not to express this affection too often.

'I think you love that little baby – he makes you happy. Catherine has other things on her mind – she doesn't want to take a role as a war widow. You bear some resemblance to your sister with your red curls and we have been very discreet about the goings-on in this house so far. Who is to say whose baby it is? Arthur paused whilst he thought up more reasons to persuade his wife to adopt his plans. He allowed his imagination to run wild as to what they could achieve.

'He's a healthy little chap; he can be our son and heir. Why not? You shall have a wonderful new house in the north. The child could be enrolled at Manchester Grammar School. I hear it's very good. After the war ends, I could start up my own business: Mortlake and Son. I shall have made all the right connections by then. What do you think?'

Beatrice replied slowly as she was trying to work out if this plan was feasible.

'I'm not sure what my parents will say. Perhaps they want Catherine's baby to stay with them. But yes, Arthur, I would love to bring up Huw and treat him as our own. He is such a dear little soul. Catherine really doesn't seem to be interested in mothering him. Already he feels like my own child.' Beatrice hesitated for several moments as if slotting the last pieces of the puzzle into place. Rapidly changing expressions on her face depicted the various emotions flowing through her mind. Eventually she turned to Arthur, a smile spread over her calm face, and said:

'I agree with you, Arthur. We would make much better parents. We could give him a good life. What part shall I play in your plans? How are you going to persuade Father?'

'You leave that to me, Beatrice my dear; I will deal with your father. You just keep quiet and get ready to move. You shall have your little baby and I shall have a son.' For all his sternness, Arthur Mortlake adored his wife; he had seen how she longed for a baby of her own, and he had the money to keep her happy. If Catherine came back and made a hullabaloo in years to come, her erratic behaviour could signify madness and he could declare her deluded and have her certified. But for now, things were looking rosy.

*

'We need to have a discussion about the baby.' Arthur' face took on a serious look as he spoke to his father-in-law in an undertone so as not to disturb the ladies. He had cornered Fred Waterman in the drawing room where afternoon tea was being served. Florence, his mother-in-law, and Beatrice, his wife, were cooing at the baby, trying to make him smile and passing him backwards and forwards between the two of them for cuddles. Florence and Fred were on a day trip from Cardiff to see their new grandson. There was no mention of Catherine's absence and no questions were asked as to her whereabouts.

'Come away into my study and we'll see if we can sort matters out.' Arthur's face hardened; he had been anticipating this awkward moment for a while. He was worried whether Fred would see it from his perspective and agree with his plans.

This study was a place for men to discuss important matters, all dark wood and leather. The air was tobacco scented and there was not a frill to be seen. Arthur felt relaxed in there, more in control of the situation than when his eyes were dazzled by the flowery calico-covered furniture of the ladies' drawing room. He must have all his wits about him to follow his plan through.

'Cigar, Fred? I have some fine Cuban beauties here.' Arthur's voice took on a friendly tone, as he held out a wooden box of fat brown cigars, looking like sausages in a row, with small label bands round their middles to prove how expensive they were.

Fred took one, held it to his nostril appreciatively to compliment his host, brought his clippers out of his waistcoat pocket and snipped off the end. He put a light to the cigar and took a long drag. Fragrant grey smoke encircled his head and he actually smiled. 'Fine stuff, Arthur, not bad at all. You will have to tell me who your supplier is. I wouldn't mind a box or two myself.'

The proprieties observed, the ritual of cigar lighting performed properly, there was nothing to stop the two men moving on to the reason why they had come to the study in the first place. However, both men seemed reluctant to broach the subject of Catherine's baby son. They took up positions at either end of an enormous sofa of substantial leather staring out at the stately garden beyond. The sofa was not comfortable, like sitting on a bull, stiff and bulky. Unspoken words hung above their heads. They puffed away on the cigars, their thoughts dancing in the room like floating dust motes.

Fred finally spoke out; feeling as he did that his position in the family gave him the right to express his opinions first. 'Well, Arthur, this baby – what is to become of it? Have you any ideas? Does Catherine still want to keep the baby? Why is she not here now looking after him? Should we get the little chappie adopted? There is the matter of scandal to be considered of course. We are a well-respected family in Cardiff. We have kept it concealed so far but what of the future?'

Arthur had reached the moment he feared. He must not make a mess of this or all would be lost, and Beatrice would be heartbroken. 'We have talked it over, Beatrice and I, at great length and have come to a decision. We would like to offer the little chap a home for now in our residence as we have no children of our own yet.' Arthur's face grew red at this statement. 'There is plenty of space for him. Beatrice would make a perfect mother – just look at how well she handles the baby.'

Fred smiled – all tension disappeared. 'That might be the perfect solution for the time being. If Beatrice takes on the mothering whilst Catherine settles down and leaves her madcap lifestyle behind. It could work well. It wouldn't be permanent of course. Catherine might find her mothering skills yet.'

Arthur smiled back and nodded, as if in agreement. This was what he had expected. The family wanted him and Beatrice to act as nannies and then release the baby at Catherine's whim. But he had a plan – he had made a fortune out of analysing the way others were thinking and acting accordingly. He remembered the saying that "Possession is nine-tenths of the Law" but he needed Fred's cooperation for that to take place. Now that he had heard Fred's views on the subject, he felt that he might be able to make his plan work.

'Tell you what, Fred. Why don't you leave the little fellow with us? Nora could remain with us as well. She is proving to be a good little nursemaid – been looking after Huw a lot recently. Then when Catherine is ready, she can collect him.' Arthur repeated his offer as he felt the need to firm up the situation before Fred thought it all through. He was not a wealthy businessman for nothing. He wanted to hear a definite 'yes' before he left the study.

'Perfect,' said Fred, 'the solution to a knotty problem. Also, it will give Beatrice the opportunity to practise for when her own little ones come along. Catherine will have the time to rid herself of her own fantasies and then she can tell people that she is a war widow with a son; plenty of those about. Florence is not of an age to be bringing up small babies. Besides which, she has her charity committee to run and the entertaining of my guests. We can't have wailing babies about.'

Arthur nodded again. He had his own opinions about Catherine. Her inclination to wildness had always been there, and childbirth seemed merely to have exacerbated it. He doubted it would go away. She would never settle down. He was absolutely sure of that. Who could say what would happen now that she had accepted that Ben was dead? She might go completely mad, out of her head with grief, a very unstable nervy girl in his opinion, full of ideas and plans but too unsettled to carry them out to the end. Did Fred even know she had rushed off to France?

Not like Beatrice steady and reliable but sad inside, longing for a baby. And if it was up to Arthur, by God, she was going to get one. Huw was a solid little fellow, chubby, healthy; just the sort of son that Arthur had always envisaged. And they knew his provenance – he would be reluctant to adopt an unknown child as Beatrice had suggested. There might be bad blood there. No, this was the perfect solution for them. They were nearly home and dry. Fred and Florence clearly did not want the child to stay with them whilst Catherine travelled all over France searching for the grave of her lover.

Arthur concentrated on not allowing his face to reveal any emotions. His plan was falling into place. He concealed his feelings of jubilation. Fred must not have any idea of what he had planned. Beatrice had filled the 'temporary' nursery with all sorts of fancy equipment that would be transported to the north, to the lovely new house. Arthur had been preparing discreetly to make this move. It all depended on Beatrice staying strong enough to deceive her parents, with no second thoughts to betray them. He instructed her that she must act out a part of a helpful sister and dutiful daughter, pretending that she had no intention of holding on to the baby in the long term.

'That seems to have settled the matter to our satisfaction,' said Fred. 'Let's re-join the ladies and let them know what we have decided. You won't have any trouble persuading Beatrice, Arthur?'

'I'm sure she will agree, she is a good wife and daughter and always eager to please.' Arthur smiled and shook hands with Fred as if to seal the agreement.

Arthur looked over at Beatrice as the men entered the room and very gently gave a small nod to indicate that his tactics had worked. They would soon be off to Manchester with the baby. 'It's all sorted, Beatrice. The baby will remain in our household for the present, we will keep Nora with us as the nursemaid. We will look after him until Catherine is feeling better. Would anyone care for more tea?'

*

Beatrice did not argue at any stage of Arthur's planning. She had always felt left out, treated differently to her two sisters: the eldest daughter who must behave whilst Catherine and Annie were allowed to wander about all over the place. Annie had settled down now and was engaged to be married – lots of fuss over wedding preparations. Catherine, meanwhile, had caused an enormous amount of turmoil but still everybody thought she should be humoured, pampered even.

Why had Beatrice not been allowed to develop her own character and search for her true self as Catherine had? And now her sister had this beautiful baby that she left in the hands of others most of the time. All Beatrice had ever wanted was to be a wife and mother so that it was so unfair that she could not produce a baby of her own. Nobody except Arthur had considered her feelings in the matter. Give her a baby. Take away a baby. No, she would not do it. She wanted to keep Huw. Already he knew her as well as his true mother. He smiled at her and cried when she left the room. Arthur had come up with this marvellous plan and she was going to help him.

Huw was her baby now.

Chapter Thirty-One - 2017

Lizzy was dropping off a cliff, travelling through fluffy clouds of mist. She leant back, closed her eyes and cuddled into the cushions. The moment passed and she sat upright, her eyes aghast with shock. 'Catherine was my grandmother? How and why? Who was my father? Who are the people I think are my grandparents?'

'Give her another cup of tea, Irene, one with lots of sugar – she's in shock. We should have told her more slowly, given her time to take it all in. Mavis looked as if she was about to say *I told you we should not have told her the final secret.*

'She'll be fine. Give her a moment or two.' Irene had been on a Red Cross course and took charge of the situation. 'Give her a moment or two. It was her right to know. I am very surprised that none of her family had put her straight.'

'Tell me,' Lizzy whispered, 'tell me the whole story please. Put me out of my misery.'

'I don't really know where to begin,' said Irene, which was not true as she immediately launched into the tale. It soon became obvious that she wanted to tell the story in a certain way and, like the tea serving ceremony, it could not be rushed.

‘I think it began that day when Nan left home to work for Matron in the hospital,’ Irene started, then she let the story unfold in her soft Somerset burr – the unravelling of the tangled mystery in its entirety.

‘This is the story Nan passed down, not written down, but told by the fireside. She always believed that somebody would come for the tin and we must be ready. She would be so pleased to know that you are here.’ Irene beamed at Lizzy.

‘This is what we know: Daisy and Catherine Waterman met when they climbed up that steep hill together and arrived at the door at the same time. Your grandmother was very kind to our Nan, when she could have easily ignored her altogether. That was the way in those days, servants were nobodies and a ragged little urchin like Daisy was then, meant nothing to most folk.’ Irene paused to see if Lizzy was absorbing this information.

‘Catherine took a liking to our Nan, probably because she was so small and obviously had a hard life. I think it was at that point that Catherine realised how privileged she was with her comfortable family life and she tried to help our Nan, Daisy, as she settled into her new life. Daisy was always by her side when she was not working, sometimes standing in the shadows when Ben was around. That’s how she came to know that Catherine had fallen in love with Ben. She guessed that Catherine was in the family way. Nan came from a family with lots of children. She knew the signs, you see.’

Irene paused again to study Lizzy’s face, which changed expression at each new revelation.

'When Catherine made the decision to follow Ben to France, she confided in our Nan and left the *Craven A* tin with her. It held letters from Ben's family plus a few of them sepia photos. That's how we knew what Catherine looked like. There's a beautiful photo of her taken in a studio somewhere and one of her with Ben. Laughing away they are, as if they had not a care in the world. That tin stayed with us until the present day, just in case anyone came asking for it.'

'Catherine's special little tin, the one she kept in her pocket, got lost. It slipped off her bed and was left behind. Our Nan found it when she was setting the room to rights and she hid it in what she thought was a safe place, a hole in one of the cupboards in the back kitchen. It would have been a good choice if Matron had not called the ratcatcher and ordered him to get rid of all the rats and board up any holes they had made. Nan was terrible upset when she couldn't retrieve the tin. She thought she had let down Miss Catherine.'

Irene had found her voice now and nothing short of a hurricane would have stopped her.

'Miss Catherine returned when Ben went missing at Vimy Ridge, but not to Kingcharlton. She went home to her family in Bristol. That much Nan learned later on. Catherine did come to see Matron, once the baby was born, to let her know that she was going back to France. Daisy was ill at home with scarlet fever. Her whole family had it. So, Catherine could not visit her because she might have caught the disease and carried it home to her baby. But before she went, she sent boxes to the cottage full of lovely food. There were other gifts as well, boots and clothes. She put a lot of thought into those presents for a lady who has just been told her lover was dead.'

Irene finally ran out of breath and Mavis took over.

'Later when Daisy went back to work, Matron took her aside one day and told her all about the baby, with a strict warning to keep it to herself. Catherine said that the baby had been left with her married sister, Beatrice Mortlake. They seemed to be having difficulties in having a child and were delighted to have this baby given to them. Catherine called him Huw, Ben's second name. Later Nan learned from Nora, the maid who looked after Huw, that her sister and brother-in-law had changed his name to Nicholas Mortlake. They had stolen the baby away to Manchester. But that's another tale.'

'My father, Nicholas Mortlake,' whispered Lizzy. 'My father was Catherine's baby and Ben was his birth father?'

'Why yes, my dear, that's the top and bottom of it. We didn't know whether to tell you or not. We thought you might get tired of searching and that it was better to leave stones unturned. But when we saw how interested you were in Catherine and Ben, it seemed right to tell you. If I were in your position, I would want to know. Some people wouldn't but I think you are strong enough to deal with it. I am going to stop now. That is enough for you to take on board. Come back and see us if you have more questions and we will try to help you. Here is the tin we were telling you about. We're glad to be handing it back to its rightful owner.'

It was Irene who handed a brown paper parcel to Lizzy and kissed her cheek. She smelt of face powder mingled with Devon Violets perfume. The parcel was securely wrapped with yards of sticky tape as if to prevent its secrets from escaping. Lizzy guessed they didn't want her to unwrap it now in their house. Opening the tin should be a private moment. It would be a very emotional experience the sisters suspected.

'Have we done the right thing, my dear?'

'Yes, you have,' whispered Lizzy.

'Shall I walk up the road with you? You look a bit wobbly.'

'No, I'm okay. Thank you so much for solving my mystery. You have given me so much information, so very kind of you. I will be back soon to ask you more.'

Lizzy walked home in a daze, clutching the small parcel as if she was afraid it might escape, and all that information would be lost. She was longing to see the letters from Vancouver and study the photos with a magnifying glass. There was a distinct possibility that she would be able to trace her relatives in Canada and all because these two caring sisters had liked her enough to share their secret. The realisation that this precious information might have been lost to her forever slowly dawned with a stunning effect. She felt weak and dizzy, in need of a chaise longue to collapse on.

*

The parcel lay on Lizzy's coffee table transmitting disturbing vibes around the room. Lizzy could feel them circling like invisible ghosts. Although she was desperate to look at the material inside, she was frightened to begin the process. Perhaps she would wait until the next day. She found two headache tablets and broke them into four pieces, easy to swallow. The water from the tap felt ice-cold swirling down her burning throat. *Oh no, not tonsillitis,* she prayed. Any emotional upset often brought on this form of torture. Lying on the sofa, listening to her heart slowing its pace, she must have fallen asleep. When she opened her eyes again, it was quite dark and Wellington was lying at her side licking her arm. He padded out behind her as she slid open the French windows to lie on her purple lounger with a large glass of red wine. *Almost a chaise longue for a fatigued lady* she thought

The moon was full; it was one of those gigantic moons that occasionally hang in the sky like a golden balloon. Lizzy was visited by a primeval need to be in touch with Mother Nature as she gazed at the moon and stars shining overhead in a dark sapphire sky. She needed to feel the earth below her feet and listen to the various sounds of mysterious nocturnal animals to soothe her agitated mind. Pulling on a thick woolly shawl, she filled the old cracked chiminea with the logs that had been piled up against the wall in a careful stack. One of Gerry's last tasks was to prune the apple trees in their back garden, so this was his handiwork. As the logs crackled and the first plumes of smoke wafted upwards, her nostrils caught the unique perfume given off by burning apple-wood and it was as if Gerry was there with her, helping her to understand.

The scent and sounds emerging from the clay fire-pit brought back memories of laughing children, fireworks exploding with bangs in clouds of coloured stars, the spicy tang of gingerbread laden with black treacle, baked potatoes hot from the bonfire charred and almost inedible, and the smell of cordite hanging in the air. Those were happy days in the garden among the apple trees. Life had seemed simple then. What would her family say to this latest bit of news, to learn that they have relatives in Canada?

Could it be true that Catherine was her grandmother and Ben her grandfather? How would her family tree look now, with all these shifting relationships? Did her parents know? The whole universe had altered with this news; it was a strange new world. She would have to take another trip to the wartime cemeteries and search for details of her newly discovered grandfather on the white marble memorial. She knew that Ben had died at Vimy Ridge but what had happened to her grandmother and where was she buried? Lizzy's quest was not completed yet.

Chapter Thirty-Two

Lizzy awoke with the feeling that something important had happened; something that could not be ignored. For a moment or two, her mind was still asleep. Slowly the memory of the previous day's encounter with Mavis and Irene returned. All that information they had been keeping from her – should she be cross with them or grateful that they had at last revealed the truth? Was it the whole truth? It was enough to deal with at the moment. How to proceed?

'I know!' she shouted at a startled Wellington, 'Let's phone Tom and see if he can help us with this. We should get some addresses and names from this new tin.'

Leaping out of bed she ran downstairs to put the kettle on, her mind buzzing like a hive of bees ready to swarm. Like the travelling bugs seeking a new home, she would have to choose the right direction. Would her grandfather Ben have written to his parents about Catherine and the baby? Did Ben even know about the baby? Did he die without knowing that he was about to become a father? Tom would bring some practicality into all this uncertainty. He answered her mobile on the second ring.

'Hi there, Lizzy. I wondered how you were getting on.' His voice as usual steadied her frantic thoughts, inducing a feeling that anything was possible if she calmed down and proceeded in a sensible manner.

'Tom, I need your help. It's a personal matter. I have been given some startling news. I need your sensible advice. Mavis and Irene have produced another tin, a bigger one with lots of letters from Ben's relatives – so they say. They also gave me the biggest shock of my life. I'm all over the place; my head is spinning. Can you come round now?' She ran out of breath and sat down exhausted.

'All this sounds very intriguing. I'll be round in about half an hour. I've a few errands to run. Is that soon enough? It's not an emergency, is it?'

'No, it's not Tom. That will give me time to tidy up a bit. We might be in for a long session. I'll pop over to the Co-op for some rolls and cake.'

Tom was as good as his word, arriving sixteen minutes later. Once he had got past Wellington's warm welcome, he smiled at Lizzy. 'What's up then, lass? More secrets revealed by the Somerset sisters? Makes me think of a witches' coven – all the drama and mystery. Why couldn't they tell you straight out instead of keeping you in suspense?'

Lizzy smiled back. All would be put right, now that Tom was here. He was such a good friend. 'You won't believe what I have got to tell you now – the real secret that they have been holding back - the secret they have kept, guarded over the generations and years. It can't be easy to let go. It had been drummed into them as children that this was a precious secret and that they had to respect Catherine and Ben's memories. Plus, they didn't want to upset my mother whilst she was still alive. Come through to the kitchen and I'll put the kettle on.'

Tom followed Lizzy and stopped in amazement at the kitchen table, set up exactly like the day they met. There was another tin in the place of honour – a bigger tin, red and white with a cheeky black cat on the front.

'Try opening that one, Tom,' Lizzy chuckled, 'I think you will find it a lot easier than the other tin, plus it's got lots of useful information inside.'

'*Déjà vu,* that's the feeling I have,' murmured Tom, 'or am I in that film, *Groundhog Day*? Where did this tin come from?'

'Apparently Catherine found she had too many letters to fit in her tiny tin, because Ben put her in charge of his family letters from Canada. He had kept them in this cigarette tin, given to him by one of his soldier buddies. When she left for France to follow Ben, she entrusted it to Daisy. The tin has been with her family ever since.'

'What made them part with it now?'

'They thought I ought to know the whole story and besides, as Catherine and Ben's grandchild, it is really my property as their heir. I had taken my tin to show them, and they were fascinated to see the tin that was lost so many years ago.'

Tom stared at Lizzy in amazement and disbelief.

'Hold it right there – Catherine and Ben's grandchild? This is the big secret they have been guarding? You're the child of the missing baby – that baby would be your father? Wow, I never expected that. Sit still for a moment and tell me the whole story. I'm flabbergasted.'

'It's a long, complicated story, Tom; we knew some of it but not the complete tale. It may have lost some accuracy down the years. I'll tell it to you as best I can remember but I might have got it a bit mixed up. What a shock. They said to go back if I had any questions.'

Lizzy relived the whole episode with Tom, the sisters excited at sharing their secret, her amazement at their revelation, the complexity of the situation. It took time to relay all the facts in the correct order but finally Lizzy ran out of words and Tom looked as if he could not deal with any more information. 'Why don't we see what's inside your new tin?'

Lizzy unpacked the tin with care, the contents were in far better condition than in her little pastille tin. The letters all seemed to be in the same handwriting save for one or two. It was clear that most of the letters came from Ben's mother.

'Look Tom, most of these letters have the same address in Vancouver. We could try contacting them and share our side of the story. How exciting.'

'How do the Hollis sisters know all this in such detail?' asked Tom. 'Some of this took place in Cardiff and Bristol.'

'I don't know,' squeaked Lizzy, 'but they seemed very certain about their facts and it sort of makes sense. I've laid awake most of the night trying to put all the information in order and figure out what it means. I can see why they didn't want to reveal their secret whilst my mother was alive. They really are lovely people, very kind despite their bluntness. I shall have to visit them again and ask all these questions. They did mention Nora, Huw's nursemaid, in passing, but I am not sure what part she played in this drama. It's a mystery. Right now, I want to see if I can make contact with these relatives in Canada. Will you help me, Tom? I'm so excited I don't know whether I'm coming or going.'

'With pleasure, my dear.' Tom beamed. 'How exciting. You might end up flying out to Canada. You're becoming a well-travelled lady.'

It was surprizing how quickly the response from Canada arrived. Lizzy had decided that sending a handwritten letter would be more appropriate in the circumstances. For one thing, the letters were sent a hundred years ago – Ben's family might have moved in that time. Also, a handwritten letter might seem more genuine – not a scam. Peter had looked up the address on Google Earth so they could see what the house looked like. It seemed very respectable. The letter was composed in a way that should not cause any alarm or instant rejection. It must have worked, for the missive that appeared on Lizzy's mat was exuberant – full of email addresses and phone numbers. It appeared that Ben's relatives were delighted to find out what happened to Ben whilst he was in Kingcharlton. They wanted her to come over for a visit and tell them all about the secret of the tins.

*

Later on, Lizzy sat on the patio with a glass of red wine, her weekly treat now instead of a constant companion, thinking about the Canadian friends eager to meet her. Swirls of excitement mixed with apprehension swept through her body at the thought of flying halfway round the world – what about that long ten-hour flight? Polly, her old school friend might help her; she had a daughter living in Vancouver. Perhaps they could go together.

She hadn't seen her since Gerry had died, when Lizzy had cut herself off from all her friends. Maybe this would be a good time to renew the acquaintance. If Tom were more forthcoming, she would have been tempted to ask him if he fancied a holiday in Vancouver. She didn't want to intrude. Perhaps one day he would share his troubles with her.

Chapter Thirty-Three

Prince Edward Island lay below them. The route had surprised Lizzy. They had flown out of Heathrow and headed north. For some reason, she had expected the British Airways plane to fly west and cross England, Ireland and America to reach Vancouver. What she had not expected was that they would fly over the top of Canada, over the snowy tundra wastes, then drop down, making the final approach into Vancouver airport from the west.

From her vantage point in the small social area at the rear of the plane, she had a brilliant view of the countryside below, causing frissons of excitement. Other people were peering out of the small windows now land had been sighted. What an adventure. She had never flown before because Gerry suffered from panic attacks at the thought of flying, and here she was undertaking a ten-hour flight into the unknown. Although she was incredibly excited at the thought of meeting her newly revealed relatives, she felt some trepidation as to what she would think of them and they of her.

Her friend Polly was flying with her, taking the opportunity to visit her daughter in Vancouver, also volunteering to help her find her way around. It was

Polly who advised her: 'Don't spend hours agonising over what clothes to take, just pack jeans, honey; everybody wears jeans, no need for pomp and ceremony. It's very casual wear, always with jeans.'

Lizzy didn't argue; she didn't believe her though, and secretly packed some decent outfits. *Nobody wears jeans all the time.*

They flew in over the dark waters of the harbour sprinkled with twinkling lights like sea-bound stars, bordered by tall, illuminated glass buildings before their plane glided down towards the airport. Lizzy snapped her suitcase into walking mode and arranged her carrying bag more comfortably over her shoulder, making sure she had her passport at hand. Polly had warned her that the customs officers with their intensity, were quite scary. She looked up at Polly – the last familiar face she would see for a while. The butterflies in her tummy were performing triple somersaults.

'Are your relatives going to meet you inside the building,' asked Polly, 'or outside in the taxi rank?'

'They told me they would be waiting at the barrier with a cardboard sign. I think that I shall know them by sight. We have been *skyping* and *face-booking* each other, since I finally got in touch with them. They sound like a really friendly bunch but I'm glad you are here with me, Polly, in case it goes horribly wrong. After all, I don't really know them. It's so hard to tell from the contact we have had so far. If nothing else, it will be a new experience. If we don't get on, I can spend the next ten days mooching about with you.'

Polly gave her a hug. 'Don't worry, sweetie. I certainly won't leave you with them till you give me the nod that you are okay. You have my mobile and the address of my daughter where I will be staying. Take care of the card I gave you earlier for a reliable taxi in case you have to leave quickly.'

Lizzy and Polly had gone through customs and were approaching a barrier when they became aware of a boisterous group of people shouting, waving and holding up a board with the name *Lizzy Redland* painted in huge psychedelic letters – the relatives were obviously pleased to see her. Would she have a Canadian doppelganger? With Ben's genes in her blood one of them might look like her. She had inherited her grandmother's wild red hair according to the Hollis sisters.

'Good luck now – have fun.' Polly gave Lizzy a final hug and released her to her new family.

The merry group encircled Lizzy, offering bunches of flowers and hugs. The entourage of cars travelled through the city and ended up in a house on the outskirts. She was ushered through the front door as if she was walking on the red carpet. Somebody carried all her luggage for her and took her coat. Feeling somewhat overwhelmed with hospitality, she felt slightly lightheaded and longed for the world to stand still whilst she got her bearings.

'Would you like some coffee? There's tea if you prefer that.' The owner of the voice was Tricia, one of her new relatives who would be her host for the holiday. 'I'm sure you must be very tired after such a long journey and all. Let me show you your bedroom and you can freshen up. We thought it would be nice for you to meet everyone at a family meal tomorrow. But if you want to say "Hi" now, we'll be waiting downstairs for you.'

'Actually, I feel very excited. I'm sure my adrenaline will drop sooner or later, and I will need a nap. But for now, I'll make myself tidy and come down and meet everybody, it was so kind of you all to turn out to greet me.'

The people downstairs were limited to very close relatives of Ben. Everyone she met was so welcoming and friendly that Lizzy was having a wonderful time until fatigue took over, causing her to droop. At this they took the hint and left with promises to 'see you all tomorrow.' Her hostess shooed her off to bed. 'Don't force yourself to get up too early, have a lazy morning in bed. Come down when you are ready. I've made up a hostess tray in your room with coffee, tea and some biscuits. There is an en-suite washroom so you can rest up awhile after that long journey.'

Lizzy felt ready to sleep for days but there was one more important task to perform. Sitting on an extremely comfortable bed, she texted Tom – ARRIVED SAFELY – IT'S LOOKING GOOD – MORE LATER. She sent the same message to her family, in their *WhatsApp* group. It was then that she remembered the time difference of eight hours. She would have to figure that out for communicating with family and friends back home.

Looking through the contents of her suitcase, Lizzy was glad that she had brought some decent clothes. If they were having a family meal in a smart venue, she would need to look tidy. Even if they were all wearing jeans, which she very much doubted, it wouldn't feel right to be in casual clothes if the party was in her honour. She was going to be "ship shape and Bristol fashion" in her outfit. She showered, put on some make-up, and thought of the hundred and one questions she wanted to ask.

As they entered the private room set aside for them at the restaurant, there seemed to be a huge assembly of smiling faces to welcome her. Tricia introduced Lizzy to those people she had not already met. 'You won't remember all the names, but it doesn't matter at all.' It seemed that Ben's family was very large. Life must have been good here with temperate weather, fertile land next to the sea, and the rivers teeming with fat salmon.

As the guests stepped forward, Lizzy tried in vain to take notes of all their names and their position within the family. It seemed that a great number of them had brought photos, now displayed on a long dining table. They ranged in size, shape and condition from small black and white like those in the memory tin to modern-day colourful large prints. Lizzy took her time to peruse some of these, grateful that her relatives had taken the effort to bring their memories along. *Was this what her life would have been if Ben had returned and taken Catherine back to a farming life in Vancouver?* She would have liked the time to sit down and study each photo carefully for clues to her grandparents' history. Someone, she was not sure who, mentioned that they would take a photocopy of all of them for her. That could be sorted out later.

Flicking through the albums, she stopped when she saw a photo of a stout stately man with an ornate watch chain slung across his expansive chest. Dangling from the heavy chain was a small square object familiar to her. Her heart missed a beat – how strange to see her little silver fob in an unfamiliar photo.

'Look at this little fob,' she blurted out to the group of bystanders. 'It's just like the little one I found inside my mystery tin. It's a lot shinier and cleaner than my *Vesta* box.' At the sound of her raised voice, there was a surge forward to inspect the photo. This was a solid connection to Ben.

'That must be the one that Ben inherited from his grandfather – the one he gave to Catherine? The one you found inside the Memory Tin, Lizzy? We wondered what had happened to it – jewellery of that nature was always handed down to relatives,' a woman called Roberta said in excited tone, pointing with a long red fingernail, tapping it on the photo. Very glamorous, with stylish clothes and haircut, she seemed to be the family historian.

'That photo is of Ben's grandfather and we believe he left the fob to Ben when he died as they both had the same initials and BT was engraved on the front of it.'

'I have the fob with me now,' said Lizzy, 'let's compare it. 'She delved in her shoulder bag bringing out a jewellery box which she opened to reveal the shining silver fob nestling on pink tissue paper. The box travelled all around the room, from hand to hand, for ratification of the item. The verdict was: "That's the one. That fob sure did belong to Ben Trueman." Many an eye glistened at the thought of young Ben and his short life. They seemed to be glad that he had found some happiness with Catherine Waterman and happy that the mystery of his last few weeks had been solved.

Lizzy then brought out the Memory Tin – the little battered pastille tin with its poignant contents and the room fell silent as she recited the way the tin had fallen at her feet and the struggle to open it with her friend Tom. She placed the tin in the midst of the table, with all its contents spread around it like children round their mother. The guests in the room marvelled at the neat way, Catherine had packed so much into the little container, the neatly folded tissue thin letters, the tiny black and white photos of the couple with just enough room left for the *Vesta* match-tin: a tin within a tin, so to speak.

A husky voice boomed over her shoulder behind her. 'I'm B.T. too, popular initials in our family.'

Lizzy turned round to gaze into the eyes of B.T. and liked what she saw. A kindly face with an earnest expression sat on top of broad shoulders. Taking Lizzy's hand is his large paw he shook it heartily.

'Yes Ma'am. I am B.T. also, but I'm Bryan not Ben. I'm a sort of second or third cousin once or twice removed from Ben or something like that. My grandmother was a second cousin of Ben, not a kissing cousin as they say round here. But they do say we look somewhat similar.'

Lizzy took a good look at the figure in front of her. His lion's mane of tousled chestnut coloured hair was drawn back into a ponytail; deep-set brown eyes were watching her reaction with a quizzical expression. His thick bushy eyebrows twitched when he smiled, and he had a dimple in one cheek. Did he resemble the black and white photo in her tin? Maybe he did and maybe he didn't. Did it matter?

'I could show you round Vancouver if you like. I'm retired now – got plenty of spare time on my hands. It would be a pleasure.'

Lizzy hesitated. As she had only just arrived, she was uncertain of what her hostess had arranged. It seemed a bit early to accept a random invitation and yet she did not want to seem unfriendly. She didn't want to sign up for an excursion that she might have to call off.

'You don't have to say yes now. I can see how tired you are after that long flight. Give it another day or two, and phone me if you would like me to take you around. Here's my number.' He handed her a calling card and she popped it in her bag.

Later in the week after a few days of meeting and greeting in a relaxed manner, Lizzy felt ready for some tourist-type exploration of the city. She remembered B.T.'s invitation and fished his card out of her handbag.

'Hi Bryan, I think I am ready to take up your offer of a tour of the city. Shall we choose a date?'

His voice was deep and husky with a cute accent. 'Sure thing, little lady. I have my list made out ready to show you all the sights. How about putting it in your diary?'

*

'But I don't want to see all the sights,' she said to Tom when she finally got the times right for phoning England. 'I want to wander around and take my time.'

'Just tell him then,' said Tom. 'It's a pity to go all that way and not see what you want to see.' His steady voice dismissed her agitation and presented the obvious solution to her problem. She must find a way to persuade Bryan to include some of the places she would really like to visit. He seemed very kind but maybe a little overwhelming in his enthusiasm.

'That's a good idea, Tom. I'll put forward some suggestions of my own. Polly recommended a part of Vancouver called Granville Island; it's a huge market on the waterfront where they sell all sorts of local produce and artefacts. You can catch a ferry across the river. That's what I want to do.' Lizzy was sure that anything that Polly had recommended would suit her fine. They had spent many days out together in the past and liked the same hobbies. Lizzy was blossoming, confident in what she wanted to do and not afraid to present her point of view.

However, telling Bryan what she would like to see was one thing and him listening and readjusting his list was another. There was a lot of, "but you don't want to see that" before they reached an amicable agreement.

Granville Island did not disappoint – the shoal of huge salmon lying on beds of crushed ice amazed her. They looked as if they had swum in on the tide to rest on an icy shore. She enjoyed meandering around little booths selling all sorts of food from around the world and tea stalls where you could sample many different brews, from fizzy pea-green to good old Irish. Bryan was still very anxious to take her to "see" most of the tourist attractions that Vancouver had to offer but she wanted to take her time to enjoy the little things, to sit and absorb the atmosphere. She felt no urge to rush about; immense pleasure came from being beside the water with a latte in a takeaway cup, watching the ferryboats carry passengers from one side to the other. Tall skyscraper buildings stared at her across the water with blind glassy eyes, and cars roared on the soaring freeway overhead. Snowy-topped mountains in the distance completed a chocolate-box scene, offering the opportunity to try the ski slopes. So much to absorb in a very short time, she did not want to waste a precious moment.

'Would you like to visit the mountains?' asked Bryan. 'We could book a trip to look at the ski slopes or take a trip up the water to Alaska. You really gotta see the musk oxen up there with their soft hair. The descendants of the original indigenous tribes produce the most fabulous traditional artefacts with their spinning and weaving. Closer to home there are the famous black squirrels in the park. We could ride through on a pony and trap.'

'Maybe when I come over again. I'm sorry. It's very tiring and what I want to do is to share memories of Ben with other relatives.' Bryan's manner was so genial despite his tendency to arrange their entire day out, that she agreed to a few of his suggestions. It was then that she made the mistake of letting slip that she had plans to attend the Remembrance Day ceremony in Ypres in November.

'Wow, that sounds wonderful. Can I come too? Let me pay for us both.' Bryan's eyes lit up like all his birthdays had come at once.

Lizzy felt ambushed. Her English reserve surfaced immediately. 'I couldn't possibly allow you to do that. We hardly know each other.'

'Sorry, I'm just so excited. Besides, I feel I know you well already,' Bryan pleaded. 'There's a sort of a connection because we share the same genes, somewhat diluted. I have the money. I can afford it. I have a good pension from the Fire Service and nobody to spend it with.'

'I understand what you're saying, but it's a bit of a surprise. Let me consider it for a while.' At the back of Lizzy's mind was the travelling experience with Peter Catchpole. This was another such bombastic man and she wanted to do things her own way. On the other hand, a companion on such a trip could be useful – someone to eat with and discuss any problems.

'Let me see if they have any places left. It gets booked up really quickly, you know.' Lizzy was not good at making instant decisions, but she had learnt that delaying the process would give her time to decide what she wanted to do.

Bryan's cheery grin dropped off his face to be replaced by one that was similar to a quivering bloodhound. 'Just let me know, honey. Tell me what firm you are travelling with. I can book it all up from the Internet. I could come over beforehand and we could travel from your place.'

'I'll have to think about that. I have not been a widow for long. I have had no-one staying at the house since I lost my husband. I lead a very quiet life. I'm not really up to entertaining guests yet.' Lizzy was unsettled by the bluff "Let's sort it out now" attitude of the plain-speaking Canadians.

Bryan laughed out loud. 'Oh no, I didn't mean that. I wouldn't want to be an unwelcome guest. There are plenty of hotels nearby. I have looked it up and Bath looks like a nice place to visit. I could take myself on the tourist trail, but perhaps you would join me for a meal or two, candlelit dinner – only joking. I will let you into a little secret. I visited Kingcharlton years ago. My late wife and I took a special holiday to England as a ruby wedding trip. We thought it would be fun to see this little town that Great Uncle Ben had visited. We didn't have any success as nobody much would talk to us. They seemed suspicious and closed up tight as clams when we mentioned his name. There wasn't the interest in the First World War that there is now. I didn't want to mention it before, in case it produced the same effect on you.'

Lizzy tried to interrupt him to say that she was willing to share whatever information she held with him, but Bryan was unstoppable. It was plain to see that he wanted to get all his feelings out in one go. He was certainly very different to Tom in that respect.

'I want to learn all about your research – you have awoken my desire to visit England again. I was hoping you would show me those special places. The story of Ben and Catherine seems so romantic and yet so sad. I have been plotting our family history but there is a gap where Ben Trueman left for England. And now I find a continuation of his line and a whole stack of little branches and twigs to fill in with all our English relatives. I tell you; it's put new life into the old dog.' Bryan paused for breath; he was going blue in the face with such a long speech.

'It seemed like a gift from the gods when you contacted us and what a story you have to tell. It would make a good novel. What do you think? I'm talking too much again, aren't I? Sorry. I can't help myself I am so excited. Whaddya say to all or some of my suggestions? Or do you need more time?'

Lizzy took a long look at his cheerful face, surely honesty exemplified. 'Let's talk it over, work out the practicalities. I didn't say you couldn't stay. It's just that I am out of the practice of entertaining since my husband died – I have let things lapse. My house is a mess.'

'Let's go grab a coffee and chat.' Bryan seemed to have the need for constant snacks throughout the day. He needed a lot of sugar with all that energy. She could hardly keep up with him.

Why not? Lizzy thought, whilst Bryan was ordering their lattes and pastries. *I've spent a lifetime being nervous. From now on I'm going to seize every opportunity to have new experiences.* Tom was right about that. There were still a few niggling doubts but what could go wrong? It would be just a nice simple holiday with a friend.

Chapter Thirty-Four

The pavements of Ypres were covered with fallen leaves, made slimy by a fall of rain. As Lizzy and Bryan crossed a wooden bridge, Lizzy stumbled. Suddenly she was falling backwards, her arms whirled like windmills; she landed on her back with such a wallop that the breath was knocked out of her. More than the pain, there was the embarrassment of lying flat on her back in front of so many people, all dressed up for the Remembrance ceremony. If only she had taken Bryan's arm when it was offered earlier but she felt she was being drawn into a very cosy situation too quickly. That might have been better than making a fool of herself. Had she spoilt the day for them? Lizzy was speechless with shock, her face the colour of putty. Several people stopped to help but Bryan scooped her up, set her back on her feet and took her in his arms to support her – another embarrassing moment. She was hugged against a comforting jacket where she could hide her face. They must look like a married couple having a cuddle.

'Thank you. I can't believe that just happened. I know I have heels on these boots, but only low ones. I've never had any trouble walking in them before.'

As she spoke, her feet started to slide again. Her eyes were moist with tears.

Bryan held her close. He smelled of shaving soap and musky aftershave. 'I think it's the wood they used to make the bridge, plus the fact that it has been raining. Look, it's really slippery.' Bryan slid a size ten brogue back and forwards over the bridge to demonstrate. 'My shoes have good solid soles, that's all it is. Come on, we will find somewhere for you to sit and recover, get you a stiff drink.' He released her from his bear hug and taking her arm very firmly in his he led her off the treacherous bridge onto firm ground.

'Here, this looks like the right place for you at the moment.' Bryan propelled her into an *estaminet*, buzzing with people chatting and clasping drinks. 'We'll get that brandy. It'll put the colour back in your cheeks.' Bryan steered her to a space on a wooden bench close to a crackling log burner. 'Warmth and brandy, just the medicine for shock. You just sit still and wait until you feel better.'

Lizzy huddled up and watched Bryan make his way to the bar. What would she have done if he had not been with her? She still felt very peculiar, lightheaded and far away. Being held against his jacket was a good place to be, he was a kind man.

'What about the parade? We'll miss it if we are inside; miss the magic of the march and the ceremonies. Let's carry on as we were going to.' Worried about spoiling their plans, she attempted to stand up, but her legs felt unsteady. There was no option but to sit back down and follow instructions. Pleased that the decision had been made for her,

Lizzy watched the smouldering logs glittering in their black cavern. Maybe having to sit in the cafe was not such a bad thing after all – this day had the feel of the creeping insidious chill of the coming winter.

Lizzy could feel her face returning to its normal warm colour as she sipped the brandy and listened to the conversations taking place all around her. When Bryan asked if she would be happy for him to stand by the door and watch the procession pass, she stood up gingerly. She buttoned up her coat to combat the cold outside, checking that her poppy had not been lost when she had fallen on the bridge.

'I'm coming too. It would be too awful not to be out in the crowd, on this day of all days. If you give me your arm I can manage. The brandy has worked marvels. Let's go.'

The street outside was crammed with people searching for a good view. Lizzy was almost moved to tears. 'Isn't it wonderful that so many people have come to pay their respects? Look at those young boys and girls wearing what must be their great-grandparents' medals. If I had inherited my English grandfather's medals, I would march too.'

'It's very impressive,' Bryan's voice was husky with emotion. 'I'm so glad you let me accompany you. I wouldn't have missed this for a pirate's treasure chest.'

Once the tail end of the procession had moved out of sight, the crowd began to disperse. Lizzy turned to Bryan. 'I know where to go now; there's this big triangle of grass set aside for people to plant little wooden crosses – the ones with written messages. I think I can find it. It's on the way to the Menin Gate.'

'Is that the place where soldiers sound the Last Post with bugles each evening?' Bryan was deeply engrossed in a pamphlet he had picked up in the hotel. 'I really want to see that, to film it and take it to show the folks back home.' Bryan took her arm once more and she made no protest. She was not going to risk falling again.

They had no trouble locating the place for planting their tribute; a sea of crosses with red poppies spread out on the green grass. Lizzy chose a spot and planted three crosses, one for Ben and one for Catherine: her long-lost grandparents side by side at last, and also one for her English grandfather, her mother's father who had fought at Arras and Ypres. She wiped her eyes as she pictured Ben and Catherine in Kingcharlton so long ago. It had been such a complex process to trace what had become of them and it was nearly finished. Peter had contacted her to say he was on the track of Catherine's grave.

'Do you want one of my crosses to plant, Bryan – I have brought some extra ones in case? I've got a marker pen for a message. You could put it here next to mine. After all Ben was your relative too, no matter how weak or strong the link was.' Bryan accepted the cross, scrawled a message, and then planted it beside those of Lizzy. She was sure that he also shed a tear. It would be difficult not to, in such an emotional environment.

Bryan took her hand in his as they stood in silent contemplation of the waves of poppies and crosses. Lizzy had no idea what Bryan was thinking but she was imagining her grandparents looking down on her from somewhere, some other universe. She really believed they would both know that she was standing there thinking of them.

*

The haunting sequence of notes of the bugles rang out over the silent waiting crowd. Lizzy's emotions were running high – her whole body was trembling so much that she clutched Bryan for support. It was impossible not to be moved whilst enveloped in such a communal cloud of grieving for their brave men who had suffered and died. Her English grandfather had handed down his medals to the family. She would have felt so proud to wear his medals in the very place where he had walked the streets and smoked a Woodbine or two. But at some stage amongst the family quarrels the medals had disappeared.

Bryan noticing her distress, whispered, 'Don't cry, honey. I'm sure that Ben was awarded a medal or two. Somebody in our family will have them stored away – the grandmas I suspect. I promise I will find them, so that next year we will march together with you wearing Ben's medals. So, don't be sad.' He seized her in his big bear-like arms and hugged her.

'Will there be a next year for us to visit? Do you want to come again with me? You're not bored?' Lizzy felt comforted in the warmth of his embrace and was content to stay there for the while.

'Of course, I want to come again, especially with you. I will be prepared then as I know how this special day is celebrated. I'll start hunting for those medals as soon as I get home.' Bryan patted her on the back as if sealing the deal. He released her and they walked on.

'Right, time for food, I'm feeling real hungry. What do you fancy?' Bryan was peering in all the premises they passed to see if there were any empty seats.

Most of the crowd must have had the same thought; all the eating-places were filling up rapidly. They walked from one end of the town to the other and eventually found a couple of seats in an old inn. Although it was like a cave inside furnished with dark panelled wood, it had plenty of comfortable seating. From somewhere at the back of the building, the most mouth-watering aromas of cooked food wafted out making their hungry tummies rumble. They settled for lasagne with frites, accompanied by two large glasses of Belgian lager.

'Real comfort food,' Lizzy mumbled after taking a delicious mouthful of hot pasta dish. 'I didn't realise how hungry I was.'

'I never forget where meals are concerned,' Bryan said washing his food down with a swig of lager. 'As my old dad used to say, "An army marches on its stomach." This is really tasty.'

Chapter Thirty-Five

Dusk was falling over fields and ancient hedgerows as Bryan and Lizzy plodded up the hill. They were heading for the place where once the workhouse had stood watching over the valley with its foreboding glassy eyes. Their conversation was convivial – they laughed a great deal as they had dined well at the local hostelry and were feeling mellow after finishing their meal with Irish coffee in tall glasses. Lizzy was reluctant to try such a strong drink but Bryan encouraged her, saying: 'Go on: you have to try one new thing every day to keep a lively mind.'

'You Canadians are so positive and proactive.' She tripped on a protruding kerb and righted herself. 'We English are naturally cautious and see the faults in everything, particularly where the weather is concerned. Goodness knows how we ever got ourselves an empire.'

The ancient road, just wide enough to accommodate a haywain pulled by a pair of carthorses with feathered feet, was falling to pieces. A margin of cobbles bordered the uneven surface of tarmac where persistent weeds had pierced the black surface. It was a very different sight from the neat and tidy surface travelled by Catherine and Daisy when they climbed to the workhouse gates that stormy evening. Overhead were modern electric lights, still spaced out at intervals as in Catherine's day, but now the old Edwardian lamp posts had been converted. Gone was the hissing gas ignited by a lamplighter with a flame on a pole. Now modern lights served the road, controlled by the mere flick of a switch. However, the overall effect was still the same as the couple walked in and out of the spotlights.

Bryan broke the silence of the Somerset evening. 'It's a steep hill for a twelve-year-old to climb in winter, slippery in bad boots.'

'Why, what a good memory: you remembered the tale of how my grandparents met and the part Daisy played in preserving our family history.' Lizzy was delighted that he had been interested; she was beginning to become fond of this distant cousin. She would miss his cheery presence when he returned to Vancouver.

'I can't forget how passionate you were when you told the tale, over and over again to all the family. I thought you would have been tired of repeating it but each time another person asked it was like a new tale. That story of Ben and Catherine's romance and their love child would have been lost for ever but for your persistence.' Bryan was clearly very impressed.

Lizzy was glad they were in a dark piece of the road for his constant compliments made her blush. 'I was so pleased to have solved the mystery of the missing baby. Bringing the news to your family was a bonus. They needed to know what happened to Ben when he spent time in England and I benefitted from hearing his history before he arrived in Kingcharlton.'

She was reminded of the day they had shown her the photo of Ben's grandfather wearing the silver pocket watch with Catherine's love-token silver fob dangling from the chain. She was wearing the fob on a silver chain and fondled it as she walked. They paused at the brow of the hill listening to the water pouring over the weir into the murky depths that had once served as a millpond. The huge wooden water wheel had been renovated and now stood in the foyer of a smart block of flats created from the mill buildings.

'So much of old Kingcharlton has gone. I'm sure this road will be destroyed soon. It's as if nobody cares about the past; the history or the place.' Lizzy sighed, a deep expression of discontent that racked her whole body. 'It's changed so much: Kingcharlton is becoming overwhelmed with too many houses in what used to be a medieval village. I'm thinking of moving away. It hurts too much to see the old landmarks go one by one. My kids are all settled happily. I want something different from life. I want to move on. I feel much happier now. I have options: new interests and friends. I am not that dull boring grieving woman anymore. I want to grasp life with both hands and experience everything I am offered.' Lizzy stood gazing at the lights shining in the windows of the new flats in the old mill building. *Life goes on,* she thought. *It's an eternal circle.*

Bryan turned to face her and took her rather chilly fingers in his large warm paws.

‘Hey, if you are into grasping things, how about grasping my hands?’ Bryan joked. ‘How about grasping all of me while you’re at it. I have grown very fond of you, Lizzy. You want to move, try new things? Come to Vancouver with me and make me the happiest man in the world.’ He turned towards her studying her face trying to gauge her response.

‘I hate the thought of leaving you behind here; the time we spent together in Ypres was magical. We could find a peaceful spot, an old-fashioned village, not crowded; a traditional little place like bygone Kingcharlton. Whadda you think, sweetheart? You’re not going to make me get down on my knees, are you? I’ll never get up again.’

Lizzy was stunned. This was not how she had expected the evening to end. But the more she thought about it the more it seemed like a viable option. She had loved Vancouver, the glorious ocean, the snowy mountains in the distance, the history of the settlers, and the feeling of freedom. But did she want the commitment – that was the big question? She had become accustomed to the luxury of being a free spirit.

There was a subdued silence; the evening air throbbed with anticipation.

‘I don’t know what to say,’ whispered Lizzy, ‘I wasn’t expecting that.’ She felt so guilty as she caught sight of Bryan’s embarrassed face in the glow of a lamp.

‘Please don’t look like that; it was a surprise but such a compliment. It’s just that life has been moving so fast this last year, I don’t know who I am any more. Can you give me some time to think it out? I need to wrap my mind around this. We don't have to rush into anything, do we?' Lizzy wished she had seen this situation arising. All Bryan's behaviour had been that of a possible suitor.

'But of course, you must have time. Clumsy me. You have had a hell of a whirlwind experience of family relationships. You take as long as you want, but I meant every word I said. Fate has brought us together, and if not as lovers, I will settle for good friends. Let's sleep on it.' Bryan had sobered up and the mood of the walk had altered.

Lizzy tucked her arm in his and they ambled back to her house. Both were in a thoughtful mood and parted for bed soon. By some unspoken mutual consent, Bryan went to the guest room she had prepared for him.

*

After a restless night for both of them they met in the kitchen. Bryan who had been up early, placed two mugs on the wooden table and stood back to face her.

'I've been thinking,' he said, 'there might be a way round all this. I don't want to lose your friendship.'

Lizzy blurted, 'Me too. I was worried you would hate me for hesitating about your offer. It's not the case that I am not fond of you but it's a huge step: relocating to Canada. There would be so much work involved tying up the loose ends, and I was just beginning to relax and enjoy life again. I don't want to rush into any serious relationship without a lot of thought. And there's Wellington to consider, he's getting so ancient. I couldn't leave while I still have him. I need time to think.'

Bryan leant across the table and patted her hand. 'Don't worry, sweetheart, I won't pressure you any. I got carried away last evening, idiot that I am. I've lain awake all night, mentally kicking myself for spoiling the best thing that's happened to me in years. When Diane died, I went into a low mood like you and I must tell you that I thought I would never step out of the shadows and into the sunshine, but I did. Now I realise I must give you time. What we need is a slow and steady courtship to get to know each other properly.'

Lizzy thought he was assuming rather a lot – courtship was a heavy word, but she said nothing – after all there was a great deal of distance between Canada and England.

Chapter Thirty-Six

In the lead-up to Christmas Lizzy realised that a meeting with Mavis and Irene was long overdue. They would want to know about her adventures in Canada. There was a nagging concern at the back of her mind that the sisters might be thinking she had abandoned them. They had been so helpful, these two sisters who had carefully guided her through the history of her hidden relatives. Gossip was the chocolate cake of life for them. They would want to know all the details of the latest chapter in the continuing saga of Catherine and Ben.

After the usual elaborate tea ceremony had taken place, Lizzy brought out all her treasures and laid them out on the cleared table.

'Look,' she said, 'I've had the photos made into a book, so you know who all the people are.' The sisters loved the photo-book, thinking that they could set Mavis's grandson Jason the challenge of making their myriad family photos into books. Once the photo book had been fully explored and the people identified to the sisters' satisfaction, Lizzy took her time talking them through the minute details of each day she had spent in Canada.

'What were they all like, Lizzy, were they kind to you? Did they like the story of Catherine and Ben?' Lizzy regaled them with stories of the abundant hospitality of her Canadian family.

'Everyone loved the tale – they had been wondering how Ben had spent his time in England before he went to France. They were very interested in the romantic way Ben had fallen in love with Catherine, especially as she came from Wales where her family roots were similar to those of the Trueman family before they emigrated. With her being a nurse, it made it into a proper wartime romance. They loved that part of the yarn.' Lizzy smiled at the memory of all those eager faces.

'What about the baby? Did they know about the baby?' The sisters were clearly keen to know this part of the story.

'One of the returning soldiers had mentioned it to Ben's mother but there was no way that they could find out if it was true. By the way, I met the man who came asking about Ben, the one you told me about a while back. He had wanted to see if he could find out more about Ben's life in Kingcharlton and was very disappointed to find nothing at all.'

Lizzy immediately realised that she had made a *faux pas* as the sisters' faces dropped. They must have remembered the man they had turned away. She quickly moved the conversation from Canada to other matters.

'There's a question I have wanted to ask you for a long time. When you told me the complete story, I wondered how you came by all those facts. You filled in all the gaps from the knowledge I had gathered.'

'It was the maids' network,' Mavis chuckled. 'Most households had a maid of some sort. They were often treated as if they weren't there or were too stupid to understand what they overheard. All sorts of snippets of information came their way and were saved, as they had little else to think about.' Mavis had a very superior look on her face as she talked about the secret network. She continued to explain.

'On their precious days off when they met the other maids, they shared their news and pieced it together like a patchwork quilt. They would most likely marry a local lad and their daughters would go into service and carry on the custom of gossip. It passed down through the generations in the spoken word. There was nothing ever written down. All sorts of secrets were kept.'

Lizzy could see the logic of this. When she was teaching in school, it was always the dinner ladies in the kitchen who knew what was happening throughout the school: any changes or new headmasters, somehow this knowledge leaked through to them before becoming official news.

'But the baby was moved to Manchester out of the area, away from the gossip. How could you know what had happened to him, seeing as the Mortlakes had renamed baby Huw Waterman to Nicholas Mortlake? How did you know they had moved him to Manchester? They were in the north for so long, surely you lost track of him. How did you put together that part of the story?' Lizzy felt that this knowledge must have meant links outside the village.

‘Aha,’ Irene said with the air of one producing the trump card. ‘But they moved back to this area eventually and brought Nora with them. She filled in the gaps of what had happened over the years. Nan kept the story of Catherine and Ben very much alive in our minds. We were never allowed to forget them. She always grieved for the little tin that went missing. She would be so pleased to know you had taken it to Canada to show Ben’s relatives.’ The two sisters beamed with pleasure at Catherine, her *faux pas* forgiven.

‘Who’s Nora?’ Lizzy was sure that she had not heard that name before.

‘Nora was the little Irish maid who was assigned to look after Catherine when she came home in an interesting condition. They went together to Bristol where the baby, your father, was born. Nora stayed with the Mortlakes when Catherine returned to the battlefields and never came back. When the Mortlakes moved to Manchester Nora went with them, to help them settle in, as she was so good with the baby.’ Mavis smirked with pleasure at Lizzy’s amazement at their prowess in keeping track of the lost baby’s history. Irene wearing a similar smile of superiority chimed in next, wanting to share the glory of the situation.

‘They gave her a proper position as Nicolas’ nanny, under Mrs Mortlake’s supervision of course; as Nora was a simple-hearted soul. When he grew up, she stayed with the family as a general maid. The Mortlakes later moved to Birmingham, when Arthur became part of the management at Cadbury’s chocolate factory.’

'That's why father had a Brummie accent,' said Lizzy. It seemed strange to hear her father spoken about as if he was a distant stranger in a story and not her parent who had lived another life with her. He had never spoken much about his life before he married her mother and she had not thought to ask.

'When they opened a Fry's factory in Kingcharlton, Arthur transferred to a new management position there, as Beatrice took a longing to be back in Bristol. They took a house not far from their original place. That factory brought a lot of employment to Kingcharlton. It was very modern for those day, the posh new redbrick building, the magnificent approach with the long winding road lined with chestnut trees, the community hall for entertainment and the playing fields for sports.' Mavis went into raptures over all the activities that took place there. Lizzy could see how the Fry family had enhanced the lives of the townsfolk. Irene chipped in, as Mavis took a sip of tea.

'You should have seen the workers streaming out when the factory-hooter sounded – they blocked the whole road. Every family seemed to have someone working there. They were allowed a portion of the waste confectionary to take home in those days as a bonus.' Irene licked her lips as if remembering the taste of the free chocolate.

All these random thoughts wandered through Lizzy's mind as she walked slowly back home till she felt dizzy with speculation. Her house was built on land that had once been used for medieval strip farming and she had the weird feeling that she was walking in that time. The intervening years disappeared as she imagined rows of oats, beans and barley instead of the grey pavements beneath her feet.

Chapter Thirty-Seven

Lizzy was reflecting on the ups and downs of the past year when a cacophony of voices heralded visitors. What a change in a mere twelve months. She was hurrying to see who was at the door whereas last year she would have hidden among the cushions on the sofa, reluctant to welcome guests. Red and blue glass diamonds set in the front door distorted the figures huddled there so Lizzy squinted through a clear diamond to make sure it was family and not early carol singers. Her eye met the bulging fish-like eye of Jackson, six years old and bright as a ray of sunshine on a winter's day. He shrieked with laughter. 'It's Nanny! It's Nanny looking out at me! She's in there, Mummy.'

Jackson bounced in, his family following, bringing with them a bubble of happiness and cheerful chatter. The boys were soon crunching crisps in front of the television, following their favourite cartoons whilst the adults stood in the kitchen watching the coffee percolate and exchanging their news. Lizzy's daughter Claire and her partner Ivan then turned to more serious matters.

'There's something we need to ask you, Mum,' Claire said, 'it's about the Christmas arrangements for this year. Nicola and I have been discussing the festivities and we thought we'd like to stick to last year's arrangements, but this time it would take place at our house. Is that all right with you, Mum?'

'Suits me,' Lizzy chuckled, 'I enjoyed being a guest last year. The food was delicious. There's just one thing I would like to change. Can we invite Tom as well? He has no family close by. I felt so guilty when I realised he had been alone, especially after all the kindness he has shown me, looking after the allotment and introducing me to the local history group.' Lizzy hadn't even broached the subject with Tom yet, but she had a feeling he would say yes. Claire nodded her assent.

'Nicola is rather worried that you might feel we were taking away your role as the matriarch of the family, but I think you enjoyed last year's activities. It's our turn to spoil you after all those years of hard work. Tom is very welcome, especially if he brings some of those famous sprouts from his allotment. They taste so much better when they're home-grown.' Claire looked to her mother for reassurance that she was happy. 'What about your birthday? Same as last year when the whole family dressed the tree – that went very well, didn't it?'

'I'm quite happy with all the arrangements, but I have another favour to ask. I've decided to have a proper tree this year, one with the spicy smell of pine needles. Could we all go to the garden centre? You could help me choose a spruce with needles that won't drop off straight away? Those needles all over the floor drove your father mad, that's why he always insisted on an artificial tree. But now I have only myself to please, I'd like to have a real one.'

'Of course, Mum, that sounds brilliant. That old tree was getting very battered. We'll take it to the tip on the way.'

'I'd like new lights as well,' Lizzy continued, 'because I have a plan: all white lights inside the house and those red globes that look like huge holly berries hung in the bushes in the front garden. Some new tree ornaments would be good. I'm giving my life a makeover.' Secretly, she still had reservations about her old favourites being discarded but she was determined to make some changes and move forward.

'I can give you some new decorations, Nanny. We made them at school. I'll bring them round on your birthday.' Jackson had been eavesdropping on the adults' conversation. His big brother Brody was still absorbed in the cartoons.

'That's lovely, Mum,' Claire rushed in before sad memories spoiled the moment. She knew how her mother felt about her decorations. 'Next Saturday or Sunday suit you? We'll pick out a tree at the weekend, help you install it in the front room, then on your birthday we can all dress the tree together.'

'Fine by me,' Lizzy was grinning. 'I'm feeling happy at the very thought of it.'

A massive spruce was filling the bay window of the front room, when Lizzy had more visitors. Nicola had brought Lily carrying a surprise gift.

'Wow, that's a whopper, Mum. You've gone from one extreme to another. Love it. We've just been to the school's Christmas Fair. Lily's bought you an early birthday present with her pocket money. She insisted on bringing it to you straight away, as she remembered you needed "new decorations".'

Lily was clutching a large polythene bag, which she held up to show Lizzy. 'Look, Nanny, some new decorations for you.' Clearly, she was very happy with her purchase though it looked like a bag that had been destined for the rubbish bin.

Nicola made a discreet face at her mother, a sort of "I couldn't stop her" grimace. Lily led the way into the front room and emptied the bag onto the wooden coffee table. Out fell a rag-tail assortment of scuffed old baubles and strings of red and green beads all tangled together with tattered tinsel and battered knitted figures. Lily was delighted and began to sort them out, squealing with excitement at each new treasure. She gazed at Lizzy, waiting for her approval.

'Oh Lily, how lovely,' Lizzy enthused. 'What a great idea to bring them for the tree. Did you buy them all by yourself?'

'Yes, Nanny. Daddy gave me the money and I chose.' Lily held up a golden tinsel star and looked thoughtfully at the top of the tree.

'You know you have to wait for the others before you can start decorating, don't you?' Lizzy bent down to look Lily in the eyes.

'Yes, Nanny, just looking.' Lily stared at her grandmother with pure innocence spread all over her small face and changed the subject.

'Look at this – it's a kissing twig.' Lily held up a ragged sprig of plastic mistletoe; a few dejected white berries clung to forlorn-looking stems. But Lily was entranced and held it over her head.

'My teacher told us about mistletoe – you hang it up in the house and people kiss under it.' She giggled at the idea of grown-ups kissing. 'It's a Christmas tradition. Where shall we hang it, Nanny?' She looked hopefully round the room for a suitable place.

'Maybe a bit later, Lily, we need some sticky stuff or a nail to hang it on. Shall we leave it for the moment whilst I make Mummy a cup of coffee? There are some new biscuits in the treats' drawer – Penguins and Wagon Wheels. Why don't you see if you can find them?' Nicola and Lizzy retired to the kitchen to make coffee and discuss further plans for the festive season.

'We'd better go and see what Lily's up to, Mum. You know she's desperate to be the first person to put something on the tree.' The two women peeped round the door and sure enough Lily had draped the mistletoe over one of the lower branches.

'Leave her be,' Lizzy whispered, 'it's not easy being the youngest of four.' They crept back to their coffee.

Lily appeared with the mistletoe in her hand a few moments late. Obviously, she was keeping to her word of not decorating the tree yet. 'Where shall we put it, Nanny?'

'You know, Lily, you can buy bunches of real mistletoe from the flower shop at this time of year. That piece does look rather old and droopy. We could get some fresh, sweetheart?' Lizzy's tones were persuasive, and Lily loved shopping.

‘No, I want this one – I like it. Please put it up, Nanny.’ Lily was becoming agitated.

What could Lizzy do? She took the ugliest bit of mistletoe in the whole wide world and fixed it to the top of the kitchen doorframe with sticky tape. ‘Don’t worry, sweetheart. Don’t cry. It’s up now – look.’ She kissed Lily on both cheeks.

‘There you go – we’ve kissed under the mistletoe.’

*

Tom was a great hit on Christmas Day. Whether it was because he was such a helpful guest, bringing his delicious sprouts fresh from the allotment or his willingness to join in all the family games, it would be difficult to say because he excelled in all quarters. When they saw their mother smiling and enjoying the day, Lizzy’s daughters gave each other a knowing look.

At the end of the day when all the other guests had departed, Tom produced an envelope and handed it to Lizzy.

“What’s this?” Lizzy peered inside. Tom had already presented her with a huge box of chocolates and a bouquet of wintery flowers.

‘Take a look, I thought you might like a night out.’ Tom looked uncertain of his gift’s reception. ‘I took a chance – unusual for me – I remembered what you said about the dances you went to in the village hall – what fun they were.

Lizzy pulled out the contents of the envelope – two tickets for a New-Years-Eve rock and roll evening to be held in the British Legion Hall with a live group playing a wide selection of music.

‘Thank you, Tom, what a lovely present. But I don’t know if I can remember all the steps – it’s so long ago.’

‘You’ll be alright, the music will set your feet, tapping. We can wait till everyone’s a bit tipsy and then nobody will be noticing us. Tom’s face was now wreathed in smiles. Can we say that’s a date to put on the calendar then?’

Chapter Thirty-Eight - 2017/8

On New Year's Eve, Lizzy pulled back the lace curtains to see if the snow was still falling. It had been a surprise when the first flakes twirled in the sky. Snow was a rarity in this part of the world, but it was not settling yet. The sky had a silent menacing white colour with an eerie glow.

The gate clanged as Tom wrestled with the handle. She stood watching him through a crack in the heavy folds of velour as he walked up the path to the front door. She swished the curtain aside to wave and he smiled at her.

She was suddenly struck by the change in his appearance. He looked quite dapper in a black overcoat, and trilby tilted at an angle. A red scarf wrapped round his neck and a huge black umbrella neatly furled completed the look. But when she glanced at his feet, she laughed – he was wearing his allotment rubber boots – scrubbed clean but hilarious. His indoor shoes must be in the black bag over his shoulder.

'Are you still game for this, lass?' The sound of his voice gave her a warm cosy feel inside. Being with Tom was always a pleasure but she was still not sure how he felt about her.

‘Have you got some boots – might get worse. There’s room in my bag for your dancing shoes.’ He was always practical without being boring, ‘We don’t want to walk home in a snowdrift in light shoes. I could have brought the car, but it might get slippery later on.’

‘We don’t need the car – we want to see the year in with a glass of wine or two. I’ll fetch my boots now,’ Lizzy said as she handed him her newly purchased gold sandals. Her daughters had whisked her off into town for a shopping expedition. They had persuaded her to buy a neat little fitted dress – a beautiful shade of deep jade green sparkling with sequins in the same colour – not fussy but it suited her so well. They also pushed her into a hairdresser for a trim and trace of colour – glowing red and gold streaks that transformed her grey tresses. She had gazed at herself in her wardrobe mirror for a long time, astonished at the effect a few purchases had made. She liked the new image – it meant she was moving on.

Wellington had wobbled out to greet Tom whilst she was fetching her boots and coat, but once he realised that he was not included in this outing, he snuggled up in his cosy place by the radiator and was soon snoring gently.

The air outside was fresh and somehow exciting. Small flakes drifted onto their shoulders, lingering on their black coats for a while as they trudged down the road. When they reached the Legion Hall, the cloakrooms were full of boots, jostling side by side. Gaudy lights inside seemed brilliant against a host of decorations glittering in red and green, a riot of colour. Lizzy pulled off her woolly hat, checking her hair in the mirror. She looked flushed; her cheeks reddened by the cold outside. In one corner a DJ's table was set up to play old rock and roll numbers, creating an atmosphere for the live group to follow. Some couples were already on the floor, dancing to Little Richard, Jerry Lee Lewis, Chuck Berry and other favourites. Lizzy watched the intricate patterns the couples were weaving – a series of set moves. A moment of fear grabbed her. Would she let Tom down? Could she even remember the basic sequences?

Despite the crowded room, they managed to secure a couple of seats with a good view of the band and the floor. Lizzy relaxed, took a sip of her drink, savouring the mix of dark rum and diet coke with its following kick and inward glow. As she took a few more sips she felt less edgy. She knew that when the group set up, she would be drawn by the music to have a go even if she made a fool of herself.

A chord on a guitar rang out. Four "lads", though they were in their sixties, took to the stage – double bass, rhythm guitar, lead guitar and drummer all in matching outfits. Suddenly there was raw music, loud and compelling, powerful, tuneful – sexy – full of energy – her feet were tapping. The rum had obliterated her nerves so that when Tom looked at her, a question in his eyes, she nodded and followed him onto the dance floor amid the gyrating couples.

Tom swept her into his arms, twirling her around like a matador with a scarlet cloak. Here was a new Tom, masterful and strong, catching her when she faltered. They were swept along by the flow of the music, like a blossom swirling in a river.

After a bout of energetic dances, the music slowed down. Tom looked at her again and then he pulled her closer to move together to the rhythm of the band. She was conscious of his aftershave – a magic enticing perfume of tangy citrus and wood smoke. It seemed as if they were communicating by movement not words. It felt good to be held by him, they fitted snugly together. After a couple of numbers she was loath to let him go, to return to the wild dancing again. She felt shaken – mixed up. Would something happen tonight – later on? Surely he must feel the same way she did.

The dancing paused for the chimes at midnight when the singing of Auld Lang Syne took over. Tom turned towards her as if to kiss her, but the excited crowd dragged them into a conga and the moment passed. The DJ took over once more for those who wanted to linger and dance the night away. Lizzy agreed with Tom it was time to go home. She felt elated, enclosed in a cosy bubble of happiness but ready for her bed.

'Take my arm, Lizzy, we'll hold each other up.' Outside the snow was deep. It was comforting, staggering along, close to each other. The snowflakes were huge, a dense cloud dancing around them, filling the sky. Luckily it was not far to her house.

'Fancy a hot chocolate, Tom?' her husky tipsy tones rang out.

'Okay, just the one,' he joked.

They shrugged off their damp coats and wet boots. The house was toasty warm. Wellington came forward, ecstatic to see them again as if they had been away for months.

Lizzy left Tom patting Wellington in the hall and danced her way into the kitchen to assemble cups, spoons and hot chocolate sachets. Tom wandered in after her with offers of help, but she had made the drinks already. As she turned to face him with two mugs of steaming hot chocolate, she saw him standing in the doorway directly beneath the piece of plastic mistletoe that her granddaughter had insisted should be pinned up. *Fate works in a mysterious way,* Lizzy thought, as she gently placed the mugs on the work-surface and walked over to Tom. The rum flowing through her veins gave her Dutch courage.

By way of explanation, she pointed out the mistletoe to a mystified Tom, raising her face to him for a traditional kiss. He could choose how he responded. It could be light-hearted like friends if that was how he felt about her, or something more serious if his feelings were as strong as hers. Their precious friendship must not be ruined through putting him in an awkward situation. She could feel the room pulsing with emotions.

He leant forward. His lips were warm – soft and enticing. His touch was light, delicate, unsure, feeling his way. He retreated; she leant forward and brushed his lips lightly, hardly daring to breathe. Had she got it all wrong – a tipsy woman on New Year's Eve – a cliché of her own making? The world stopped spinning for a moment that felt like a lifetime...

Then his arms went round her drawing her closer. She could feel his heart beating. His lips brushed hers again, gently at first, and then hungrily. It was going to be okay. The world started spinning once more.

Needless to say, Tom stayed the night. Fireworks were exploding outside in the snowy night and inside in Lizzy's cosy bed. The first day of 2018 was perfect. More fireworks in bed, until Lizzy realised the family would be turning up for lunch. There was a leg of lamb waiting to be cooked with all the trimmings. Lizzy sighed. Tom was amused: 'Come on, lass, we'll do it together. It's a while since I helped prepare a family meal.'

They drifted around the kitchen in happy bliss, chopping and mixing, stopping every so often for more kisses. Wellington weaved his way in and out of their legs. He wanted to share the happiness of his two favourite people.

None of the family seemed surprised to find Tom helping to cook the lunch. Nicola and Claire gave each other a wink and a suggestive rising of eyebrows. Their husbands were too busy discussing the football match they were going to watch later on, to notice anything unusual.

As they assembled round the table, rather squashed but cosy, Lizzy raised her glass. 'A toast to Catherine and Ben, my long-lost grandparents – without them I would not be here. Happy New Year, everyone. I have a feeling that it's going to be a good one.'

Wellington woofed and waited for the titbits.

Chapter Thirty-Nine

It was with a heavy heart that Lizzy sat down to write a letter to Bryan telling him that she and Tom were now a couple. She had no idea how to start and sat with pen in hand waiting for the words to come to her – the words that would finish what might have been a relationship. She had become very fond of this Canadian relative but in no way did it match what she felt for Tom. In reality she had just been waiting for Tom to open his heart. She picked up her pen, wrote a few words, screwed up the page and started again.

She could have sent an email but computer messages seem so harsh and cold. This was no way to convey her feelings. She thought a letter might be more delicate, but that was not working. She would have to confront him face to face – she was being a coward, not wanting an emotional scene but Bryan deserved more than a letter. They had *skyped* and messaged each other but Bryan had never brought up the question of her moving to Canada or of his feelings for her. She thought he must have realised that the lack of conversation about their relationship must have warned him that there was to be no happy ending for them. At least she hoped that this was so. She was not conscious of leading him on but maybe she should have seen how he would have perceived their situation.

She turned her laptop on. Like her grandparents before her, she must be courageous enough to do the right thing. Best to bite the bullet and get on with it.

Chapter Forty

'What do you want to see first, my love: grandfather's tribute or grandmother's grave?' Tom and Lizzy were seated in the car, wrestling with a map showing all the war cemeteries.

'I think we ought to visit the monument at Vimy Ridge first as Ben doesn't have a proper grave. But he has been remembered on the monument – his details engraved in stone with all the men who died whose bodies have not been found. I want you to see it for yourself. That would leave more time for Catherine's grave afterwards: that might need some attention. Most likely it has been neglected all these years in a village churchyard with nobody knowing where it was.'

The magnificent monument of Vimy Ridge stood glistening snowy-white against a sapphire sky like a giant stalagmite. The elaborate figures of the solemn men and women carved on the walls simply defied description of their sublime beauty.

'You can see this monument for miles,' said Lizzy. 'As we travel round in the car, you will see it in the distance many times. It's surprising what a small area the battles were fought in. Agincourt is not far away. A useful arena for centuries of fighting.'

'Well, you should know all about it, love – you're the expert,' Tom laughed.

They located Ben Trueman's name on the marble edifice. Lizzy traced his name with her long fingers, thinking of the grandfather she had never known. What would he have made of her? She imagined him jolly and bouncing her on his knee. A neat little wreath of poppies lay on the back seat ready to be placed alongside more formal tributes. Tom extracted his mobile phone from his pocket to take some photos for the family album. She wanted to show them to Mavis and Irene who had helped her to trace her grandfather.

'Ready, Lizzy? Are you feeling okay? You look a bit pale. Do you want to leave Catherine Waterman's grave for another day? It's all very emotional.' Tom gazed at her ashen face and hoped her emotions were not overwhelming her.

'No, I must go now to see what state her grave is in. I've waited so long for this moment I'll explode if I don't go now. Don't worry, I'll be okay. I'm ready to meet my grandmother.'

The graveyard was small, tiny compared to the other cemeteries they had visited – a village graveyard placed alongside a sturdy weathered church. Lizzy and Tom wandered around the grey slabs, hand in hand, translating the French inscriptions with what remained of their school-day French. Lizzy was better at translating written words than speaking. They stopped suddenly. A little apart stood a white stone engraved with the familiar English words and markings of the headstones ranked in rows at Tyne Cot.

'This is it then, you've found it.' Tom put his arm round Lizzy who was standing deep in thought gazing at the words *Catherine Waterman* – here was her grandmother at last. When Peter informed them that he had finally tracked down the place where Catherine was buried, Lizzy had visions of a neglected grave barely legible, abandoned in a village churchyard. This stone was clean, sparkling white and easily read, surrounded by flowering shrubs. Had somebody tended this grave so lovingly for a hundred years? She unwrapped the flowers to place on the grave. She had brought them with her, expecting the surrounding ground to be unloved and devoid of any tributes. Instead, there was barely a space among the shrubs to lay her posy down. As she stood amazed at the scene, she was startled to hear someone speaking in French behind her. 'This is a relative, my dear?'

They had not noticed the woman who had crept up behind them, barely five feet tall and dressed in black. She had the appearance of someone who had lived in this village for a very long time and could tell them a story or two.

'You have been searching for someone dear to you, and now that you have found them, you are sad. My name is Francoise Benet and I live over there.' She pointed to a cottage at the corner of the graveyard, close to the lych-gate leading to the church.

Lizzy and Francoise began a conversation composed of faltering French and thick guttural dialect. But they understood each other rather well. Tom, watching the two women eager to communicate, speculated that sometimes emotions convey more than words.

'Is it you who has looked after the grave? It's so beautiful – thank you.' Lizzy wiped her eyes under the careful gaze of her new friend whose twinkling amber eyes did not miss a thing.

'Not just me, the whole village looks after the graves of those who came to help us in wartime. My parents were part of this, they told me the tale. This nurse, taken by the terrible flu epidemic – she was a relative?' The old woman's face was rosy and wrinkled like a well-stored apple.

'She was my grandmother. I never met her, but they say we looked alike. Thank you for looking after the grave – it's so pretty.' Lizzy wiped away the tears that were streaming down her face. A snowy snippet of handkerchief was thrust into her hand by kind fingers, which also gave her a little pull on her arm.

'You have had a shock. Would you like to come to my house to drink some coffee? I have some madeleines fresh from the bakery.' Francoise seemed to take it for granted that they would say yes.

Tom suspected that this little old lady had noticed them entering the graveyard, had gone to the bakery whilst they were searching, wanting to be the first to discover the history of the foreigner who lay in their graveyard.

The cottage was small, neat and cosy. The madeleines were already displayed on a plate of faded willow pattern with a crocheted cover over them. An ancient coffee pot was steaming on the stove, emitting a gorgeous aroma of real coffee and three cups were waiting on the table. *Aha,* Tom thought, *I was right about the advance preparations. Just what Lizzy needs right now.*

Francoise regaled them with the history of the village and all that she knew about Catherine. 'We were honoured to have the grave of one of the nurses who tended those poor souls with terrible injuries. It was so cruel that she died of the fever that took so many when the war had ended.'

Realising that some of the story was being lost in translation, the two women gazed at each other, frustrated at the intricacies of language. Francoise's face suddenly lit up – she burrowed in the pocket of her capacious apron to produce a mobile phone. Picking out the numbers slowly, she held it to her ear. A rapid conversation followed. Tom and Lizzy could not understand a word apart from 'tomorrow, tomorrow lunch-time.' Francoise finished her call, and the mobile phone was returned to her pocket.

'My grandson,' she said 'He will come tomorrow at lunchtime. He speaks English well. Will you return? – I will make lunch for us all – he will translate so that the story can be told properly.'

'Yes, we will,' they both said with beaming faces.

Tom and Lizzy spent some time in the cottage, consuming all the madeleines with many cups of the fragrant coffee from the battered old pot. Lizzy's colour slowly returned but eventually they thought it was time to leave Francoise in peace. Her eyelids were drooping, she probably needed an afternoon nap. With promises to return the following day at noon, they left Francoise standing at her door waving. Then they wandered happily down the dusty road – hand-in-hand – a wonderful ending to the story of Catherine and Ben, and their lost baby.

Later in the evening, sitting in the local *estaminet* with generous glasses of cognac glistening like liquid amber in front of them, they reflected on the day and their benefactor. The village elders were playing dominoes in one corner, the soft burr of their voices soothing and unintelligible. The landlady was seated behind the bar, knitting and chatting with a couple of customers on high stools.

Silence overcame them; the rich cognac was making them sleepy and rather tipsy. The cosy ambience encouraged Lizzy to take a chance on asking a question that had been puzzling her for some time.

'Tom, can I ask you something?'

'Anything you like, my dear.'

She hesitated – it was hard to put into words though she had thought about it often.

'I have had feelings for you almost since the moment I met you, and sometimes I felt you had the same feelings but you never said anything. Why was that?'

Tom was silent for a moment; then he spoke in a thoughtful way as if teasing out a tangled knot of delicate silken thread, slowly and with great care.

'You are quite right about the feelings. I was attracted to you from the beginning but you seemed so vulnerable – so lost in your grief you didn't know your own mind. You would have accepted comfort from any source, and I wanted to wait until you had regained your balance and could make a rational decision.'

He stopped under the weight of such a long speech for he was a man of few words. 'Does that make sense? Do you understand – I didn't want to hurt you, though believe me there were times when I wanted to sweep you into my arms and cover you with kisses.'

Lizzy nodded, overcome with love for this dear man who seemed to know her so well. They had travelled together on a quest from the opening of Catherine's memory tin. All this time, Tom had been waiting for her to settle down and declare her love for him.

Lying in the bedroom of their holiday *gîte*, Lizzy was awake but relaxed. Golden light from a lamp outside shone through the window throwing shadows of dancing leaves on the whitewashed walls. She gazed at Tom's sleeping face and murmured, 'Who would have thought it this time two years ago.'

When she closed her eyes, visions played out behind the fluttering lids. She remembered every step of her journey from finding the tin to seeing her grandparents' graves. She thought of Tom and his steadfast kindness to her and the thrill of New Year's Eve. She thought of her family, happy to accept Tom into the fold. As she drifted off into happy dreams, she thought how curious and yet how wonderful life was.

Epilogue - 1918

Fred Waterman stood in the hallway of his house in Cardiff, which had once been full of happiness and laughter as his three daughters flitted to and fro, staring at the dreaded telegram in his hand. He had gone to the front door himself when he saw the telegraph boy walking up the path. He opened it straightaway on the doorstep and responded to the boy's questioning face with a shake of the head. Absentmindedly he reached into his breast pocket and brought out a small coin for the waiting lad. There was no reply to this message.

How should he break the news to Florence was his only thought. She had been so very upset over the baby's departure to Manchester and Beatrice's indifference to her pleas to at least keep the baby close in Bristol until Catherine returned. But it seemed as though their oldest daughter had ceased to be the docile character she once was, putting her husband's wishes above her parents.

He looked at the telegraph crumpled in his hand. It must be dealt with. He opened the door of the drawing room and went to stand in front of Florence.

'My dear,' he said, 'I have some bad news I am afraid. You must be very brave. Catherine has succumbed to the Spanish flu and died in France.'

This was the first blow; the second followed swiftly when Fred contacted Arthur to make arrangements for baby Huw to be brought back to the Cardiff homestead. Then Fred realised the depths of Arthur's duplicity. Florence was distraught over the loss of her daughter and wanted to take Catherine's baby back into their household. Arthur refused to comply and told Fred flatly that the baby would be staying with him and Beatrice in Manchester.

'But he's a Waterman. He must come to us,' pleaded Fred, tears in his eyes.

'No, he is a Mortlake. I registered him as our son, when Catherine failed to do so. You don't want to raise a great scandal, showing how she abandoned her baby son. You will just have to let it lie. We are in a position to give him a very good life.'

'Catherine is dead. Annie is planning to go out to India with her husband and I have no family here. We would like to bring Huw back into our household. He could inherit our money and maintain the family business – keep the Waterman line alive.' Fred's voice was tremulous, that of an old man receiving shock after shock.

The voice of Arthur was calm but firm, in contrast to his companion.

'He is not Huw Waterman anymore. He is Nicholas Mortlake who lives in Manchester with his parents, Arthur and Beatrice Mortlake, who are bringing him up in a good Christian home and will be giving him a decent education. You cannot uproot him now; it would be totally unfair to him and to us. Furthermore, just think of the scandal that would surround Catherine's good name. You would not be able to keep your esteemed position in Cardiff.'

Fred was a broken man, destroyed by death and the tribulations of warfare. He had looked to Catherine's son to restore him, but Arthur would not budge. Fred blamed himself for not being more alert when Arthur had appeared so helpful and sensitive to the situation. He had never really liked or trusted Beatrice's husband. At the time, he thought they were being very generous to take on the burden of someone else's child. He never thought that Arthur could be so audacious as to steal Catherine's baby.

They had been surprised when Arthur and Beatrice had moved up to Manchester soon after taking full charge of baby Huw, but Arthur claimed it was necessary to accept the offer of a more satisfactory position in the north. They should have been suspicious then. Arthur had abandoned a good position in Bristol. Fred now realised the depth of the other man's deception. It had all been planned out. He had thought that he was managing the situation but he had merely walked meekly into Arthur's plan to kidnap his grandson.

Arthur responded in what he considered to be a reasonable tone. 'Look here, Fred. The boy has been registered as Nicholas Mortlake. We have fulfilled all the legal requirements. He is our son now.'

They never spoke again. Fred and Florence both died not long after, of sorrow perhaps. The matter was never spoken of in the family. Baby Huw was not present in the photo albums or written up with the other births in the front of the Waterman's bible, sitting black and sombre on the mahogany sideboard. Future generations had no way of knowing that he ever existed.

*

But the good people of Kingcharlton knew. Daisy and her family and the poor people in Woodbine Cottages knew. Matron and Nora knew, but not to gossip about. Many people in the village thought they knew something, if not all the details. But nobody spoke of it outside the Daisy's household and that was only discreet references. The *Craven A* tin was resident for many years on the top shelf of the pantry, wrapped up in a clean tea towel until it was finally moved to the loft. By that time the family did not believe that anybody would be calling to reclaim it. Catherine's tin lay buried for a century until it fell at Lizzy's feet. Daisy's story as told to her descendants slowly unravelled the mystery of the missing baby. And so, a family history was restored.

Printed in Great Britain
by Amazon

43050545R00199